Last Hope

A Gideon Johann Western
Book 3

By
Duane Boehm

Last Hope: A Gideon Johann Western Book 3

For more information or permission contact:
boehmduane@gmail.com

This book is a work of fiction. References to real people, events, establishments, organizations, or locales are intended only to provide a sense of authenticity and are used fictitiously. All other characters, and all incidents and dialogue are drawn from the author's imagination and not to be construed as real.

ISBN: 1-51513-724-4

Other Books by Duane Boehm

In Just One Moment
Gideon Johann: A Gideon Johann Western Prequel
Last Stand: A Gideon Johann Western Book 1
Last Chance: A Gideon Johann Western Book 2
Last Ride: A Gideon Johann Western Book 4
Last Breath: A Gideon Johann Western Book 5
Last Journey: A Gideon Johann Western Book 6
Last Atonement: A Gideon Johann Western Book 7
Wayward Brother: A Gideon Johann Western Book 8
Where The Wild Horses Roam: Wild Horse Westerns Book 1
Spirit Of The Wild Horse: Wild Horse Westerns Book 2
Wild Horse On The Run: Wild Horse Westerns Book 3
What It All Comes Down To
Hand Of Fate: The Hand Of Westerns Book 1
Hand Of The Father: The Hand Of Westerns Book 2
Trail To Yesterday
Sun Over The Mountains
Wanted: A Collection of Western Stories (7 authors)
Wanted II: A Collection of Western Stories (7 authors)

In memory of Grandma Boehm for all those things in which it is hard to find the words

Chapter 1

Sheriff Gideon Johann of Last Stand, Colorado and his part-time deputy, Zack Barlow, were finishing a breakfast of salt pork and hardtack after their first night on the trail. They were traveling west towards Silverton after Gideon had received a telegram from that town's sheriff requesting help with a gang of outlaws headed towards Last Stand. The thieves had robbed the mine's pay wagon, killing two men in the process.

The two lawmen had camped on the same spot where the previous year Gideon and his now wife, Abby, had spent their first night together after his absence of eighteen years. On that night, he learned that he had a daughter. He had also confessed that his absence had been the result of running from the guilt of accidentally killing a boy during the war. Healing had begun on that evening. He still got misty thinking about that night, and was lost in thought when Zack interrupted his reverie.

"I forgot how hard of a bed the ground makes. I guess I'm getting spoiled," Zack said.

"Wait until you're thirty-eight years old and see how hard it feels. I'm as stiff as a board. This married life has about ruined me," Gideon said with a smile.

"Have you got your new place about finished?"

"Yeah, it's done. I guess you haven't been over since I got the corral finished. When we get home, you need to ride over after Ethan is done with you for the day and have dinner with us. And speaking of Ethan, how did he take it that you had to head out with me?" Gideon asked as he threw his saddle blanket onto his buckskin horse. Ethan was Gideon's best friend, and Zack's primary employer.

"You know how Ethan is, being a preacher and all. He's much too polite to grouse about something that he agreed to, but I could tell it troubled him that we would get behind on branding the new calves," Zack answered as he cinched up his chestnut gelding.

"Let's head out. And we need to keep our eyes peeled today. I expect we will cross paths with the gang if they are still headed this way."

"Do you think it could be Big Nose George?" Zack asked. Big Nose George Parrot had killed Zack's father in a stagecoach robbery and the young man had sworn revenge if ever provided the opportunity.

"I've never heard of him coming down into Colorado. I wouldn't get my hopes up," Gideon said.

The two men rode for an hour with little conversation until Zack blurted, "Gideon, I need to talk to you about something."

Gideon looked at Zack and had a bad feeling about where the conversation was headed. He had no idea what the subject would be, but he was pretty sure he didn't want to be a part of it. "What's on your mind?" he asked wearily.

"Did you know that Joann wrote me and told me that she wants us to just be friends?" Zack asked.

Joann was Gideon and Abby's daughter that he had learned of that night at the camp spot. Her visit the previous fall had sparked a brief romance between her and Zack before she returned to the Wyoming Territory.

Gideon's shoulders sagged and he slowly blew out a breath of air. "No, I didn't. I'm sorry to hear that."

"Does Abby know?"

"Now if I didn't know, how am I supposed to know if Abby knows?" Gideon said, annoyed at the question.

"I bet she's got some rich rancher's son courting her, and I bet you're glad that your daughter is going to end up with somebody like that instead of me," Zack accused the sheriff.

Gideon closed his eyes and shook his head. This was not the first time the subject of Zack being worthy of his daughter had been broached. "Sometimes I just want to reach over and slap a turd out of you. You're riding with me because I trust you to have my back when the bullets start flying. Do you really think that I'd wish unhappiness for you? I would think that you would know me better than that with all we've been through together. I think Joann is a mighty fine girl, but I don't see where she has anything on you, and I don't know why in the hell you don't think more highly of yourself. Joann would do fine by you. Unless she is engaged, the battle is not over yet. If you want her, don't give up that damn easily."

Zack rode on silently, sulky for a bit before saying, "I guess we better be watching for outlaws."

For the next hour, the two men said nothing as they rode along, still annoyed at each other. The road ran straight and mainly level with an occasional hill, making for easy travel. To the south, the land was flat with good grass and an occasional Gambel oak grove, and to the north began the gradual rise to the foothills, timbered in a mix of pine and aspen. As they topped a big hill, they caught sight of four riders coming in a hard lope their way. Behind the riders, another quarter of a mile farther down the trail, were three more men in pursuit. The four men also saw Gideon and Zack, and with an arm wave from the front rider, the men turned and rode into the timber towards the foothills.

"I'd say that we just found our robbers, and I wish it was in a better spot to capture them," Gideon said.

"What do you think we should do?" Zack asked.

"Let's make a circle to the south and come in behind that stand of trees. I expect the posse will do the same from the other direction and we can meet them and come up with a plan."

"Sounds good to me," Zack replied.

"And just in case something happens, I want you to know that if I had anything to do with choosing a son-in-law, I'd pick you," Gideon said.

"I hope you get your wish. I'd hate to have to break in another old codger for a future father-in-law," Zack said as they both put their horses into a gallop.

The posse beat Gideon and Zack to the stand of trees and busied themselves scanning the woods across the road for signs of the outlaws. The sheriff of Silverton walked over to greet them. "I'm Sheriff Mitch Clemons, and you must be Sheriff Gideon Johann. Thanks for coming," he said.

Gideon climbed off his horse and shook the sheriff's hand. "Yes, I am, and this here is my deputy, Zack Barlow. I hope we can be of some help. Did they stop in the trees or keep on going?"

"We saw them scurrying about. I think they plan to hold us off until nightfall and then sneak off into the hills. Do you have any suggestions?" Sheriff Clemons asked.

"I'd say that you and I flank them on each side, and our men can start shooting from here to keep their attention. It's about the only thing that I can see to do," Gideon said.

"I thought the same thing. It worked in the war, and let's hope that it works here. Don't forget that these men are cold-blooded killers," the sheriff warned.

Sheriff Clements gave the instructions to the men and they began firing into the woods while the two sheriffs maneuvered around to each side. As Gideon moved, he had to stay crouched in the grass and scrub brush, and it brought back memories of his days of fighting on foot in the war before he became part of the cavalry. The outlaws were now returning fire with the deputies, and as Gideon crept around to the side, he spotted the general location of three of the outlaws from the smoke of their guns. He darted from tree to tree until he could see one of the outlaws thirty yards away taking aim towards the road.

Gideon contemplated calling out for the man to surrender, but realized that there was no chance for that to happen. If he did that, the outlaw would undoubtedly dive behind a tree and negate their flanking tactic. He took aim at the man's left side below the arm and fired. The outlaw jumped straight up in the air and twisted towards Gideon with a look of shear panic before falling on his face. Gideon stood frozen as a wave of emptiness washed over him. In his old life, he wouldn't have given a second thought to shooting an outlaw, but not anymore. Life was too precious to him these days, and he took no pleasure in extinguishing another man's existence.

As Gideon looked away from the prone body, he saw another outlaw taking aim on him. He spun back behind the tree as a bullet whistled by him. Cursing himself for his carelessness, the instinct of self-preservation rushed through him, followed by the fury that had made him such a relentless soldier. He crouched down and peeked around the tree, but the shooter was no longer to be found.

Gideon didn't like the idea of the outlaw knowing his location, and he not the outlaw's, so he began working his way around to the rear of the woods. Every few steps he would stop and listen. The shooting was slowing down and he didn't hear anybody moving through the trees. He came upon the robbers' tied up horses. Deciding to move them, he set his rifle down to untie the reins just as one of the men came sprinting his way. Gideon was as surprised as the other man appeared to be. The outlaw raised his rifle as Gideon drew his pistol and fired three shots in rapid succession. Each shot drove the outlaw farther back until he fell, shooting his gun straight up into the air as he hit the ground. Gideon walked over to the man and gave him a good kick to make sure that he was dead before taking the horses around towards Sheriff Clemons' flank.

"Sheriff Clemons, I killed two of the outlaws and I have their horses. What about you?" Gideon yelled out after taking cover in a swale.

"I killed one of them. I guess we still have one to go," Sheriff Clemons responded.

From the middle of the trees, a voice called out, "I'll surrender. Just tell me what you want me to do."

Sheriff Clemons yelled, "Leave your guns behind and walk towards my voice with your hands on top of your head and sing nice and loud all the way. I'll have a bead on you."

The outlaw followed the orders, singing "Shall We Gather at the River" in a voice so pitchy that Gideon wondered if Sheriff Clemons might shoot the singer just to end the song.

Gideon headed towards the sheriff after the lawman had called out for him. He found the sheriff waiting patiently with his rifle still aimed at the outlaw.

The outlaw said, "Well, if it isn't Gideon Johann. I never thought I'd see you wearing a badge. In fact, I figured you'd be more likely to be in my line of work."

Gideon looked towards the man, surprised at hearing him say his name. He studied him for a moment before saying, "Fred Parsons, when in the hell did you become an outlaw?"

"You know this man?" Sheriff Clemons asked.

"He was one of the best soldiers I ever rode with," Gideon replied.

"He seems to have a different calling these days," the sheriff remarked.

"I decided there had to be an easier way to make a living than staring at the ass of a cow," Fred said.

"I'm afraid your easy days are over for good. You'll likely hang for this," Sheriff Clemons said.

"You know, Gideon, I once saved your life, and if you hadn't ducked around that tree at the last second, I would have killed you a few minutes ago. Funny how life works."

Gideon felt the emptiness in the pit of his stomach again and fought off nausea. The bond built between men that fought together in war was almost indescribable. There was no solace in bringing Fred to justice. He wanted to get away as quickly as possible and put today out of his mind. "There's not much funny about today," Gideon said.

"Did you know that Finnie is in Animas City? He's the town drunk. I tried to get him to straighten up and join us, but he is content scooping horseshit and drinking himself to death," Fred said.

Gideon turned to the sheriff. "You don't need me anymore and I want to get out of here. Good to have met you. I'll send your deputies up here."

Sheriff Clemons shook Gideon's hand. "Thank you for your help. Maybe I can return the favor someday. I'll make sure that he is cared for properly."

"I hope they spare your life and that someday you're free again. God have mercy on you," Gideon said and walked away.

Zack and the other deputies were waiting in the road with the horses as Gideon walked up to them. He pointed the deputies towards the sheriff.

Gideon turned to Zack. "I have to go to Animas City. I need to check on an old war buddy. You can either head back or ride with me - your choice."

"Will I still get paid?" Zack asked with a grin.

"Sure, it's not my money. I could use the company anyway," Gideon said as he mounted Buck.

After riding for about twenty minutes, Zack said, "You're awfully quiet for wanting company. Are you still sore at me?"

"No. The man we arrested was also one of my war buddies. He's the one that told me that Finnie was in Animas City. It makes for a sad day all away around," Gideon said.

"I'd say so. Tell me about Finnie."

Gideon, despite the circumstance, grinned at thinking about Finnie. "Finnegan Ford came to this country when he was fourteen. He has an Irish accent so thick that it takes a while to understand him, but the man is funny. He was the one that kept us smiling through the bad days. And now I guess he is a drunk."

Chapter 2

Never having been to Animas City, Gideon sized up the place as they arrived. It looked a lot like Last Stand, but with more hustle and bustle as miners scurried about in an apparent hurry to buy supplies. He and Zack rode up to the first saloon and tied their horses to the hitching rail.

"I don't know what to expect. Finnie could get pretty cantankerous when he got drunk back in the day. We will see," Gideon said.

The Last Stand Last Chance Saloon was the only saloon that Zack had ever been in, and when they walked into this place, he had to force himself to keep from gagging. The place reeked of stale beer and body odor. A cloud of smoke hung so heavily in the air that it looked as if there was a morning fog. Most of the men appeared to be miners with the brawn to match their work. The saloon girls were uglier than Zack ever imagined women could be and still get hired for such a job.

At the end of the bar, a man loudly sang "Whiskey in the Jar". His heavy Irish accent and drunken slur made the words indecipherable and only his excellent singing voice made the song recognizable. It occurred to Zack that the man was likely Finnie. The singer did look the way he had imagined Gideon's friend to appear. The man was short and squat with shoulders like an ox. His hair was strawberry blond and he wore bushy sideburns that accented his long pointed nose and cleft chin. A layer of dirt coated him, and his clothes were mostly worn out.

Gideon tapped Zack on the shoulder and pointed at the singer. They walked up to the bar with Gideon standing next to the man. The Irishman stopped singing and looked at the two men.

"What's the best drink in here?" Gideon asked.

"If you came in here for the taste, you've sadly made a serious mistake. All the drinks in this sorry establishment taste as if they've already passed through the body once and are only fit for getting drunk," Finnie said and took a sip of his whiskey.

"You remind me of this little sawed off Irishman that I served with in the Second Colorado Cavalry. He was an irritating little shit," Gideon said.

Finnie set his glass down on the bar and turned to study Gideon. He tilted his head and rubbed his chin before breaking into a grin at the recognition of his friend. "Gideon Johann, you old dog. You're still as pretty as a baby suckling a teat. How many years has it been? You're sure one I never thought I'd see again," he said as he held out his hand and shook Gideon's vigorously.

"It's been too long, Finnie, too long. How did you end up here?" Gideon asked.

"I came here to make my fortune, but things did not go as I had planned, and I lost my desire for it after that," Finnie said as if the memory still pained him.

Changing the subject, Gideon said, "Finnegan Ford, this here is my deputy, Zack Barlow."

The two men shook hands as Finnie looked at Gideon and pointed at the badge. "And where might you be the sheriff and what brings you out this way?"

"In Last Stand. Unfortunately, I helped capture Fred Parsons. He's liable to hang for his part in a murder and robbery. He's the one that told me that I'd find you here."

"I remember you talking about your hometown. Always sounded like a nice place. Old Fred, he tried to get me in on that nonsense. Not for me. I've sunk considerably lower than my prime, but I still know right from wrong. It must have pained you to go after our old war buddy," Finnie said and took another sip.

"I didn't know that it was him until we caught him. It certainly was a surprise and not something that I would have ever expected. It was a sad day for sure. I guess people change," Gideon said.

"Yes, we do, Gideon. Yes, we do," Finnie said sadly.

"Finnie, I want you to come back to Last Stand with me. I can get you a job and you can make a new start for yourself."

Turning surly, Finnie said, "What's the matter, doesn't Last Stand have its own town drunk?"

"Don't be that way. We always had each other's back, and I just want to help you get a fresh start. You'd do the same for me.," Gideon said.

"You mean like keeping your secret all these years?"

"It's no secret anymore. Most of the town knows about me killing the boy in the war. It was only in the last year that I finally put that behind me. People helped me start over and I want to do the same for you," Gideon pleaded.

"Gideon, I'm glad you're doing well now. I remember what a burden it was for you, and I appreciate your kindness, but it's too late for me. The bottle is my best friend now. I'm content and there's no need for you to trouble yourself over me. It's been good to see you again," Finnie said and turned back towards the bar to end the conversation.

Gideon stood stunned, still looking at Finnie. He had expected difficulty in convincing him to leave, but he hadn't figured to be dismissed so easily. Gently taking Finnie's arm, he said, "Please come with me. You are better than this."

Finnie jerked his arm away. "Be off with you. I don't need your damn pity," he yelled at Gideon.

A man standing on the other side of Finnie moved around him to face Gideon. He began poking Gideon in the chest and said, "Your badge don't carry any weight around here, and Finnie don't want to see you. So leave him alone."

Gideon was about to try to calm the situation when Finnie spun the man around and caught him on the jaw with a vicious right-hook that knocked the troublemaker unconscious before he hit the floor. "Don't touch my friend," Finnie screamed.

Chaos ensued as three of the fallen man's friends jumped into the fray. Gideon, Zack, and Finnie were exchanging blows with the men in an all-out brawl. Finnie had been trained as a boxer in his youth and used his skills to thrash his opponent. Gideon held his own against a much larger man, but Zack, whose fighting experience was limited to schoolyard tussles, was getting pummeled. In a rush to come to Zack's aid, Finnie aimed a punch to his man's stomach and as the man doubled over, he delivered a haymaker to the face that put the man down. Finnie yanked Zack's assailant around and walked the man back with a flurry of jabs that forced the troublemaker to turn tail and run out the door.

"Someone needs to teach you the art of boxing," Finnie called out to Zack.

The constable arrived, drew his gun, and yelled, "That will be enough fighting. Stop at once."

Seeing the badge on Gideon, the constable said, "I'm Constable Ryan. Who are you and what happened here?"

"I'm Sheriff Johann of Last Stand, and I was having a spirited conversation with my friend Finnie here when these men decided to stick their noses where they didn't belong. We were just defending ourselves," Gideon said as he wiped blood from his lip.

Constable Ryan holstered his gun and looked at the bartender. "Is that about the size of it?" he asked.

The bartender, drying a glass, and looking around warily at the combatants, said, "More or less."

"And what was your spirited conversation concerning that it attracted so much attention?" Constable Ryan asked Gideon.

"I was trying to get him to come back to Last Stand with me. He seems to think that Animas City is more to his liking," Gideon said.

"Finnie, you're a good fellow and all, but trouble follows you like stink follows shit. You need to go with your friend or I'm going to arrest you for being a public nuisance," the constable said.

"You can't arrest me and nobody else. I have my rights," Finnie protested.

"Yes, you do, and the judge may agree, but he just left the day before yesterday and won't be back till who knows when, so you will have to sit in jail until you get your day in court," Constable Ryan said while failing to conceal his grin.

"I'm being railroaded out of town. I fought for the Union and this is how I'm treated. It's a fine day for democracy," Finnie complained.

Gideon grinned at the constable as if they had pulled off a great feat. He put his arm around Finnie, saying, "You'll love Last Stand. It's a fine town and the sheriff there won't run you off."

"You think it's funny now, but you might not later. I might tear your whole town down, and I know you won't shoot me and you sure can't lick me," Finnie said.

"Do you have a horse?" Gideon asked.

"Yes, yes, I've a horse. No saddle, but I reckon I can still ride bareback. You best buy me a bottle 'cause there's no way I can travel that far without some liquid encouragement," Finnie said.

"I always carry a bottle. Let's get out of here," Gideon said.

"Zack don't look so good," Finnie announced.

Zack sat at a table with one hand covering an eye and the other rubbed his mouth. Color was gone from his face. "I'm all right," he mumbled.

"Let's get him outside," Gideon said as he and Finnie each took an arm and walked the wobbly young man out the door.

In the sunlight, Zack's beating became apparent. Both lips were badly busted and swelling, and his left eye would soon be black to go with the scrape on his right cheek. He bent over, bracing his hands on his knees as he sucked in deep breaths.

"For as big as you are, you sure aren't much of a fighter," Finnie said.

"If you would have gone with us in the first place, I wouldn't have had to suffer this embarrassment. The end result would still be the same and I'd be feeling a whole lot better," Zack said.

"True, true, my boy. And since I'm going to be dragged to your town anyway, I'm going to teach you how to fight. It pains me to see a man as useless as you are in the art of boxing," Finnie said.

Zack gave Finnie such a look that Gideon wondered if the young man was contemplating shooting the Irishman on the spot.

Wishing to end the conversation and get started back to Last Stand, Gideon said, "Let's get your horse. We have some riding to do."

Chapter 3

Abby Johann missed Gideon more than she even expected. His absence to help the sheriff of Silverton had caused their first time apart since they married the previous fall. The last few months had been the happiest time of her life. She looked around their new log cabin, and thought about all the memories that they had already made there. The cabin would never be as nice as the house that she had left behind when she divorced Marcus Hanson, but the cabin was a home and that was something the house never could have been.

They had purchased a hundred head of cattle, and Abby had taken on the job of overseeing them when Gideon was busy with his job as sheriff. Riding out each day to check on the herd had become one of her favorite pastimes. She had always loved riding, and the cattle gave her an excuse to get out of her normal household chores each day.

As she pulled on her riding pants, she could not get them buttoned. At that moment, she knew that it was time to quit deceiving herself. She was pregnant. For the last few weeks, she had noticed the symptoms, but wouldn't allow herself to admit it. Continuing to pretend any longer would be futile. Tears of joy pooled in her eyes as she imagined herself rocking their new baby. She could think of nothing more wonderful than having another child with Gideon. Abby's aunt and uncle in the Wyoming Territory had raised their daughter Joann, but this time they would share the experience together.

She did worry that the news would overwhelm Gideon. He had been through so many changes in the last year. After he had been found near death outside of Last Stand, he was a bitter and angry man that had been running from his past for so long that it had become a way of life. Sometimes she still marveled at the changes in him. He rediscovered the person that he had been when she knew him in her youth and became a loving father to Joann and Winnie, her daughter from her marriage to Marcus.

Using some twine, Abby tied her pants together and threw on a light jacket to hide the gap in her breeches. It wasn't as if she expected to see anyone anyway. After saddling her favorite horse, Snuggles, she walked him out of the barn and saw Gideon riding up the road. Flushing with apprehension, she had planned to use the ride to decide how to broach the subject of a baby, and now had to decide whether to break the news or wait.

Gideon put Buck into a lope at seeing Abby, and dismounted before the horse came to a stop. As he gave Abby a hug that lifted her feet off the ground, he said, "I missed you."

"I missed you too. I've gotten used to a warm bedfellow," Abby said.

"Speaking of such, I thought I'd find you in bed ready and waiting."

Abby giggled. "Yes, I should have since I have nothing better to do around here than lie around naked. I guess we best hire servants so that I can just be your love toy. You are a vain man," she joked.

"You are not going to believe what has happened to me. We caught the gang that robbed the pay wagon, and the only one that survived the shootout was Fred Parsons. I've told you about riding with him in the war. I still can't believe he became an outlaw. He'll likely hang for it. It's a sad day when you have to arrest someone that once saved your life, but he made his choice, and I guess he will suffer the consequences. Anyway, he told me that Finnie Ford was a drunk in Animas City, so Zack and I rode there to bring him back. That's why I've been gone longer than expected. I know you've heard me talk a lot about Finnie. It turned into quite the ruckus to get him to Last Stand. On the ride back, I would only let him have enough whiskey to keep the shakes away. He raised such a fit on the way that I know that Zack thought I was crazy for doing it, and I'm probably the last person that needs to try to help someone, but I couldn't turn my back on him knowing full well that he needed help," Gideon said.

"I do remember you talking about both of them, and I think you are the perfect person to help him. You know what it's like to be down on your luck, and now you are strong enough to do for him what others helped do for you. I'm proud of you," Abby said.

"You might not think so after you meet him. He's a rascal and he really is in a bad way."

"I'm sure I'll come to like him, and if not, I certainly know how to set him straight."

"Did you know that Joann sent Zack a letter saying that she just wanted to be friends?" Gideon asked.

"While you were gone, I got a letter from her telling me all about it," Abby replied.

"I love that girl to death, but she is fickle. She could do a lot worse than Zack Barlow. I bet she has a new beau."

"Of course, she does. She is smitten by the son of a rich rancher up there in the Wyoming Territory. You can't interfere with something like this. She'll resent you if you do, and as headstrong as she is, it would only hurt any chances that Zack still has. It's not as if she is married yet. Just give it some time," Abby said.

"I guess you're right, but I still don't like it. I was hoping they would hitch up and she would move down here," Gideon said with resignation.

Abby took Gideon by the hands. "Honey, I have some news for you too."

"And what might that be?" Gideon asked warily.

"We're going to have a baby," Abby squealed.

Gideon's face went blank and his mouth moved to speak, but no words came out at first. "Really? We're going to have a baby? I know that you've talked about wanting one, but I really thought you were too old."

Abby pulled her hands away from Gideon and placed them on her hips. "Gideon Johann, I'm thirty-five years old for crying out loud. I'll make you think too old. If I ever hear that out of your mouth again, you'll be the one that can't have any more children. You'll be hanging out there with your steers commiserating about when you had a pair," Abby said.

Gideon grinned sheepishly and pulled his hat down over his eyes. "I guess that wasn't the proper response for impending fatherhood," he said before throwing his hat in the air and grabbing Abby. "We're going to have a baby. Can I tell anybody?"

"I think we better wait to tell Winnie. She's been through enough change for now, and I suspect it will crumble her little world for a while until she gets to hold the baby. You can tell Ethan and Sarah, and of course Doc will need to know, but let's wait until things are further along before we announce it," Abby said and gave Gideon a hard kiss.

"You make me so happy. I can't believe it."

"You're probably still worried I'm going to castrate you. Let's go check the herd," Abby said with a devilish grin.

Chapter 4

The morning after his return home to Abby, Gideon awoke in a fine mood. Not only was he overjoyed at the thought of impending fatherhood, but he had also learned that the new situation didn't preclude him from getting some loving. He was so full of gusto that he gobbled his breakfast down as if he were in a race and put Buck in a lope all the way to Ethan's place.

Ethan was tightening his cinch to go ride, having sent Zack ahead to start a fire for branding the new calves. "You didn't do much of a job looking out for my ranch hand. Zack's low enough over losing Joann, and he'll never get him a woman if you keep getting him beat up," he said before Gideon had reined Buck to a halt.

"Ethan, Abby is going to have a baby," Gideon said, ignoring the complaining.

"Well aren't you the gobbler strutting his feathers. Congratulations."

"I'm a bit giddy over the news. I sure wasn't expecting it," Gideon said as he dismounted.

"I'm really happy for you. You deserve it," Ethan said and shook Gideon's hand.

"Thank you. Sometimes I can't believe this is really my life."

"You better get in there and tell Sarah. The missus might get a bit irritable if she is left out."

Sarah had become the sister that Gideon had never had. He had even taken to calling her Sis. Her belief in him when he didn't believe in himself had meant more in some ways than even Ethan's support. Ethan had believed in him from the memory of what he had once been, where Sarah believed in him from what she had seen in the here and now.

"Gideon, what a pleasant surprise. What brings you out this way?" Sarah said as the two men entered the cabin.

"Sis, I got some news," Gideon said, failing to hide his smile.

"And what might that be?"

"Abby's going to have a baby."

Sarah let out a squeal and ran to Gideon, giving him a hug. "I did a better job of straightening you up than I ever could have imagined. I'm so happy for the two of you," she said with a laugh.

Ethan, watching in amusement, said, "Of course, Sarah gets all the credit. She takes credit for everything."

"I wanted you two to be the first to know, and please keep it under your hat. I have to get to Last Stand and make sure Finnie is not tearing it down. I brought a war buddy back to town that is down on his luck. I probably bit off more than I can chew, but I had to try," Gideon said.

"Zack told us all about all that. He sounds like quite the character. Good for you for trying," Ethan said.

Sarah, beaming like a proud parent, said, "Oh what a difference a year can make in our lives."

"That it does. I'll see you guys Sunday," Gideon said as he took his leave.

Gideon rode into town, stopping at Doc Abram's office before checking on Finnie. The doctor was one of Gideon's few confidantes and he valued his opinion. Doc was busy cleaning his spectacles when Gideon walked through the door.

"Who's that little fellow that has been in and out of the jail all morning?" Doc said as a way of a greeting.

"That there is Finnegan Ford. I fought in the war with him, and he is down on his luck so I brought him back here. He's a good man that's lost his way. I wanted to talk to you about him. He's a bad drunk and gets the shakes when he doesn't have his whiskey. I gave him enough on the ride here to keep it at bay, but I wanted to know how I should handle it," Gideon said.

The doctor put his glasses on and peered at Gideon. "You're going to have your hands full if he is that bad of a drunk. You won't be able to watch him all the time, and that's when he will slip, but you were doing the right thing in giving him enough to calm him. If you can keep him sober, the episodes of the shakes will gradually subside. But keeping him sober is not likely."

"Well, thanks for the encouragement," Gideon said sarcastically. "I guess you don't agree with my bringing him here."

"Don't you go putting words into my mouth. I can speak for myself just fine and I didn't say one damn thing about thinking it was a mistake, but if you don't want to hear the truth then why in the hell did you come in here?" Doc said, ripping his spectacles off his face.

"I'm sorry. I guess I wanted to hear you say that it was going to be fine and that I could help him."

"You can help him, but I think it will be hard and there will be setbacks. When a person is to the point of getting the shakes when they don't have it, they're a bad drunk," Doc said.

"Abby is going to have a baby," Gideon blurted out.

"Now that's more like it. You should have told me that first. We need to celebrate," the doctor said, reaching into his desk drawer and pulling out a bottle of whiskey and two glasses.

"It's a little early, don't you think."

"It's never too early to celebrate news like that," the doctor said as he poured the glasses and pushed one towards Gideon "To a healthy Baby Johann." The two men clinked their glasses together.

"Thank you, Doc. Keep it to yourself. I know that it will stress the seams of your jacket to keep a secret, but we'd prefer it," Gideon said after drinking the toast.

"I can keep a secret anytime that I want to do it. I just don't usually want to," Doc Abram said and let out a laugh.

"I need to get over to the jailhouse and check on Finnie. I'll see you later," Gideon said before walking out the door.

Gideon found Finnie pacing about the office. A bath, shave, and new clothes had transformed the Irishman.

"That's the best twenty dollars that I ever spent," Gideon said on seeing him.

"You didn't spend it. You loaned it," Finnie reminded him. "I wondered if you were ever coming back. I don't know a soul here, and you barely left me enough whiskey to get by. I should've let that constable throw me away."

"Calm down. I don't remember anything making you nervous in the old days," Gideon said.

"These aren't the old days and I'm not that person anymore. I know I'm a drunk, but I've come to accept it. And I have you to thank for dragging me to a strange place, then abandoning me, and yet act like you are doing me some big favor," Finnie said.

"I went home to see my wife. I did not abandon you. Do you want to tell me what happened that you ended up this way?"

"No, I do not. Maybe someday, but not now. I hope that you have a plan, because I don't have a clue what I'm supposed to do with myself."

"Let's go for a walk."

The two men walked down the street to outside of the Last Stand Last Chance Saloon. Motioning Finnie towards a nearby bench, Gideon said, "You sit there while I go inside. I won't be long."

Mary, the saloon owner, was another of the few people that Gideon considered his friend. She was standing behind the bar as he walked into the saloon. "Gideon, what do I owe this pleasure," she said as a joke.

"It is a pleasure to see me, isn't it?" Gideon replied.

Mary looked Gideon over carefully as he walked up to the bar. Feigning vainness was not a normal trait of Gideon and it surprised her. "What's got you spurs jangling so loud – oh my God, I know. You're going to have . . ." she said before Gideon could get his hand against her lips.

"Tarnation, woman, is there anything about me that you can't figure out? You make it darn hard to surprise you," Gideon said, thoroughly annoyed at Mary. From the first time that he had met her, it was as if she could read his mind. Her gift never failed to amaze and irritate him.

"All right, I didn't realize it was a secret," she said before leaning over close to his ear. "Congratulations."

"Thank you. I need a favor if it is at all possible."

"And what might that be?"

"I'm surprised that you can't tell me," Gideon replied before explaining the situation with Finnie.

"So where do I fit into all this?" Mary asked.

"I was hoping that you could hire him to come in for a couple of hours before you open to clean the place. He's staying in the jail so he just needs some money for food and to keep his horse fed. He'll probably need a glass of whiskey to get him through it, too. I'm going to try my best to dry him out, but it's going to have to be gradual," Gideon said.

"Are you sure he's still the same person that you knew in the war? People have a way of changing," Mary said, smiling wryly at the inference to Gideon's turnaround.

"He may have lost his way, but I don't think he would ever lose his honesty. He's waiting outside if you want to meet him. With your ability to size men up, I'm sure that you will be able to decide for yourself," Gideon said, still annoyed that she had figured out that he was going to be a father again.

"Go get him and let me meet him."

Gideon returned with Finnie. Mary's youth and beauty surprised the Irishman. She was a far cry from any other woman that he had met running a saloon. He looked longingly at the bottles behind her, and did his best to hide the trembling of his hands.

"Pleased to meet you," Finnie said to Mary.

"Listen to that accent. Your voice is as soothing as a baby's coo. Glad to meet you," Mary said.

"I don't know about my accent, but I must say that your beauty certainly puts a shine to this here saloon."

"And a charmer, too."

Motioning towards a bottle, Gideon said, "Why don't you pour us a drink. I'm a bit dry."

Finnie did his best not to gulp the drink. He let it savor in his mouth before swallowing. "You sell a considerably finer whiskey than my last saloon of choice. My compliments."

"So can you have yourself over here to clean by eight and not steal my whiskey?" Mary asked.

"I have already brought shame to my mother, God rest her soul, for the life I live, but I would never dishonor her name with a son that is a thief," Finnie said.

"I'll see you in the morning then," Mary said and gave Gideon a wink.

Chapter 5

Gideon persevered through the first week of Finnie's stay at the jail, but the Irishman made for an irritable companion. Finnie's allowance of three drinks a day kept the shakes away, but did nothing for his disposition, and tested the sheriff's patience. To Gideon's relief, Finnie picked up a couple other odd jobs to keep him out of the office and away from temptation.

The two men were killing some time before Finnie left to clean the Last Chance. They were arguing on the proper way to cut catfish for the frying pan. The debate was getting lively when Blackie, from the livery stable, walked into the jail.

"What brings you this way?" Gideon asked, relieved to have a diversion.

"I walk past the alley of the Lucky Horse every morning, and today Cal Simpson and his bartender were putting a rolled up rug into the back of a buckboard. From the way they were carrying it and the way it bowed in the middle, I think it had a body wrapped in it. They never noticed me and I scurried on over here," Blackie said.

The Lucky Horse was the other saloon in Last Stand. The place was rowdy and frequented by a rougher crowd. Gideon disliked the rum-hole and its owner, and only went there when his job demanded it.

Gideon leaned back in his chair. "Do you really think that it was a body?"

"Well, I guess it might not be, but something sure was in that rug," Blackie said.

"I'll walk over there and have a look. You two need to keep this to yourselves," Gideon said.

Finnie jumped up from his seat, tugging his hat down tightly on his head. "I'm not some yappy schoolgirl. You know that I can keep my mouth shut," he said in his thick accent before disappearing out the door.

Gideon found the alley empty except for its usual stack of garbage and the pungent smell of piss. Traces of the wheel prints from the buckboard were clearly visible. After walking back to the jail, he mounted his horse. The track was easy to see to determine which direction they had left, and he caught sight of the wagon a half-mile from town moving at a brisk clip. Deciding to see what their plan was, he hung back out of sight and followed at a leisurely pace.

After about another mile, Gideon found where the wagon had turned down an old logging path. He tied his horse just off the road and pulled his Winchester from its scabbard. Gideon walked down the logging trail until he spied the wagon. As he snuck in close enough to get a view, he saw the two men digging a hole, and was content to let them work up a good sweat.

"Are you men digging for gold? I've been standing here watching and you're sure attacking that ground at a feverish pace," Gideon said with his rifle held leisurely at his waist and pointed in their direction.

The two men froze at the sight of the sheriff. Cal Simpson, the saloon owner, had been hostile towards Gideon since his appointment as sheriff, and glared back as if hoping that looks could kill. "We're out here burying my dog," he said.

"It's a long ways to travel for a dog burial," Gideon said as he walked to the wagon and confiscated their rifle. "Unroll the rug."

Cal continued to stare at Gideon while the bartender gazed at the ground.

"All right, it's not my dog. One of my whores was addicted to morphine, and she took too much and died. We're out here burying her. There's no law against it," Cal said.

"What's her name?" Gideon asked.

"Minnie Ware," Cal answered.

"What's your name?" Gideon asked the bartender.

"Leo Jones," he said, still not looking up from the ground.

"We usually bury our dead at the cemetery. Seems kind of shady to me," Gideon said.

"You know how those church ladies can be. I didn't figure they would want some whore buried in the cemetery," Cal said.

"I never knew you to be so thoughtful, Cal. I might just come up with a whole new opinion of you, but I think that we had better have old Doc determine the cause of death. I wouldn't want anybody to get away with murder."

Cal began to protest, but Gideon cocked his Winchester and motioned with it for them to get back on the wagon. He followed the wagon back to town and then forced the two men to carry the rug into the doctor's office.

The doctor entered the front office after hearing the commotion. Looking surprised at seeing the rug placed on his floor, he asked, "What in darnation is this all about?"

"I'll be back in a minute to help you. I'm going to lock these two up first," Gideon said.

"You have no right to lock us up. What law have we broken? You don't get to make the rules up as you go," Cal protested.

"Cal, you're about to use up all my goodwill. You can either march across the street or I can knock you silly and drag you myself," Gideon threatened.

After giving Gideon one more go to hell stare, Cal headed out the door. Gideon locked the men up and returned to the doctor's office. He and the doctor unrolled the rug and lifted the body onto the table.

Minnie Ware was naked with bruising on her face and body. Gideon had never met the whore and didn't even remember seeing her around town. The girl looked to be about twenty years old, petite, and pretty. Seeing her made him think about his own daughter. Joann wasn't much younger than Minnie was. Since learning that he had a daughter and building a relationship with her, he had become much more aware of the plight of young women. He touched the dead girl's face, wondering what the story was that she ended up a whore.

"Cal said she died of a morphine overdose," Gideon said.

Doc Abram held up one of Minnie's arms and lightly touched a bruise. "That morphine must have made her beat the hell out of herself then. Looks like strangulation to me. You get on out of here and let me do a proper examination. I'll look you up when I know something."

Gideon walked to the Lucky Horse. He found the front door locked so he walked around to the alley and let himself in through the back door. The place looked empty until he tried a side door and found two whores sitting at a table drinking coffee. Gideon didn't know the prostitutes. The two women exchanged glances at seeing the sheriff.

"Ladies, I would like to know what you know about Minnie Ware's death?" Gideon asked.

Each of the whores waited for the other to speak before the one on Gideon's left finally interrupted the silence. "The three of us always have a drink at the end of the evening, and when Minnie didn't come down, I went to her room and found her dead," she said.

"Do either of you know anything about her or from where she came?" Gideon inquired.

"None of us go around and brag about our past life. It's best not to tell where you are from so that nobody goes looking your family up and spreading the news that their daughter is a whore," the one on the left said.

"Who did you last see her with?" Gideon asked.

The question caused both women to look down at the table.

"A lot of the times we are upstairs with a man when one of the other of us gets a customer so that we don't see them. We already talked about it and neither of us knows," the same whore said and started picking at her fingernails.

"What about Cal and Leo?"

"Cal wasn't here last night, and Leo is so scared of women that he don't come within ten feet of us," the other whore said and giggled.

"So the only thing that you two know is that you found Minnie dead. Is that about the size of it?"

The girls looked down again, both nodding their heads. Gideon felt sure that they knew more than they were telling, but saw little chance of getting it out of them.

"Take me to her room," Gideon commanded.

After the whores led Gideon to Minnie's room, he dismissed the women. The room appeared tidy and clean except for the bed, which looked as if there had been a wrestling match in it. A small amount of blood spotted the sheets. He looked on her vanity and in her drawers, but found no sign of morphine or any papers to help figure out her past life. Giving the room one last glance, he decided that Minnie Ware had been murdered and that those that might be of some help had no intention of cooperating.

Gideon walked back to the jail and sat down at his desk. He was still sitting there an hour later, lost in thought on how he was going to solve the murder if no one was going to talk, when Doc Abram entered the office.

"She was definitely strangled," Doc said as a greeting. "Somebody worked her over good and then strangled her. She had had sex, but I'm not sure that means much considering her line of work. Two of her fingernails on her right hand were broken and there was some blood under them. I'd say that the killer is sporting some pretty wicked claw marks. Other than that, she was a healthy young woman."

"The other two whores in the saloon said that they found her last night, but nobody is talking," Gideon said.

"I'd say that's about right. It didn't happen this morning."

"Looking for somebody scratched up is about the only thing that I have to go on. Maybe I should just round me up every man within riding distance and give them a look over because I don't think anybody is going to talk," Gideon said.

"I can't help you there. Good luck. It doesn't look good on the town to have such notoriety," Doc said before taking his leave.

Gideon walked back to the room that housed the prisoners. Cal and Leo sat on their beds, looking up as he entered.

"I can charge both of you with concealing a murder. I want some answers," Gideon said.

Cal stood up and walked to the door. "I wasn't there last night and didn't find out about her until this morning. I don't know nothing."

"So I've been told, but your bartender was there."

Leo stood up and brushed his pants to remove dried dirt from the grave digging. "I don't watch who the girls take upstairs. That stuff is all between Cal and the whores. I stay away from them. I've seen what the French pox can do to a man, and I stay clear of it."

"Who was in the saloon last night?"

"I haven't lived here long enough to know anybody's name. It was just a bunch of cowboys," Leo said.

Gideon unlocked the door to their cell. "I'm going to let you two go for now until I decide if I'm going to charge you with anything. Don't be leaving the area, and if you come by any information that can help find the murderer, you best come see me."

Cal Simpson glared at Gideon as he walked out of the cell.

Gideon asked, "Do you have something that you want to say?"

The two men headed out the door without saying another word. Gideon walked to his desk, finding Finnie sitting in his chair and looking at wanted posters. With the way the day had gone, the sight almost annoyed Gideon, but his friend looked so much better than when he found him that he decided not to complain.

"Are you planning on becoming a bounty hunter?" Gideon asked.

"No, I think I've found my calling as Mary's maid. She sure is a taskmaster, but she is very pleasant about it. She's quite the sweet young lass, but it's a sad day to know that I've slipped from being a respected soldier to cleaning saloons," Finnie said wistfully.

"When we get you weaned off the bottle completely, I will get you a job on a ranch. These ranchers always need good ranch hands. A lot of them tend not to be very reliable."

"Don't be counting your chicks before they hatch. That bottle still has a powerful hold on me. It's only out of respect to you that I haven't slipped. And besides, I can't rope. Fist fighting and shooting a gun are the only things that I was ever much good at," Finnie proclaimed.

"Whatever it takes for you to stay sober, you just keep on doing it. I got a murdered whore over at the other saloon, and I need to work on that. I'll see you later," Gideon said and walked out of the jail.

Gideon walked to the Last Chance. The time was a little after one o'clock, and the lunch crowd had thinned. He seated himself at his usual table, catching Mary's eye as he did so. She wasted no time in walking over to him.

"Do you want a beer and lunch?" Mary asked.

"That sounds good. I also need to talk to you if you can spare the time," Gideon said.

"I can do that. You look troubled. Had a bad day?"

"I thought that you knew me better than I knew myself. You tell me," he joked.

"I'll be right back. Put a smile on that face for me."

Mary returned with a lunch of boiled ham, potato slices, and a beer. She sat down beside him and patted his arm. "What's troubling you?" she asked.

"Before we get to that, how is Finnie working out?" Gideon asked.

"He needs a shot of whiskey when he gets here and a shot on his way out the door, but I certainly get my money's worth on his labor. He's quite the charming Irishman when he's not pining for a drink," Mary said.

"I'm glad to hear that. He was quite the character in his day. I hope we can get him dried out, and he can find himself. Kind of like I did," he said before sipping his beer.

"Have a little faith in him. I think he wants it."

Mary had been a whore in the Last Chance before its saloon owner had been murdered. The deceased proprietor had surprised the whole town by willing the saloon to her. Gideon wondered how she would take the news of one of the town whores being killed.

"Mary, one of the girls at the Lucky Horse was murdered."

"Oh, my God. Do you know who did it?"

Mary's face betrayed how badly the news shook her, and with all that she had been through in her life, it took a lot to do that.

"I don't have a clue and I'm not getting any cooperation from anybody over there. I can't even find out who was over there last night. That's why I need your help. I was hoping that you could get the news out and see if anybody mentions being over there. Maybe somebody saw something."

"You know this hits close to home, and I know full well how some men are. I will do whatever I can for you. You know that," Mary said.

"I know. I hate to keep dragging you into these things. I guess I need to get the city council to start paying you for all the spying that you do for me," Gideon said, trying to lighten the mood.

"I hope that you can get to the bottom of this."

"Me too. I don't have a good feeling about it," he said and took a bite of ham.

Chapter 6

Two days had gone by since the murder of Minnie Ware, and Gideon was no closer to solving the crime than on the day he started. Mary had talked to a couple of cowboys that had been at the Lucky Horse that night, but neither of them had seen anything unusual, and there was no reason to doubt their stories.

Frustrated by his lack of progress, Gideon decided to head home early in the afternoon and take Finnie along to introduce him to Abby. She had been after him to bring Finnie home for dinner, and the meal gave Gideon an excuse to get out of town in hopes that beginning fresh the next day would lead to a break in solving the murder.

Finnie was a reluctant guest and took considerable persuading to talk him into coming. Gideon had expected such a dustup and it was one of the reasons he had postponed the introduction until now. The Irishman groused on the ride to the cabin, nervous that he was no longer fit to meet Abby. Gideon finally reached back into his saddlebag and pulled out his whiskey bottle, letting Finnie take a bigger swig than he would have liked in order to calm him. The drink seemed to help as he quieted down and complimented Gideon on his fine looking cabin and barn.

Gideon's Redbone Coonhound jumped off the porch and started baying at Finnie.

"Good Lord, that dog is loud. I never knew you to coon hunt," Finnie said.

"Nobody can sneak up on us with Red around, but I don't hunt him very much," Gideon said.

"I would think not."

"Looks like Sarah is here," Gideon said at recognizing Ethan's horse and buckboard tied by the barn.

The two men walked into the cabin, finding Sarah sitting at the table beside Abby, patting her arm while the expecting mother sobbed.

Alarmed, Gideon started rapidly firing questions. "What is it? What's wrong? Is it the baby?"

Abby gulped a breath of air before speaking. "I've been thinking about what you said, and maybe you're right that I'm too old to have a baby, and we don't even have a cradle or anything. I gave all Winnie's baby things away. I never thought this would happen again," she said between sobs.

Gideon avoided looking at Sarah, but he could feel her glare boring a hole through him nonetheless. As he concentrated on calming his wife, he said, "Abby, you know how much I want this baby. I was just shocked at the news and did not choose my words well. It has been a year of huge changes for me. And I will make you a cradle. It's not as if the baby is due tomorrow. We have lots of time."

"I'll be in my fifties when this baby moves out," Abby said and put her head down in her arms and began wailing.

Gideon glanced at Finnie. His friend looked as if he might bolt for the door. Gideon thought about following him if he did. In all the years of knowing Abby, he had never seen her cry over much of anything. She could get mad as a wet hen, but seldom shed tears. He worked up the nerve to glance at Sarah.

Sarah smiled at him knowingly. "Gideon, I know you don't have any experience with this, but expecting women can be emotional. I don't know what it is about pregnancy, but it makes our moods go wild. We can be crying one minute and giggling the next. One time when I was pregnant with Benjamin, I cried because Ethan mentioned that his shirt needed a button sewn on it and I thought that he was picking on me. And you might want to choose your words more carefully from here on out," she said.

Abby began composing herself, raising her head up and wiping the tears away. "I'm so sorry for my behavior. Please introduce your friend to us," she said.

"Abby and Sarah, this here is Finnegan Ford. Better known as Finnie," Gideon said.

The two women greeted him, before Finnie said, "I've spent many a night by a campfire with Gideon listening to him talk about your beauty and charm, and I must say that it was no exaggeration."

Abby giggled at the compliment. "Well aren't you sweet. I don't think there's much about me that could be taken for beautiful or charming at this moment. I wish I would have made a better first impression."

"Nonsense. If I were you and knew I'd be birthing a child of Gideon Johann, well I'd cry to," Finnie said as Abby and Sarah let out giggles, enjoying a laugh at Gideon's expense.

"He means well," Abby said to everyone's amusement.

"You have that glow of an expectant mother and I must say that you have done wonders for Gideon's disposition. It's such an improvement that I have to look at him twice some days to make sure it is really him," Finnie said.

Gideon stared at Finnie as if he were looking at him for the first time and decided that the Irish rogue could charm a rattlesnake out of its rattle. He wasn't sure if the behavior of Abby or Finnie was the more shocking of the two. Realizing that the next few months were going to be challenging, Gideon looked at Sarah, hoping to find some comfort, but found her grinning at him mischievously.

Winnie, just back from school, came bursting through the front door and stopped abruptly upon seeing her mother's red eyes and the crowd of people in her house. "Is something wrong?" she asked.

"No. No, everything is fine. Winnie, this here is Mr. Finnie. He is Gideon's friend from the war. He's having supper with us tonight," Abby said.

"You're as pretty as your mother. Nice to meet you," Finnie said.

"Oh my goodness, I love your voice. Pleased to meet you," Winnie replied.

Sarah stood. "I need to get home. Benjamin will be home too and it will be dinnertime before you know it. I've been inviting Zack to eat with us most nights. He's been so down since Joann wrote him that I couldn't help but feel sorry for the poor boy. When I look at his pitiful face, I'd like to get ahold of your other daughter."

"Me too," Gideon remarked before Sarah said her goodbyes.

For the next few hours, Finnie regaled Abby and Winnie with stories of Ireland and the amusing times spent with Gideon in the war. He had Winnie convinced that back in Ireland, he had slain dragons and knew leprechauns. By the time they finished supper, Winnie was enthralled with him. Abby had giggled so much that Gideon wondered if his wife might be ready to trade him in for the Irishman. The war had provided scant opportunity for interaction with women, and Finnie's ease and charm around them was something Gideon would have never guessed in a million years.

After the meal, Finnie said, "I have enjoyed your fine cooking and company, but I believe I best take my leave before night falls. I'm not familiar enough with the lay of the land to navigate the dark."

"Why don't you stay the night? We can ride to town together in the morning," Gideon said.

"A good guest always knows to leave at the highpoint and not wear out his welcome. I'm much obliged for your hospitality, but I best be on my way," Finnie said as he arose from the table.

Gideon walked outside with Finnie, retrieving his whiskey from the saddlebag and handing it to his friend. Finnie took a long pull from the bottle before wiping his mouth on the back of his hand.

"That's a fine woman that you have there. You were a damn fool to wait so many years to come back here," Finnie said.

"I don't think you're in any position to give advice on how to live one's life."

Finnie let out a chuckle and climbed up on his horse. "You have a point there. Thank you for this evening. I really enjoyed myself. I'll see you in the morning," he said before riding away.

Gideon walked Buck to the barn and brushed him down after unsaddling him. As he worked, he kept thinking about Finnie and his surprising ease with women. During the war, Finnie had bragged that his accent could melt the heart of the hardest-hearted woman, but his friends had all accepted the boast as the usual exaggerations that go on around the campfire. Gideon decided that it wasn't only the accent, but his unexpected charm. The thought made him chuckle as he put the horse in his stall and poured oats into the feeder before heading back to the cabin. Abby was lighting the lanterns as he entered.

"Your friend is quite the character. He was nothing like I expected," Abby said.

"He surprised me too."

"Gideon, I'm sorry I made a spectacle of myself, but now that I'm pregnant, I can't help but to worry about it. I know that many women have babies into their forties, but most of them have produced a whole herd of kids along the way. Do you realize that I will have three children that are each spaced nine years apart? That's a long time between babies. What if it is different this time?" she said as she dropped into a chair in the main room.

Gideon sat down in the chair beside Abby. "All this worrying won't change a thing. The only thing that you can control is taking care of yourself. Finnie is not the only person that is showing me a different side. Where is my girl that goes through life meeting any challenge at hand? You're still the girl that held off a gunman that came to kill you and Joann. No matter what, we'll be fine. Let's just be happy that we've been blessed with this baby and take it as it comes. I think you are worrying for nothing."

Tears welled up in her eyes as she smiled at Gideon. "You're right. Getting a second chance with you and having this baby are blessings. I'm looking at it all wrong. I love you," she said before climbing onto his lap.

"Yeah, you better do that now while you have the chance. You might not fit here much longer," Gideon teased.

Abby pinched his nose and said, "There's lots of things around here that might not fit much longer if you keep that up."

Chapter 7

The morning after Finnie's introduction to Abby, Gideon walked into the jailhouse to the sound of a whiskey bottle sent rolling across the floor from opening the door. Finnie snored loudly on the cot that Gideon used when he stayed overnight. An arm and leg hung to the floor. The room reeked with the smell of whiskey and farts. Gideon puffed up his cheeks, blowing the air out slowly as he rubbed the scar on his cheek. He had feared that Finnie would go on a bender, but wasn't expecting it after the success of the previous night. After propping the door open and raising the window for some fresh air, Gideon set about making some coffee.

"Wake up, Finnie," Gideon called out and kicked the cot leg,

Finnie let out a moan. "Sweet Jesus, let me sleep it off."

"Get up. This isn't a hotel," Gideon said, kicking the leg harder.

Finnie sat up, bending over and holding his head in his hands. "Kicking this thing doesn't help my head. It hurts enough without your help."

Gideon handed Finnie a cup of coffee. "Here, drink this. You have to get yourself square and get to work. Mary will not tolerate you showing up late or missing work."

"Mary, Mary. I should have let that constable lock me in jail. It would be better than this. I have you to thank."

"Yeah, locked up with no alcohol at all would've worked out just fine. You would've shaken yourself to death. I don't want to hear it. You were so happy last night. What brought this on?"

Finnie took a sip of coffee, ran his hand through his hair, and looked up at Gideon. "I know that you had your burden that you carried around for years, and don't get me wrong,

I'm glad that you've found happiness, but you're not the only one that dreamed of a pretty wife and a family. I was a Catholic, you know. I always thought I'd have a passel of kids. Riding back from your place last night, well the lonesomeness set in like a lost ghost. So I took comfort in my mistress the bottle."

Gideon rolled his chair around his desk to over in front of Finnie and sat down. "Finnie, look at me. You're even a little younger than I am and there's still time to turn your life around. Just look at mine. A year ago, I wouldn't have thought that the life I have was possible. I was lying in the woods dying and I didn't care. I was ready for it. But with the help of friends and faith, all of us are capable of changing. And I will be here for you, and so will Mary and Abby, but if you don't stop drinking, you're never going to live to see forty. You still can find someone. Heck, as charming as you were last night, it might be my wife," he said and gave Finnie a slap on the knee.

Finnie smiled for the first time that morning before taking a couple of big gulps from his coffee. "You're a good friend, Gideon. I know that you mean well whether I ever come to appreciate it or not. I better get cracking. I fear Mary will serve me my balls on a platter if I show up late."

"Be good, Finnie," Gideon said as the Irishman headed out the door.

Gideon waited until mid-morning before strolling over to the Lucky Horse. He hoped that in interviewing all its employees again, one of them might slip and provide some useful information. Cal and Leo were behind the bar preparing for the day's first customers while the two whores sat at a table playing rummy. The two men were no more friendly or helpful than in Gideon's previous dealings with them. As Gideon walked over and sat down with the whores, he watched them glancing nervously at Cal. The two women would not even speak to him, but sat there as if they were mutes. Disgusted, Gideon walked out of the saloon more convinced than ever that they all knew a lot more than they were telling and that nothing would force them to talk.

With his spirit sagging with each step towards the jail, Gideon began to doubt that he would solve the murder or even learn from where Minnie had come. The idea that someone so close to his own daughter's age was murdered so callously in his town, not only haunted him, but also galled him to no end. He wondered if the underside of Last Stand thought that he was incompetent enough that they could do as they saw fit. Diverting his course, he walked into Doc Abram's office.

The doctor looked up from scrubbing his patient table. "Good morning."

"Doc, I don't think I'm going to solve Minnie's murder. Nobody is talking and I don't have anything else to go on," Gideon said as a way of a greeting.

"You know, I always say that the only true secret a man possesses is the one that he is keeping to himself. I suspect that others know who the murderer is, and it may not be this week, and it may not even be this year, but somebody will eventually let it slip," Doc said and dried his hands on a towel.

"I hope you're right," Gideon said, rubbing his scar. "I don't consider myself a prideful man, but I can't help not to take it personal when somebody thinks he can get away with murder in my town. Doc, you have your finger on the pulse of Last Stand as much as anyone does. Do you believe that the outlaw-minded around here think that they can get away with murder under my watch?"

Doc shuffled over to his desk, sitting down and pulling off his spectacles. "The last few years of Sheriff Fuller's watch, things began to slide around here. He was just plain getting too old for the job. As soon as you took over, the shenanigans came to a stop. People respect you, and some fear you, too. This murder was a crime of passion. There was no thought to it. It was on impulse. Now quit doubting yourself or I'm going to put my foot up your ass. You're doing a fine job."

Gideon grinned at the doctor. "Your bedside manner has gone to hell in your old age, but thank you."

"I wish that is all that had gone to hell," Doc muttered as Gideon left.

As Gideon walked across the street towards the jail, he saw Finnie waving him down from up the street.

"What is it?" Gideon asked as Finnie neared him.

"Mary says that you need to come to the saloon. That's all I know," Finnie said.

"You're looking better than you did this morning," Gideon said as he followed Finnie towards the Last Chance.

"I had to beg and plead for a drink this morning to knock off the ills of last night. I caught holy hell the whole time I was drinking it too, but the whiskey did help. Mary started making faces before I had set two steps into the place. For one so young and pretty, she can be a mean one," Finnie remarked.

Gideon chuckled. "Have her tell you sometime about how that chunk of wood got blown out of the bar."

"I doubt I want to know," Finnie said as they entered the saloon.

Mary was bartending. She walked over to the end of the bar to meet Gideon. "I don't know if you know him or not, but that cowboy sitting at the table over there is Cass Walker. He works for the Kaiser ranch. They sent him to town to get some things. He was at the Lucky Horse that night and just learned about the murder when I told him. You need to talk to him," she said, nodding her head.

"I've seen him around, but never talked to him. I guess I better go introduce myself," Gideon said.

"He's a good one. You can believe what he tells you."

Gideon walked over to the table where the cowboy sat drinking a beer. "Hi, I'm Sheriff Johann. I don't think we've ever met," Gideon said and offered his hand. Cass shook it, and Gideon sat down without invitation. "I understand that you were at the Lucky Horse the night that Minnie was murdered. What can you tell me about it?"

"I was out in the alley taking a piss when that little banker fellow came out the back. He had a white handkerchief against his neck. Of course, the light wasn't good, so that I couldn't see much, but it surprised me. I've never seen him in either saloon before," Cass said.

"You mean Mr. Druthers?" Gideon said in surprise.

"Yeah, I think that's his name. The little, bald, thin-lipped man that runs the bank."

Gideon leaned back in the chair, blowing out a puff of air, and absently rubbing his scar. The news couldn't have been much more surprising. A running joke around town was that the only thing that Druthers needed for happiness was to fondle money. The banker kept to himself, making no friends, and showing no interest in women. "Thank you for your help. If this turns out to be something, you'll have to testify at a trial. I'll get word to you if need be. Thanks, again."

"Whatever you need, Sheriff. Sorry I couldn't have been some help sooner," Cass said as Gideon stood.

Mary still stood at the end of the bar as Gideon walked back.

"Can you believe it?" she asked.

"Well, I certainly wouldn't have guessed it. It should be easy enough to find out if he is scratched," Gideon said.

"I think the idea of him having interest in women is more shocking than him being capable of murder. I hate doing business with him."

"I'm going to go see him now and I'll let you know what I find. I don't know what I would do without you," Gideon said.

Mary grinned at him. "That's the way I like it. Keeps you beholden to me," she teased.

"That I am. And speaking of favors, do you think Finnie is hopeless?"

"That was bound to happen. I've never seen a drunk not slip a time or two before it took. Time will tell, but I think he's worth the effort."

"Me too. I'm going to go look our banker up now. Talk to you later," he said and left.

Upon entering the bank, Gideon only saw the bank teller, Mr. Fredrick. Mr. Druthers office was empty and there were no customers.

"Where's Mr. Druthers?" Gideon asked.

"I guess he went home for lunch. He never tells me anything – just leaves and expects me to be here when he gets back," Mr. Fredrick said.

"Has there been anything unusual about him the last few days?" Gideon inquired.

The teller thought a moment before answering. "Don't say I said so, but he's a strange bird anyway. He has been more fidgety than usual the last couple of days - pacing about the office and such. And he started wearing this silk kerchief around his neck like he's English royalty or something. Claims that Doc removed a boil from his neck, though I'd never noticed one."

"Thank you, you've been very helpful," Gideon said and turned to leave.

"Should I tell him that you wish to see him?"

"I'll find him. If he doesn't return, I suggest that you take charge of the bank," Gideon said to the puzzlement of the teller.

Gideon walked to the home of the banker and knocked on the door. He could hear someone scurrying about before Druthers called out in his monotone delivery, "I'm not feeling well and won't be receiving visitors today."

"Mr. Druthers, this is Sheriff Johann and I need to see you," Gideon demanded.

"Sheriff, I'm ill. You will have to come back another day."

"You can either open the door or I will kick the damn thing in. Now open it," Gideon hollered.

Druthers opened the door just enough to peer out. Gideon popped it with the palms of both of his hand, smacking the banker in the head and sending him reeling backwards.

"What is the meaning of this treatment?" Mr. Druthers yelled, cupping his hand on his forehead.

"Take that kerchief off your neck," Gideon ordered.

"I will not. You have no right to barge in here and start ordering me around," Druthers protested.

Gideon gripped the kerchief so swiftly that Druthers never had a chance to defend himself.

The banker began screaming, "It's knotted. You'll strangle me before it gives way."

"Take it off or I will cut it off, and your throat might get in between my blade and the kerchief."

The banker began unknotting the kerchief as quickly as his shaking fingers would work. Gideon pulled Druthers' collar out of the way, revealing three claw marks on his neck. Two of the scratches were deep and nasty looking.

"You're under arrest for the murder of Minnie Ware," Gideon said, grabbing Druthers by the arm and marching him towards the door.

"Sheriff, you don't want any part of arresting me. This here is way bigger than me. I've got friends that will get me the best lawyers that can be had to get me off. I'm telling you that you want no part of this. You'll be the one that's sorry if you do," Druthers said.

Gideon shoved the banker so hard that Druthers tumbled into the yard. "I suggest that you get up, keep your mouth shut, and march to the jail or I will kick you there like a can," Gideon warned.

Chapter 8

Word of the arrest of the banker moved through the town like a heatwave. Gossips ran into both saloons shouting the news before Gideon had even walked Mr. Druthers all the way to the jail. Patrons emptied from both establishments, as well as neighboring stores, to catch a glimpse of the sheriff and banker advancing down the main street.

Cal Simpson took particular interest in the proceedings from the front of his saloon. He motioned the bartender over to him and told him that he was in charge while he ran an errand. After slipping out the back door, Cal disappeared down a side street.

Gideon locked Mr. Druthers in a cell. "Do you want to tell me what happened?" he asked.

"You can go to hell. I'm not saying a word. You'll be the one that's sorry that this happened before it's over with, and not me. I just might have to call in some notes on all your friends when this is all said and done," Mr. Druthers threatened.

"You're awfully sure of yourself for somebody facing a hanging. It might be a little harder to run your mouth with a noose around your neck," Gideon said and walked out of the room.

Gideon crossed the street toward Doc Abram's office. The doctor had stepped outside to see about the commotion and was now talking with a passerby as Gideon approached.

"I told you that somebody would know something," Doc said.

"So you did. I guess being as old as you are provides great wisdom," Gideon teased.

"Thank goodness that there is some benefit to it."

"I'd like you to come over and look at Druthers to see if you think that it looks like scratch marks that Minnie could have made. That way you can testify to it. Oh, you'd better grab your bag too. His neck looks infected to me."

The doctor grabbed his bag and followed Gideon to the jail. Mr. Druthers sat on his bed, looking amused at seeing the two men.

"I want Doc to have a look at your neck. I don't want you getting sick on my watch," Gideon said.

"You can go to hell all over again. I don't need no doctor," Druthers said.

Gideon unlocked the cell and yanked Mr. Druthers to his feet by his shirt. He then pinned him against the bars and used his free hand to twist Druthers' head to the side, making the banker holler in pain.

"Have yourself a look, Doc," Gideon said.

The doctor pulled the banker's collar flat and peered at his neck. "It looks like scratches from a human to me. Hold him there while I douse it with some iodine," he said before retrieving a bottle and cloth from his bag and treating the wounds.

"Doc, I owe you a beer," Gideon said as he shoved Druthers back down onto the bed.

"If he hangs, we'll call it even," Doc said, staring Druthers in the eye.

After Doc took his leave from the jail, Gideon dropped into the chair behind his desk. A sense of calm washed over him for the first time since the murder. His initial inability to solve the crime had started to erode his confidence at being sheriff, but he now banished the doubts from his mind. He opened his desk drawer, retrieving a bottle of whiskey and a glass. Once he had poured two fingers worth, he took a sip and let it linger in his mouth before swallowing. He leaned back in his chair and gazed at the glass. Sleep would come much easier for him tonight.

Later in the afternoon, Gideon played checkers with Finnie. Gideon had beaten him three games in a row. The Irishman was getting wound up and cussing with each move when Ethan walked into the office.

"I was down at the feed store and heard that you had arrested Mr. Druthers. Sounds like you've had quite the day," Ethan said.

"I never would've guessed him as a murderer in a million years. I was beginning to think that it was going to go unsolved," Gideon said. "By the way, Ethan Oakes this here is Finnegan Ford."

Finnie stood and shook Ethan's hand.

"Gideon used to talk about you during the war, and he didn't exaggerate – you really are a big bastard," Finnie said.

"Finnie," Gideon chided. "Ethan is a preacher now. Watch your mouth."

The two men still had a grasp of each other's hand. Ethan said, "Gideon has talked about you since he has been back, and he didn't exaggerate on you either – you really are a sawed-off little shit."

The two men let out cackles of laughter and pumped each other's hand as if they were old lost friends. Gideon watched on in quiet amusement. The two men were so different, and he had wondered how they would react to each other. If their first meeting was any indication, they were going to get along just fine.

"Sarah said that you were quite the character," Ethan said.

"You have a most charming wife. You two gentlemen sure know how to pick the women," Finnie said.

"Speaking of men and their choice of women, we need to do something to cheer up poor Zack. If that boy gets any lower, his face is going to be dragging the ground like a hound on the trail of a coon," Ethan said.

"You need to send him into town. I promised him that I would teach him how to fight. That poor boy thinks that you're supposed to use your face to stop a punch," Finnie said.

"I tried to talk him into going to the dance this Saturday night, but he doesn't want any part of it. Sarah has been telling him that the girls at church have all been pining for him," Ethan said.

"You two sound like a couple of gossiping old ladies. I still hold out hope that Joann will come to her senses. I've put too much work into training that boy not to get some benefits of a son-in-law taking care of me in old age," Gideon joked.

"I better get home. Maybe we can all go fishing and take him and Benjamin," Ethan said before saying his goodbyes and leaving.

Gideon lost the fourth checker game to Finnie, who beamed with satisfaction at ending with a win.

"I'm going to head home. Can you bring a meal from the hotel over here to Druthers? Just tell them that you need a prisoner meal. They will know what to do and will put it on the account," Gideon said.

"I'll be glad to do it. Anything else that you need?"

"That should do it. Mr. Druthers should be fine after that and not need any attention. I'll see you in the morning."

"Tell that pretty wife of yours that I said hello," Finnie said before Gideon left.

Finnie ate at the hotel and then took a meal to Druthers as Gideon had requested. Afterward, he walked over to the doctor's office and talked Doc into a couple of games of checkers. The Irishman could not quite size-up the doctor and stayed on his best behavior in his presence. At times, the doctor seemed to him to be a good-natured old gent, and at others, a grouchy old man. Finnie wasn't sure if the doctor would find his humor amusing so he concentrated on the game and talked little.

The doctor departed for the Last Chance as it grew dark, and with nothing else to occupy his time, Finnie went to bed. Sometime during the night, the ring of the bell above the door awakened him. As Finnie sat up on the cot, he called out, "Gideon, is that you? What brings you back here in the middle of the night?"

The person walked towards Finnie, not saying a word. Finnie, not alarmed, still assumed it to be Gideon. "Gideon?" he called out once more.

As the person reached him, Finnie saw the blue steel of a revolver reflecting in what little light there was in the room. He tried to dive to the floor, but the barrel of the gun came crashing down on his head and he hit the floor unconscious.

The man turned the wick up in the oil lamp and walked with it into the cell room. Mr. Druthers sat on his bed, awakened from all of the commotion. Upon recognizing the intruder, Druthers stood and walked to the cell door. "I wondered what was going on out there. I thought you'd hire me a good lawyer to get us out of this. Never dreamed you'd break me out of here. Where am I going to go?" Mr. Druthers said before the man shot the banker three times at pointblank.

Chapter 9

Just as the sun popped up over the horizon, Gideon arrived in town. He found Finnie stretched across the floor. Gideon's anger flashed at seeing his friend passed out from booze again. He restrained himself from giving Finnie a good kick.

"Damn it, Finnie, wakeup," Gideon growled.

He leaned over Finnie, ready to give him a hard shake, and saw the blood on his brow and the knot on his head. "Finnie, can you hear me?" Gideon hollered.

Finnie moaned and mumbled, "Oh, my aching head. Did I get kicked by a horse?"

"No, somebody waylaid you good. Let's get you up on the cot," Gideon said as he helped Finnie up with considerable effort.

Unable to remain sitting, Finnie gently lowered himself onto his back. "What happened?"

"I think somebody must have busted Druthers out of here. Let me go see. I'll be right back," Gideon said and ran back to the cell room.

Mr. Druthers lay in a pool of blood so immense that it even gave the war veteran pause. Gideon had viewed many a dead man in his time, but death was something that he never got used to seeing or smelling. From the look of the mess, the banker's heart had surely kept pumping out blood a long time before he had died.

"I'm going to go get Doc," Gideon said as he emerged from the cell room.

He ran to the doctor's office and found the doctor buttoning his shirtsleeve. Doc looked annoyed and ready to pounce on him.

"Doc, somebody waylaid Finnie and killed Druthers. I think Finnie is bad," Gideon said before the doctor had time to fuss.

Without saying a word, Doc Abram grabbed his bag and followed Gideon across the street. The doctor squatted down and touched Finnie's knot, causing the Irishman to wince.

"I'll need that lamp over here for some good light. Roll me your chair over, too," Doc ordered.

"What do you think?" Gideon asked as he rolled the chair over and sat the lamp beside the cot.

"I think that you need to make us some coffee and let me do my job. A man needs some coffee to function when you get to be my age," the doctor groused.

"I can do that," Gideon said, making a hasty retreat.

"Finnie, can you hear me?" Doc asked.

"Of course, I can hear you. They didn't cut off my ears, they hit me upside the head," Finnie replied.

The doctor grabbed the lamp and held it in front of Finnie's face. He looked into Finnie's eyes and made him follow his finger with them. "Do you remember what happened?" Doc asked.

Finnie thought for a moment before answering. "I remember somebody coming in. I thought it was Gideon so I sat up on the cot like a frog on a lily pad and let them knock my head off," Finnie whispered.

By the time Gideon had the coffee made, the doctor had completed his examination. Taking the cup from Gideon, he said, "He has a concussion, but his brain isn't scrambled. That's a good sign. I don't think his skull is cracked and I don't see any other injuries. I'm going to stay here with him for a while in case he starts vomiting or has seizures. We can put a sign on my door so that folks can find me if need be."

Gideon leaned over Finnie and asked, "Did you get a look at them at all?"

"Too dark," Finnie said and closed his eyes.

"Damn, I never saw this coming. I hate that I put poor Finnie in harm's way. Druthers ran his mouth yesterday that he had friends that would get him out of this. I guess they had other ideas. There sure is something not right about all of this. This will teach me to feel good about solving a crime," Gideon lamented.

Doc Abram took a sip of coffee. "Somebody was certainly afraid of what Druthers might say. They shot him, didn't they? Something woke me up last night, but I didn't know what it was. I bet it was the shots."

"Yeah, they shot him all right. There's blood everywhere and I have a hell of a mess to clean up."

"Do you think that it was Cal?" Doc asked.

"I don't have a clue. I wouldn't think that Cal would be the friend with the money for a lawyer that Druthers talked about, and I doubt somebody with money would use Cal to do the murdering. He's not exactly what you would call a hired gun," Gideon said.

"This is going to get interesting."

"Do you think that I'm up to the challenge? I'm good with a gun, but I'm not a detective. I'm afraid I may be over my head."

"You're as capable of a man as I've ever known and there's no point in doubting yourself. It may take a while, but you'll get it figured out," the doctor said.

"I hope you're right," Gideon said, still not feeling convinced.

"I'm starting to like your friend here. We played checkers last night. I have him buffaloed. He doesn't quite know how to take me yet. It's pretty amusing. I see how he is around you and everybody else, but with me, he's all polite and mannerly. I'm going to start having some fun with him. That'll have to wait for now," Doc said as if Finnie could not hear him.

"That it will. I'm going to go get the cabinetmaker and let him get the body out of here and then get to cleaning," Gideon said before taking one last swig of coffee and heading out the door.

After returning and cleaning the cell, Gideon relieved Doc Abram long enough for the doctor to go eat breakfast. Upon the doctor's return, Gideon had all of being in the jail that he could stand and headed out on his usual walk around town. He first stopped in the Last Chance to tell Mary the reason that Finnie would not be in that day. News of the dead Mr. Druthers being carried out of the jail had already spread throughout the town, and Gideon could not walk twenty feet without having to stop to recount what had happened. The walk took twice as long as normal and by the time that he completed his circuit, he gladly returned to the jail.

Finnie sat on the edge of the cot, sipping coffee when Gideon walked into the office. He looked up and smiled. "An Irishman's head is a lot harder than you think," he said.

"You aren't telling me anything that I don't know. Do you want me to go get you some breakfast?" Gideon asked.

"Having you wait on me sounds like a bully idea. It's the least that you can do for causing me to almost get my head caved in."

"Don't make me regret that you survived," Gideon said before heading out to buy Finnie some breakfast.

∞

The sun hung well into the western sky, but Ethan wanted to check on his herds before calling it quits and heading home. His cattle had been restless for a couple of days and he intended to make sure that they had settled for the evening. He sent Zack to check the herd to the north while he headed to the western herd with the understanding that they would meet at the pond when finished to see if the beaver were building dams again.

Ethan rode across the pasture towards the cattle and saw smoke just into the woods to the side. He put his horse into trot towards it and came upon four men sitting around a campfire cooking a rabbit.

"Hello, there," Ethan called out as he climbed down from his horse. "I saw your smoke and wanted to make sure that I didn't have a brush fire on my property."

One of the men stood up and walked towards Ethan. "I'm sorry. We figured we were on free range. We're just passing through," he said.

"You're fine as long as it's just for the night. Please make sure your fire is out when you leave."

"Oh, we will. Don't worry about that," the man said. "That's a fine looking piebald you got there. Is that an Indian pony?"

"Yeah, I traded for him a few years back. He took some work to get him trained to be a cattle horse, but he's the surest footed animal that I've ever owned," Ethan said proudly.

"He's the biggest Indian pony that I've ever seen. Works out good for a big boy like you," the man said.

"Yeah, you could say that," Ethan said and chuckled.

"Would you be interested in selling him?"

"No. I got too much time invested in Pie to ever make it worth my while for that."

"I'd sure like to buy him."

"I just can't sell," Ethan said.

"Then I'll just take him," the man said, drawing his gun and firing.

Ethan did not have time even to react. The bullet caught him in the chest, sending him reeling backwards before falling to the ground.

"Why in the hell did you do that?" another man hollered.

"I wanted that horse and the damn fool wasn't smart enough to sell it," the shooter said.

"Now we got to skedaddle. The rabbit ain't even cooked," the other man bemoaned.

"Well let's saddle up and ride then," the shooter said.

Ethan couldn't get up from the ground. He listened helplessly as the men rode away. He was having a hard time catching his breath and figured he was dying. The idea of dying didn't scare him, but the thought of never seeing Sarah or Benjamin again brought tears to his eyes. He also worried about how Sarah would manage the ranch without him before taking comfort in knowing that Gideon and Zack would take care of her. Closing his eyes, he began to relax, ready for whatever came.

Zack made it back to the pond and was surprised not to see Ethan already there. Ethan had a shorter trip and should have beaten him back. Deciding that his boss may have had trouble with the cattle, he started riding in that direction. As he caught sight of the herd, he noticed the smoke off to the side. He put his horse into a lope and rode towards it. Ethan's blue shirt caught Zack's eye. He galloped to Ethan and jumped off his horse before the animal had stopped.

"Ethan," Zack cried out upon seeing the blood.

Ethan opened his eyes as Zack squatted over him.

"I don't think I'm going to make it," Ethan whispered before gasping for air. "Tell Sarah and Benjamin that I love them."

"Don't say that. I can't lose you like I did my pa. We all count on you, Ethan. You got to hold on while I get help."

Ethan nodded at him.

The chest wound made an awful sucking sound.

"Ethan, keep your hand over the wound and try to seal it. That noise it's making can't be good," Zack said.

Zack began pacing while slapping his hands onto the top of his hat. He couldn't decide whether to go get Sarah so Ethan wouldn't be alone or head straight for the doctor. Deciding that time was of the essence, he headed straight south for town.

By the time Zack made it into town, his horse was spent and in full lather. He pulled up in front of the doctor's office, saw the sign on the door, and ran across the street. Bolting through the door, he caused all three men inside to jump.

"Damn, Zack, you about gave us heart failure," Gideon said.

"Somebody's shot Ethan and he's bad. He's having a hard time breathing and his chest wound is making sucking sounds," Zack blurted out.

"Oh, for Christ's sake," Doc said, rising to his feet.

"Is anybody with him?" Gideon asked.

"No, I didn't think that there was time to get Sarah and then come for you."

"That was good thinking. You go ride to Sarah and bring the buckboard. Doc and I will go to Ethan. Where is he?" Gideon asked.

"He's over in the pasture west of the cabin, in the tree line on the west side. My horse is spent."

Doc snatched up his bag. "Gideon, go to Blackie to see if you can get me a gentle riding horse and one for Zack. I need to go to the office and get some things."

"Can you ride?" Gideon asked.

"I'll have to. We don't have time to take the buggy," Doc said.

Turning to Finnie, Gideon said, "You stay here and get to feeling better. I may need you afterward."

Minutes later, Gideon returned with two saddled horses. He tied Doc's bag to the frog on the smaller horse. The three men headed north in a lope. Doc gripped the saddle horn for all that he was worth, unsure that he could still balance himself in the saddle. They rode for four miles before Zack cut towards the northeast, already dreading telling Sarah the news about Ethan. Gideon and Doc rode another three miles, passing by the herd as the cattle raised their heads, looking at all the commotion. They spotted Ethan at the same time and veered his direction.

Gideon dismounted and ran to Ethan before the doctor even attempted to leave the saddle. Doc Abram had pain shooting from his legs all the way to his shoulders. He felt pretty sure that he had no hide left on his ass.

"Damn it, Gideon, help me down. I'm not sure that I can even walk," the doctor barked.

Ethan opened his eyes at the sound of the doctor's voice and saw Gideon kneeling over him.

"I'll be right back," Gideon said.

Gideon's legs felt as limp as noodles as he walked towards the doctor, relieved to see Ethan still alive. "I'll get your bag.

Go on and get over there," he said as he helped Doc off the horse.

"Ethan, I'm here for you. Just hold on," Doc said.

"I'm strangling," Ethan gasped.

"I'm going to take care of you. You have to stay with me until I get you fixed. Now move your hand away from the wound," Doc said as he moved Ethan's hand out of the way and ripped his shirt open, sending buttons flying.

Gideon walked up with the bag and handed it to the doctor. Doc examined the hole in the shirt before deciding that the bullet had punctured the fabric without carrying any material into Ethan. Infection from the cloth would be one less thing that would have to be worried about. He took a bottle of iodine from his bag, poured it onto a cloth, and wiped around and into the edges of the wound causing Ethan to grimace in pain.

Doc said, "I know this hurts, but I can't do anything for the pain on account of your breathing difficulties. I'm going to have to sew you up now."

Ethan nodded his head in understanding.

"Gideon, get above his head and hold his shoulders still if need be," Doc said as he pulled a spool of metal suture from the bag.

"Aren't you going to take out the bullet?" Gideon asked.

"That bullet is the least of my worries. He'll be fine with it left in there. I have to get the wound sealed or the lungs will collapse and he will suffocate," the doctor said.

"Have you ever had to do this?" Gideon asked.

"Once and it worked. Some doctor figured it out during the war. I have to get the wound airtight so that it quits drawing air through it," Doc replied.

The doctor threaded his needle and started sewing the bullet wound shut. Ethan labored to breathe, but he didn't move as the doctor sewed on him. The only sign of the pain that he was enduring was a clenched jaw and eyes squeezed shut.

As Doc tied off the suture, he said, "The worst of it is over."

Doc proceeded to cut squares of linen that he placed on the wound and poured a few drops of collodion onto it. He repeated the process until satisfied that he had added enough layers to seal the wound airtight.

"Ethan, it will take a while for your breathing to ease, but it shouldn't get any worse. Try to relax. Just stay still while the bandage dries," Doc said.

Gideon moved to Ethan's side and held his hand. "Can you tell me what happened?" he asked.

"Found four men camping. Wanted to buy Pie. Shot me when I wouldn't sell," Ethan managed to say.

"You get well. We still have too much making up for lost time for you to go die on me, you hear?" Gideon said.

Ethan nodded his head.

The sun was setting as Zack, Sarah, and Benjamin arrived with the buckboard wagon. Sarah and Benjamin scampered down from the wagon and ran to Ethan as Gideon and Doc made way for them.

"Oh my God, Ethan. What have they done to you?" Sarah cried out.

Ethan raised his arm towards her and she grasped it. "I'll be fine," he whispered.

"Pa," Benjamin said and began crying.

Ethan patted the boy's leg. "You'll have to nurse me like you did Gideon."

Doc interrupted them. "We need to get him back to your cabin. It'll be dark soon."

Sarah had thrown every blanket and quilt that she could find into the back of the wagon and now spread them. With the help of Gideon and Zack, Ethan stumbled to the wagon.

Doc hobbled to the buckboard. "I'm riding back here with Ethan. I couldn't stand to put my derrière in the saddle if my life depended on it."

The ride to the cabin was through pasture for the most part and the only jarring occurred as they crossed the creek.

Sarah and Benjamin sat on one side of Ethan, both holding his arm, and the doctor sat on the other. Ethan remained silent and kept his eyes closed. His labored breathing and an occasional grimace from a bump were his only movements. They reached the cabin, and Gideon and Zack managed to get Ethan to bed. The trip had drained the last of Ethan's strength and he no longer responded to conversation. Doc Abram examined the bandage, satisfied that it held.

"Benjamin, you sit here with your pa while I go talk with Doc Abram," Sarah said before walking out of the bedroom with Gideon and Doc in tow.

"Doc, I want to know how bad it is and don't you dare sugarcoat it. I need the truth," Sarah said.

"Sarah, I would never do that to you. He was shot in the lung and his chest filled with air. He almost suffocated. His breathing should get better, but it is a very serious wound," Doc said.

"What are the odds he recovers?" she asked.

Doc thought for a moment, rubbing his chin the whole time. "I'd say a little better than even. He's young and strong, but it will be a long haul. The lung will have to heal and there's always the worry of infection, but I'd bet on Ethan if I were betting."

Sarah put her hands to her mouth and began crying. Her body shook like a willow branch before she leaned into Gideon. He wrapped his arms around her and patted her back.

"You got me through this and we'll get Ethan through it," Gideon soothed.

Her voice sounded muffled from her mouth being pressed into her hands and against Gideon's shoulder. "Do you know what happened?"

"He told me that four men were camping on your land and they wanted to buy Pie. When he wouldn't sell, they shot him," Gideon said.

"They tried to kill him over a horse," she said and started crying harder.

"Sarah, I will find them if I have to go to Hell and back. I promise you that," Gideon said.

"I need to be with him," Sarah said and made a beeline for the bedroom.

Gideon looked at Doc. "This here has been one bad day," he said.

"That it has and I expect that it will be a bad night. I'm going to stay here with Ethan. I think that I'm getting too old for all this," Doc said as Zack walked over to join them.

"Solving Druthers' murder is going to have to wait. Do you think Finnie can ride with me tomorrow to find these characters?" Gideon asked.

"That's hard to say. He may be back to his usual self, and then again, he may feel worse. You'll just have to see how he feels," Doc said.

"Zack, you'll have to stay here and run the ranch. You can take Doc back to town on the buckboard when he's ready and retrieve your horse. I'll take the two that we borrowed back to town tonight. You'll be fine. And thank you for what you did. You saved his life," Gideon said and held out his hand to shake.

"I won't let you down," Zack said as they shook hands.

Gideon walked back to the bedroom. "Ethan, I'm going to leave now. Tomorrow I'm going to go find the men that did this. You better be sitting up in bed when I get back," he said and squeezed Ethan's hand. Ethan showed no sign of hearing him.

Chapter 10

The smell of bacon cooking awoke Gideon before dawn. Walking from the bedroom into the kitchen, he found Abby preparing breakfast by lamplight. She still wore her nightgown, and as she turned to greet him, her baby-bump was the first thing that he noticed. He found the bump more endearing every day and smiled.

"What are you doing up so early?" he asked.

"I knew that you would head out at first light and I wanted to fix you a good breakfast. I'm going to check on Sarah and Ethan first thing after I see Winnie off to school," Abby said and kissed him.

"You're going to spoil me to the point that I never want to leave this house," Gideon said, wrapping his arms around Abby.

"If you do that, we might end up with so many children that we couldn't feed them all," she teased.

"Yeah, especially now that I know that you have lots of childbearing years left," he chided.

Growing serious, Abby said, "Do you think Ethan made it through the night?"

"I never would've left him if I had thought he wouldn't. I hope that he will be a little better this morning," Gideon said before taking a seat at the table.

As they were eating breakfast, Abby said, "What are you going to do if Finnie can't ride with you? It seems to me that four men are too many to go after by yourself."

"I'm pretty sure that he will go. As fired up as he was when I brought the horses back to town last night, I think he would've headed out then if we could have tracked them."

"I hope you are right."

"I'm going to take the sorrel that we bought and the saddle that came with him. Finnie's horse would never hold up with hard riding and he doesn't own a saddle," he said.

"Would you saddle Snuggles for me while you are out there?" Abby asked.

"Don't you think that you need to take the wagon?"

"Snuggles is a much softer ride for the baby than that bouncy buckboard. I have no plans to fall off him."

Gideon grinned at her. Abby's belief in her riding abilities was legendary, and he had to admit that she rode as well as anybody that he knew. "Yes, ma'am," he said. "I better get ready. There's a lot to get done."

By the time that Gideon dressed and had the horses saddled, Abby was clothed and Winnie was eating breakfast. He walked over to the child, leaned over, and kissed her on top of the head. He had never dared to show that much affection toward her. "Be good for your momma."

"You better be careful while you are gone," Winnie said and stood up in the chair to kiss his cheek.

Abby watched the proceedings with amusement. There had been times when she thought that Gideon would never win Winnie over, and he might not have, if Joann hadn't convinced her sister to be nice to him for her sake.

"I might get jealous if you two get any closer," Abby said.

Gideon kissed his wife. "After I go to town, I'm going to stop in to check on Ethan. I'll see you over there."

The sun had risen halfway above the horizon by the time Gideon made it to town. He found Finnie sitting in his chair, clicking his fingernails on the desk.

"It's about time you showed up," Finnie said.

"I take it that you are capable of riding then. You better be sure because we have a lot of lost time to make up," Gideon said.

"I just have a wee bit of a headache. That's all. Nothing compared to my hangover the other day."

"Did you talk to Mary last night about coming with me?"

"I did. She said to go get the bastards," Finnie said with a smile.

"Go put that holster on over there and pick a rifle off the rack. I've sighted them all in with a fine bead," Gideon said before pulling a deputy badge out of the drawer after Finnie moved out of the way.

"It's been a long time since I wore a gun. I hope I can still shoot," Finnie said as he strapped on the holster.

"You better. Just so you know, I don't plan on bringing these men back."

"Me either," Finnie said.

"I have our saddlebags packed with supplies. Grab a couple boxes of cartridges for each of us and let's ride."

The two men rode towards Ethan's cabin. Finnie had never rode this direction and the land impressed him with its lush grasslands surrounded by woods with majestic mountains in the background. Fresh air cleared the remnants of his headache and invigorated him to the point of feeling stronger than he had in years. Doc and Zack were sitting on the porch as they arrived.

"How is he doing?" Gideon asked as he climbed down from Buck.

Doc stood up and walked stiffly to the steps to meet them. "He's awake and breathing better. Not as well as I would have hoped, but you take what you can get."

"Have his chances worsened?" Gideon asked.

"Goodness, no. I feel better about him than I did last night, but I wanted more. Just greedy, I guess. Go see for yourself."

"You look like that horse ride about did you in."

"It did. I'm as stiff as a board and I'm afraid to look at my ass to see if there is any hide left on it," Doc said.

"I'm going to go see Ethan and try to get that image out of my mind," Gideon said.

Finnie stayed outside with the other two men as Gideon entered the cabin and walked straight to the bedroom where he found Sarah and Abby sitting on either side of Ethan. Abby held a glass of milk and Sarah fed him broth.

"How is our patient this morning?" Gideon asked.

"I'm surely better than yesterday. I thought I was going to suffocate," Ethan whispered, pausing between words to take breaths.

"I suspect by the time that I return with Pie that your nurses here will be so sick of you that they'll stick you on top of that horse."

"He won't be the first patient around here that I got sick of eventually," Sarah teased.

"I bet not. I imagine our preacher here will be a much better patient than I was," Gideon said.

"Sorry for the trouble," Ethan said.

"You certainly didn't ask to get robbed or shot. Had you ever seen the men before?"

Ethan shook his head. "They weren't a rough looking bunch. Caught me off guard."

"Finnie and I will find them. I expect you to be up and around when I get back. You get well," Gideon said before leaning over and squeezing Ethan's hand.

Gideon then turned towards his wife and gave her a kiss.

"I'll be back as soon as I can. Don't do anything that you shouldn't. If you need help, Zack will just have to help you out, too."

Abby smiled at him. "Well, aren't you the overprotective father to be these days?"

"I'm overprotective about lots of things these days. I'll see you all when I get back," Gideon said before leaving.

Out on the porch, Gideon turned to Zack and said, "I know that Sarah is in good hands with you. I'd appreciate it if you could check in on Abby when you have the chance. I'm counting on you." He then shook the young man's hand.

"Don't get any meaner, you old codger," Gideon said to Doc and slapped his arm.

Gideon and Finnie rode to the spot of Ethan's shooting. The tracks of the men were easy to find. They had taken off in a gallop and the horses had kicked up chunks of grass as they ran. The tracks led in a southeasterly direction and they followed them for over a mile before seeing where the riders had reined their horses down to a walk.

"Looks like their horses got winded. Where do you think they are headed?" Finnie asked.

"I'm guessing that they decided that the best thing to do was to get out of Colorado. New Mexico is the shortest route for that. If they think that is going to stop me they are sadly mistaken," Gideon said and ribbed Buck to speed up the pace.

Little tracking skill was required to follow the trail. The outlaws were still riding to the southeast several miles past Last Stand. The trail was the same that Gideon had used to return to Last Stand the previous year. Plenty of spring rain had made the valleys rich in lush green grass. They rode through woods of aspen, pine, and Gambel oak at various elevations on the trail. The highest mountains surrounding the area were mostly void of vegetation and strutted out of the earth in their gray glory while the lower peaks tended to be pine covered like an old man with wisps of hair.

After three hours of riding, they found the spot where the men had camped for the night. Feeling relieved, Gideon said, "They're not as far ahead of us as I feared they would be. I thought maybe they'd ride most of the night."

"I have a hunch that we're not dealing with seasoned outlaws. They don't seem very concerned with covering a lot of ground," Finnie said.

"Well, let's go find out."

∞

Abby stayed with Sarah all morning and made lunch for everybody. After the meal, she noticed Sarah slip out the back door and followed her once she cleared the table. She found her crying on a bench out in the orchard.

"Do you want to be alone?" Abby asked.

"No, come sit beside me," Sarah said and patted the bench.

"I think Ethan is going to be fine. He's a strong man," Abby said to reassure her friend.

"I know. Sometimes I just get overwhelmed with how hard life is out here. Last year it was Gideon getting shot, then Benjamin kidnapped, and now Ethan is shot. Do you ever wonder what it would be like to live somewhere more civilized? I love it here, but sometimes it's just too much."

"I've never thought about living anywhere else. This is the only place that I've ever known, but you are right that it is a hard life at times. I'm sure that living back east or in Denver has its dangers too. Life is hard wherever you live, I think. Maybe that's what it takes to make the good times sweeter," Abby said.

Sarah let out a little laugh. "You and I should have some real sweet times ahead. I'm so happy about the baby for both of you. Who would have ever seen that coming a year ago?"

Abby giggled. "Not me. That first time that I saw Gideon here after he woke up, I could have added a few more bullet holes to him," she said, thinking back to her and Gideon's first encounter in eighteen years.

"That's one thing that I take some pride in. Once I got to know Gideon, I never gave up on him no matter what he said or did. I could always see the goodness wanting to break through," Sarah said.

"He thinks the world of you. You can keep him on his toes better than I can."

"A man can take a little chewing on from a sister better than he can a wife, especially someone like Gideon. And speaking of men, I better go check on mine," Sarah said.

"I'm going to head home shortly."

They walked back to the cabin and Abby told Ethan goodbye and that she would see him tomorrow.

Doc said, "Not so fast there, young lady. I want to have a talk with you before you leave. Let's head to Benjamin's room."

After following the doctor to the room across the hall, Abby asked, "What is it, Doc?"

"This is the first time that I've had the chance to see you since I learned that you are with child. I want to know how you feel," Doc said.

"Oh, I feel fine. I'm having more pains than I did with the other two, but nothing bad."

"Having babies is one of those things that doesn't necessarily get better with practice. I know that you don't want to hear this, but you're not in your twenties any longer. You need to make sure that you get plenty of rest. You don't need to be riding a horse much longer either."

"Doc, you sure know how to flatter a girl," Abby chided. "First Gideon thought that I was too old to get pregnant and now you act as if I'm too old to deliver a baby. I feel fine and I will be careful. You must know how much I want this baby."

"We all want you to have the baby. It's my job to make sure that it happens. Have you had any bleeding?" Doc asked.

"No, none. I'm about four months along, I think. I should have figured it out sooner, but I've never been real regular."

"All right, but you make sure that you see me if anything changes," the doctor said before they left the room.

Abby said her goodbyes and left. After she departed, Doc took out his stethoscope to check Ethan's heart and lungs once again. He worked methodically, asking Ethan to take as deep of breaths as he could as he moved the stethoscope around his chest.

"Your lungs sound much better. Better than this morning. I think you're making dandy progress. Keep this up and you'll be up and around in no time," Doc said as he carefully placed the instrument back into his case.

"Thank you, Doc. I don't think that I would be here without you," Ethan said.

"I'm just glad we got to you in time. You had me scared. I'm going to have Zack take me back to town and I'll be back to check on you tomorrow."

The doctor walked stiffly out the door and could barely climb into the wagon to join Zack. "Damn, it's hell getting old," he said.

∞

Gideon and Finnie entered a stream so clear and blue that they could see trout swimming in it. They stopped midstream to let the horses drink. "It would be a sight more enjoyable to be fishing today," Finnie said to break the monotony.

"Yes, it would, if only people could behave themselves. Makes you wonder why people chose the path they take," Gideon replied.

"I'm afraid that is a conversation that is a little too deep for a simple mind like mine."

"Well, how about we talk about why you chose the path that you took then."

"Gideon, you're as sly of a devil as I've ever seen, but don't think that I didn't see that coming. My momma didn't raise no fool."

"So are you going to tell me or not?" Gideon asked.

"I was doing some work for the Indian commissioner at the Southern Ute Reservation, and I met this little Ute squaw. When the job played out, I decided to head to Animas City to make my fortune and I talked her into going with me. Everything went fine at first and then Little Bird started missing her people and wanted to go home. There was nothing for me at the reservation, so I let her go. I missed her a heap more than I was expecting and the bottle became my new mistress. I never told that girl that I loved her, but I did. I guess I never wanted to admit it. That's about the long and short of it," Finnie said.

"I'm sorry to hear that. You could've gone back with her."

"She needed to be with her people, and there was no place for me back there. It just wasn't meant to be. Enough about me. We have some men to track," Finnie said and nudged his horse into walking.

They pushed their horses as hard as they dared for the rest of the day before making camp that night. Gideon managed to shoot a couple of rabbits and they dined on them and hardtack. Finnie had his best day of staying away from the whiskey, only needing it once as they rode and again after supper. Both of them were tired from the hard day of riding and bedded down early. They reminisced about their days of riding together in the war before drifting off to sleep.

Chapter 11

Finnie arose before dawn. He had always been an early riser when sleeping outdoors. After throwing some wood onto the fire, he had the flame hot and the coffee on before Gideon sat up in his bed.

"You're up early," Gideon said.

"Don't you remember? I was always the first to rise. Do you think we gained on them yesterday?" Finnie asked.

"I figure they had a three hour jump on us from the night that they shot Ethan. Yesterday, we didn't get as early of a start as I would've liked. We lost a lot of time when I picked you up and we checked on Ethan, but we still covered a lot of territory. So I'm guessing that we're two to four hours behind them depending on how long they rode yesterday. We can't be far from New Mexico," Gideon said.

"The sooner we find them the better. I haven't ridden this hard in years and I can feel it in every bone in my body. That cot of yours sleeps pretty good."

By the time the men finished a breakfast of hardtack and jerky, the sky to the east began to lighten. As they saddled the horses, Gideon said, "I'm not worried about checking for tracks very often. Unless they make a turn, they're headed to Santa Fe."

Gideon and Finnie rode hard all morning, only checking for tracks about every hour. The men they pursued were staying on the main trail headed toward Santa Fe. The vegetation grew sparse as the trail wound south through the mountains. Around noon, they came upon a small lake. A tepee sat beside it, billowing smoke and steam. Nearby, a saddle horse grazed.

Gideon pulled Buck up and studied the horse and tepee. "Unless I'm badly mistaken, that there is Farting Jack Dolan," he said.

Chuckling, Finnie said, "Pray tell, who might that be?"

"I was a deputy in northern Colorado and the sheriff would hire him to track for us. He's an old mountain man, best tracker I've ever known, and he taught me the finer skills of tracking," Gideon said.

"I guess the name says the rest."

"Anybody home?" Gideon called out as they rode up to the tepee.

"For Christ's sake, I might as well live in the son of a bitching hell of a city the way people are showing up around here today. Don't people know that anybody that lives in a tepee in the middle of the wilderness sure as hell don't like company," a voice swore from inside the tepee before a skinny man emerged, naked from head to toe and drenched in sweat. His pale skin could have passed him off for an albino except for the ruddy color of his hands and face. His hair and beard were steel-gray and hung wildly to his shoulders and chest.

"Farting Jack, it's been awhile," Gideon said as he and Finnie climbed down from their horses.

"Gideon. Well, I'll be damned," Farting Jack said and shook Gideon's hand. He remained standing in all his naked glory as if it were the most normal thing to do in all the world.

Gideon introduced Finnie before continuing the conversation. "How in the world did you end up clear down here? It's a long ways from Boulder."

"I got the trapping fever again and I heard that the beaver were still plentiful down here. It weren't true though. I see that you have worked your way up to a sheriff," Jack said before expelling an explosion of gas. "Whoa, that was a good one."

The two men were forced to retreat a couple of steps before continuing the conversation. "Yeah, I'm sheriff of Last Stand. That's what brings me down here. Have you seen four men ride by here? They should've had a big piebald with them," Gideon said.

Jack studied the sun. "They came by here about two hours ago. Wanted to know how far it was to Santa Fe. Told them I didn't have a clue."

"Did they seem to be in a hurry?" Gideon asked.

"I don't reckon so. Their horses weren't lathered or winded, and they were in a fine mood and took considerable pleasure in my sweat-bath."

"They took considerable pleasure in shooting a friend of mine, too. They nearly killed him and I take it a little personally. It's good to see you again, Jack, but I have to go catch those men," Gideon said.

"They weren't much of a mean looking bunch. Nothing compared to some of the men that we tracked down back in the day. You shouldn't have much trouble with them. Good seeing you again, Gideon," Jack said before returning to his tepee and ripping another thunderous fart as he bent over to go through the opening.

As they climbed into the saddle, Finnie said, "I bet he kept your posse jumping on a still night around the campfire."

"He could scatter a crowd right smartly, that's for sure. I bet we have us some outlaws tracked down before the sun has set if we move quickly," Gideon said as he wheeled Buck around.

They pushed on well into New Mexico. The land grew harsher the farther they rode until there was not much to see but rock and brush. Stopping at midafternoon, they rested the horses and dined on another meal of hardtack and jerky. Finnie had already taken two pulls from the bottle that day and needed another. All the riding had worn him down and made him ill tempered.

"You need to make that bottle last," Gideon reminded him.

"Well if you didn't have me out here in the middle of nowhere, I wouldn't be needing it so much, now would I? This is a hell of a way to make a living," Finnie complained.

"This has nothing to do with my job. This is for Ethan. I'd do the same for you."

Finnie corked the bottled back and wiped his mouth with the back of his hand. "I know you would. I've gotten soft and I need this riding to harden me. It's a hell of a thing to know that you're not the man that you used to be."

"Just be thankful that it's not too late. You're going to get there. It just takes time," Gideon said.

"Do you really believe that? There are days when I have my doubts," Finnie admitted.

"I do. Now let's ride. We'll be getting into pines before long. I expect that we'll catch them in there somewhere."

After riding a few more miles, the land greened up with good grass and thickets of pine. The sun hung low in the west as they came upon some horse dung with the shiny still not dried off it.

Gideon reined his horse to a stop at a little creek running down from the mountains. "Let's just hold up here and wait until they make camp. I don't want to take a chance that they see us and start running. We'd have a hard time catching all of them if they scattered. After it gets dark, we'll charge them just like we did in the old days. I was going to take them alive and hang the sons of bitches, but I don't think there is a suitable tree in miles. The two of us should be no match for them."

"I hope that I can still aim a pistol. It's been a long time," Finnie said.

"You'll be fine. It'll be hard to miss at pointblank. They won't know what hit them."

"What if they surrender?"

"I'm not going to shoot somebody with their hands in the air, but I doubt that'll be their first inclination. I hope not anyway," Gideon said.

After loosening the cinches on the saddles, Gideon and Finnie tied the horses at the creek before walking under the pines and making pallets out of the pine needles. The sun had set enough that the temperature began to drop from the high of the day and made for good sleeping weather. Both men were dozing in a matter of minutes and slept until Gideon awoke at dusk.

Rousing Finnie from his slumber, Gideon said, "Let's go get done what we came to do."

After riding for more than an hour, night settled in and cloud cover made a game of peek-a-boo with the moon and stars. Gideon began to wonder if he had made a mistake in stopping. Serious doubts were starting to creep into his mind as they rode on before Finnie spotted light ahead off to the right. As they rode farther along the trail, they could see a roaring campfire through the pines. They continued on until they reached the spot where the men had left the trail. The four men were camped in a clearing about thirty yards wide and fifty yards from where Gideon and Finnie sat on their horses watching them. The men were preoccupied with eating their meal and continually scooting farther away from the heat of the raging fire.

"That's them," Gideon whispered. "I can see Pie plain as day in that string of horses. Let's ease forward until we are about thirty yards out and then swoop in on them. I'll take the two on the left and you take the ones on the right."

Gideon and Finnie drew their revolvers and cocked them.

"I hope I'm ready for this," Finnie said.

"You will be. We've charged into battle enough that it all comes back. Let's give that yell the Rebs used to do to us. It used to scare the shit out of me and I'm fearless," Gideon joked.

The crackling fire and the men's conversation allowed Gideon and Finnie to ride forward undetected. Gideon gave Finnie a nod and they both spurred their horses and let out a howl that made for a poor imitation of the battle cry. The four men all jumped up from their seats, letting tin plates clatter to the ground. They stood momentarily frozen in place until one of them yelled, "Draw your damn guns and shoot or we're all dead."

Gideon aimed Buck straight at the man farthest to his left. The outlaw fumbled to pull his pistol from his belt and became frantic as the horse raced in on him. Pulling hard on the reins, Gideon slowed the horse just as it crashed into the man, sending him somersaulting backwards. The outlaw to Gideon's right held his revolver with both hands and took aim as if he were targeting a walnut instead of a human body six feet away. He remained gazing down his barrel as Gideon shot him in the forehead. The first man had managed to get into a sitting position and attempted to extricate his pistol when Gideon's bullet knocked him backwards.

Finnie's two men were standing beside each other with their pistols drawn. They realized that they were about to be trampled. The one to Finnie's left dove out of way, while the one on the right stepped to the side. Finnie was upon the man by the time the Irishman could take aim at the outlaw, and his barrel reached no more than a foot from his quarry's face as he fired. The shot sent a shower of blood and tissue into the air. Wheeling his horse hard to the left, Finnie saw the flash of fire from the outlaw's gun and let out a yelp of pain before he and the outlaw exchanged two volleys at each other. Both of Finnie's shots found the chest of the man and he fell over dead.

The sounds of crackling fire and horse nickering replaced the gunfire noise. Bodies were strewn about in grotesque positions. Finnie had his left hand under his coat, feeling around on his right side for a wound.

"Did they get you?" Gideon hollered.

"I got a bullet hole through my coat, but I guess the lead just burned me. It stung like hell though. What about you?" Finnie said as he holstered his revolver.

"I'm fine."

The man that had never managed to draw his gun, called out for help. The force of the collision with Buck had knocked him back into the shadows and Gideon walked towards him with his gun still drawn.

"I can't feel my arms or legs," the wounded man managed to say as Finnie joined Gideon at the outlaw's side.

"Let's carry him to the fire so we can see better," Gideon said.

The man screamed as they lifted him and again when they laid him on the ground. From the firelight, Gideon realized that the outlaw was no more than a boy of probably seventeen. The bullet had hit him dead center in the upper chest.

"Am I dying?" the boy asked.

"I'm afraid that you are. Is there anything that I can do for you?" Gideon asked.

"We weren't outlaws until my brother shot that man for the horse. I don't know what possessed him to do that. I've never stolen anything except for a little candy when I was a kid. We were looking for work up until then," the boy whispered between gasps for breath.

"What's your name, son?" Finnie asked.

"It don't matter. I don't want Momma to know how it ended anyway," he said and closed his eyes.

The boy's breathing continued for another five minutes, growing shallower until it stopped all together.

"Do you think that we did wrong?" Finnie asked.

"No, the rest of them could have stopped riding with whichever one shot Ethan. If you ride with a horse thief, well then you are a horse thief. They chose to ride on and this is how it ended. I do feel badly for the boy. He never lived to be old enough to let life wizen him up," Gideon said.

"It's a shame."

"Yes, it is. It would've been a shame if Ethan died or does die, too. It's best to be a whole lot better with guns than these fellows were if you're going to shoot people and steal horses."

"What do we do now?" Finnie asked.

"I guess we'd better ride all night and haul them out of here as soon as we can. I don't want to be explaining why a sheriff from Colorado is in New Mexico with four dead men," Gideon said.

They saddled the horses and strung them together with a lariat before laying the bodies across the saddles and tying the dead men's hands and feet to the stirrups. The proceedings took a good hour and the moon had risen high by the time they mounted.

"This is going to make for a long night and those bodies will be stinking by the time that we get back," Finnie said.

"You've got to admit that it beats being one of the dead ones though," Gideon reminded him.

"Just give me the bottle. I need a good swig to get through this night."

Gideon pulled the bottle out of his saddlebag and took a deep pull. "Me too," he said before handing the bottle to Finnie.

The travel was slow as they were forced to go at a walk through the night. Sometime before dawn, they came to the tepee of Farting Jack. The old man sat by the campfire cooking. On hearing the hoof beats, he let out a howl and began dancing around the fire. Gideon howled back and the old mountain man beckoned them in for some fried catfish.

"I always make out like I'm crazy if somebody approaches in the night. The meanest man in the world won't mess with a crazy person. They'll give you a wide berth," Jack said as the men dismounted.

"I expect you're right about that," Finnie said, still feeling the hairs on his neck standing up from the old man's startling howl. "I'll take the horses down to the lake to get a drink."

"I see that you got you quarry," Jack said.

"That we did. They were amateurs and had no business stealing a horse and shooting Ethan," Gideon said.

"I guess we all make bad choices that if we're lucky enough, we get to live to regret," Jack said.

"Amen to that."

The three men dined on the catfish. Finnie raved about it being the best that he had ever eaten. Jack offered them his tepee for a nap before they headed on their way, but Gideon was anxious to get out of New Mexico and to check on Ethan.

"If you ever get up near Last Stand, make sure that you come and look me up," Gideon said as they climbed into the saddles.

"I expect you haven't seen the last of me, you German devil," Jack said.

"So long, Jack," Finnie said.

"You're all right for a potato lover," Jack said.

Gideon and Finnie rode on through the morning. They occasionally met another rider, but did not speak. Each time the passerby rode on by and just stared at the bodies. In the afternoon, Gideon felt sure that they were back in Colorado and stopped at a stream. They tended to the horses before crawling under a tree and sleeping for a couple of hours. By the time that they arrived in Last Stand, they were asleep in the saddle.

Chapter 12

Zack decided to ride over to check on Abby. He wanted to please Gideon and offer her his assistance in any chore that she might need done. Abby stood out in the yard feeding chickens as he arrived.

"Hey, Zack, what brings you over here?" Abby called out as she shaded her eyes with her hand to see him.

Zack climbed down from his horse. "Gideon asked me to check on you to see if you needed help with anything, so here I am."

"The cattle are fine. They are grazing where they're supposed to be and everything else is new enough that it hasn't broken yet."

Zack stood there looking uncomfortable. "So you don't need me to do anything?" he asked as if disappointed.

Abby studied Zack trying to figure out what was going on until it dawned on her that he wanted to talk about Joann.

"Why don't you come in and have some apple pie with me? I've been craving it something fierce since I've been carrying this baby. Sarah gave me some apples from her cellar. The pie should be cool enough by now, and I sure could use some company."

Zack followed Abby into the cabin where she directed him to sit at the table while she got them each a glass of milk and a slice of pie. He politely waited for Abby to take the first bite before he tasted the pie.

Abby closed her eyes and looked as if she was having a spiritual moment. "Oh my goodness, that hits the spot. You can't imagine what it's like to have cravings when you are with child."

"No, I can't," Zack said and chuckled.

"I wrote Joann and told her that she is going to be a sister again, but I haven't heard back from her yet."

"This pie is really good," Zack said and then cleared his throat. "I hoped to talk to you about Joann."

"What do you want to know?"

"I'm not really sure. I don't know what to do. I missed her bad enough before she sent me the letter and now I can't stop thinking about her. I thought about maybe heading up to Wyoming when Ethan gets better. What should I do?" Zack asked.

Abby had to have another bite of pie before she answered. She needed to think of a good answer anyway. "To be honest with you, Zack, I don't know what you should do. Joann is so spirited that it makes her hard to predict. Maybe you can go up there and sweep her off her feet, but I'm afraid it's more likely to get her dander up and she won't have a thing to do with you. I expect that she will come for a visit when the baby is born. That might be your best chance to win her back if it's not already too late. Love is a tricky thing." The more that she talked, the more the hope seemed to be seeping from the young man.

"I'm sorry I bothered you. It's not your problem and I just need to move on," Zack said dejectedly.

"Zack, I care deeply for both you and Joann, and I want to see you both happy. I have to believe that it will work out for the best no matter how it turns out. If it's not Joann, you will find the right one someday," Abby said.

"What about you and Gideon?" Zack asked before realizing how the question sounded. "Oh, I'm so sorry. That sounded like an accusation, and it wasn't. I just meant that you two should have been together." He blushed by the time that he stopped talking.

Abby didn't know what to say. She didn't find Zack's words insulting, but he certainly had put her on the spot. "You got me there and I don't have a good answer. I guess if you are as sure that Joann is the one as I was about Gideon, you should at least go down with a fight. I wish that I had."

Gideon walked in just as the silence grew awkward. "I'm back," he announced.

Abby arose from the table and walked over to greet her husband. "I missed you," she said before kissing him.

"I missed you too. How is Ethan doing?" Gideon asked.

"He's getting better, but it's slow going. Doc said that it took a lot out of him, but he thinks that he will be fine," Abby answered.

"That's good to hear."

"Did you find them and get Ethan's horse back?" Abby asked.

"Yes, we found them and I have Pie tied up outside. I'll run him over to Ethan after I rest. We did a lot of riding."

"Did you capture them or kill them?" Zack asked.

"They're all dead. They put up a fight and they certainly weren't experienced outlaws. If you are going to shoot people and steal their horse, well then, you had better be a whole lot better at your trade than those fellows were."

"Do you want me to take Pie back? I was just getting ready to leave," Zack said.

"I'll bring him over. I wanted to see Ethan anyway," Gideon said.

"Good, I'll be able to check the herd that way and not have to stop at Ethan's cabin. I'll see you later," Zack said.

"Were you over here trying to win my woman away?" Gideon teased.

"I was trying to get advice on how to win your daughter back," Zack said dejectedly.

"Don't give up yet. Joann's fair game until she says 'I do'. And thanks for checking in on Abby," Gideon said.

"I got to go. Thanks for the talk, Abby. See you later," Zack said and headed out the door.

Abby cut herself another piece of pie. "You can't believe how I'm craving pie. I think this is the best one that I've ever baked. Do you want a piece?"

Gideon looked at her in amusement. Failing to hide his smile, he wasn't about to ask for a piece of pie with the way that she brandished the knife that she had used to cut it. The pie appeared to be a little too precious to Abby to risk depriving her of the rest of it. "I'll sit here and talk with you while you eat it and then I'm going to rest," he said, relieved that she was too preoccupied to notice the smirk on his face.

∞

After taking a nap in the jail, Finnie walked to the Last Chance to let Mary know that he had returned and that he could resume helping her in the morning. Word of the return of Gideon, Finnie, and the four bodies had raged through the town like a wildfire so that his appearance in the saloon came as no surprise. Mary was bartending as he walked up to the bar and sat on a stool.

"You look none the worse for wear. I'm glad to see that you two scallywags made it back safe and sound," Mary said.

"That we did. We lived to tell the tale one more time. I had a bullet come close enough that it burned me," Finnie said.

"You need to be more careful. I'll probably live the rest of my life and never get to hear another Irish accent like yours," she said as she dried a beer mug.

"I don't think that would be much of a loss. I haven't exactly made my mark on this world."

"You're looking a whole lot better than when you first got here. Your eyes are clearer and you carry yourself like you matter now. Do you need a drink?"

Finnie thought for a moment, trying to decide what to do, before saying, "I think I'll have a beer. I'm doing pretty good today and I might as well be good when I can. Who knows what I'll be like tomorrow." He chuckled nervously after his confession and looked down at the bar to avoid looking at Mary.

"I got a deal for you," Mary said, placing her hand on his arm. "Homer is coming to tend bar at five o'clock, and I don't think we'll be that busy tonight. You go get yourself cleaned up and I will buy you dinner at the hotel. You can charm me with that accent all you want."

Finnie looked up into Mary's dark eyes and they were staring back at him. Her gaze unnerved him a little and he was dumbfounded at the invitation. He stammered badly while trying to figure out what to make of the request. The idea that an attractive woman wanted to have dinner with him was almost beyond his comprehension. Finally marshaling the easy charm that he normally used to disarm women, he said, "Eating a fine steak in the company of a wonderful lass such as yourself will make for a most pleasant culinary experience."

∞

Gideon awoke from his nap in the afternoon, surprised to find Abby curled up beside him asleep. Watching her for a moment, he decided that she was even more beautiful now that she was pregnant. She had a glow about her. As he rolled his feet to the floor to sit on the edge of the bed to put on his boots, she awoke.

"I could get used to this. This baby is wearing me out more than Winnie or Joann did," Abby said.

"I'm sure it has nothing to do with your age. This baby is probably just being difficult since it's mine," Gideon teased.

"That's just what I thought. There's no other good explanation," she said as she sat up.

"I'm going to take Pie back to Ethan and see how he's doing. I shouldn't be that long," Gideon said before leaning over and giving Abby a kiss.

"I'll be here."

As Gideon walked out of the room, Abby still sat on the bed looking as if she was contemplating whether she would get up or go back to bed. Once outside, Gideon noticed how exhausted and thin the horses looked from all the travel. They would need a couple of days rest and extra feeding to bounce back. He rode to Ethan's cabin at a leisurely pace so he wouldn't strain the animals any further.

Gideon rode up to the cabin and saw Doc's buggy parked in the yard. Benjamin sat on the swing, gliding back and forth.

"How is your pa feeling today?" Gideon asked.

"He's feeling poorly. He was real good yesterday. I've been helping Zack run the ranch," Benjamin said proudly.

"Well good for you. I knew that you would be a big help to him. You probably have to tell Zack what to do," Gideon teased.

Benjamin smiled at Gideon. "I see that you got Pie back. Pa has been worried about you and that horse."

"I had to get him back or your pa would've never let me live it down. I would've had to resign as sheriff. I'm going to put him in the barn and feed him. I'll be right back," Gideon said as he led the horse away.

After returning from the barn, Gideon went into the cabin and saw no one. He walked back to the bedroom. Sarah and Doc were sitting in the room watching Ethan sleep. Lines of worry etched the doctor's face and Sarah had dark circles under her eyes and looked pale. Her appearance made Gideon worry. Sarah had been through so much in the last year and he wondered how much more she could take.

"How is he?" Gideon asked.

"He's running a fever today. Not bad, but it still has me worried. It's a sure sign of an infection and there's nothing that I can do for him either. He's going to have to fight it off himself," Doc said.

"I'm not going to stay. When he wakes, you can tell him that Pie is back in the barn."

"Did you catch them?" Sarah asked.

"They're all dead. We charged them and they tried to put up a fight."

"Thank you. It should do Ethan some good to know that you and Pie are back. He has been more worried about that than himself," Sarah said.

"Is Zack taking care of things? If anything needs doing, just let me know," Gideon said.

"No, he's been doing a fine job. He's come a long ways in a short time. I think staying busy keeps his mind off his woman troubles," Sarah said.

Ethan opened his eyes and saw Gideon.

"You made it back, I see," Ethan said.

"I did and you have a horse out in the barn that needs your attention. He's a little run down from all his travels. We all know how picky you are with him," Gideon said.

"That's right. I can always find new friends or a new wife, but a horse like that is hard to find," Ethan said with a smile before drifting back off to sleep.

Chapter 13

After a good night of sleep, Gideon arose anxious to get back to trying to solve Mr. Druthers' murder. He had risen a half-hour earlier than normal, fixed breakfast, and had it eaten while Abby slept. As he walked into the bedroom, he smiled at seeing her snoring softly. He wondered how his usually active wife would handle all the additional rest that the baby would require. With a kiss on her forehead, Gideon told Abby goodbye, and received a mumbled answer that he knew that she wouldn't remember.

Gideon rode Snuggles to town to give Buck some time to recuperate from their travels. As he walked into the jail, Gideon found Finnie freshly shaved and sitting at the desk. The smell of coffee filled the air, giving Gideon pause, as Finnie had shown no inclination to attempt the chore before now.

"I didn't know that you knew how to make coffee," Gideon chided.

"I got up early and wanted some. If you remember, I made some on the trail," Finnie reminded him.

"You look as perky as a colt on a spring morning."

"Well, you aren't going to believe what happened to me after you went home. I went to see Mary to let her know that I had returned, and she invited me to dinner at the hotel. We had a grand time talking and joking. She told me all about growing up in the orphanage and about the murder of her husband after they homesteaded here. Mary wanted to know everything about Ireland. I can't remember the last time that I had a nice meal with a lady. It made for quite an evening. I don't know what to make of it though. Why would Mary do that? Do you really think that she'd be interested in somebody like me?" Finnie asked.

Gideon was pouring a cup of coffee and almost overfilled it while listening to the surprising revelation. Finnie's news couldn't have been any more shocking than if the murderer of Minnie Ware walked in and confessed. His mind raced on what to say if Finnie started asking questions. He had never discussed Mary's past with Finnie, and he had no idea if his friend knew that she had been a whore or that he'd been one of her customers when he first came back to town. Thinking of himself as one of her customers made him feel sordid. Mary and he had had feelings for each other, and he wondered how Finnie would feel about that. Gideon had not had one moment of regret for choosing Abby over Mary, but as he sat down in his chair, he couldn't help but feel a tinge of jealously at the thought of Mary being interested in another man. "I don't know what to make of it. I've never known Mary to take someone to dinner. At the very least, I would say that she's very fond of you," he said.

"It sure has put the giddy-up in my step, I'll tell you that. I can't imagine what she would see in a little sawed off drunk like me though. She was probably just being nice, and I should leave it at that."

"I'm sure that her intentions will become apparent to you. Mary is not one to beat around the bush."

"Will you talk to her for me and see what's going on?" Finnie asked.

"I most certainly will not. This isn't grade school and passing notes and having friends do your talking for you. For Christ's sake, you fought in a war. I would hope that you can handle this yourself," Gideon said before taking too big of a sip of coffee and burning his mouth.

"Well, fine then. You don't have to get ringy on me. You're right though. I should handle this myself. It's just that I've never had a woman of means interested in me. I can't quite picture it," Finnie said.

"Mary's a fine woman. If she is interested in you, you had better put that bottle away for good. I won't have her suffer with that. She's had enough trouble in her life."

Finnie grinned at Gideon. "I figured you'd get all protective about her. I've seen how you two are together. She told me to my face that she used to be a whore and about you and her. So you don't have to be coy about all that."

Gideon suddenly felt as if he were the one put on the spot. "If you have all the answers, then why are you asking me questions? Figure it out for yourself. This is the thanks I get for trying to help a friend that is down on his luck. And if Abby can be friends with Mary, I don't want to hear another word about it from you," he said, indignation rising with each word.

Finnie let out a belly laugh that shook his whole body. "I love it when you get all riled. You get as defensive as an old woman trying to hide her age. I never said I had a problem with it. I'm the last person in the world that should be judging anybody. I just wanted to let you know so that you didn't feel the need to dance around the subject."

Rubbing his scar, Gideon grinned in spite of his discomfort about the subject. "I'll be glad when it's time for you to go to work and get out of here."

Gideon made his usual walk of Last Stand after Finnie headed to work. The sleepy little town was just coming to life. He stopped to chitchat with a few storeowners out sweeping the walk. After making his rounds, he walked down the alley behind Last Chance and slipped through the back door. He found Mary sitting alone at the table in the back room still in her housecoat and drinking coffee.

Mary looked up and smiled. "Good morning to you. I hear that you got your men."

"We did. It was a lot of riding and I'm glad to be back and in my own bed. Traveling doesn't have the same appeal that it once did," Gideon said.

"How's Abby feeling?"

"She's doing fine, but the baby makes her tired. She doesn't like admitting that she is older this time," Gideon said and smiled at the thought of her in bed that morning.

"I know that you're dying to ask if I've heard anything new about the murder of Druthers, and I haven't heard so much as a peep. If anybody knows anything, they know to keep their mouth shut," Mary said.

"I was afraid that you'd say that. I've been thinking about this a lot. Cal and Leo aren't going to talk and the girls are scared to death to say anything. I thought about dragging Cal and Leo to the jail to talk to them and see if you would slip into the Lucky Horse and talk to the girls. Maybe they would relate to you and tell you something," Gideon said as he sat down at the table.

"You mean one whore to another? Like we have some kind of sisterhood," Mary said.

Gideon grinned sheepishly. "You know I've never thought of you as a whore, but yes that is the gist of it."

"We can give it a try. Cal and Leo should be there in an hour or so. When I see you walk out of there with them, I can try to slip in the back and see what happens. I've never met those girls. Cal's girls keep a low profile around here. They don't spend their money shopping around town, that's for sure. I'll walk on over to the jail when I'm done so that you know that you can get rid of them."

"Thank you. I don't know what I'd do without you."

"I don't either. You'd probably be like a little lost puppy," Mary teased.

"Probably. It seems it takes you, Sarah, and Abby to all keep me in line. I must be a fierce burden to all of you."

"Did Finnie say anything to you about last night?" Mary asked.

"He did."

"And what do you think about it?"

Gideon sensed that no matter what he said that it wouldn't be the right answer. Mary would make him play devil's advocate one way or the other. "I think you're both adults and should dine with whomever you please."

"What's that supposed to mean? Sounds like you think Finnie shouldn't be seen out with a whore or that I shouldn't be seen with a drunk."

"Don't put words into my mouth. I didn't say that. I just meant that it was your and Finnie's business. Nobody else's opinion matters."

"It caught you by surprise, didn't it?"

"Yes, I must say that it did. I didn't see that one coming - not that I find anything wrong with it. Just didn't expect it," he said, trying to tread delicately.

"I made the invitation on the spur of the moment. It doesn't mean that it's going to turn into a romance or anything," Mary said.

"Mary, who are you trying to convince – me or you? Finnie's a fine man as long as he gets his drinking under control, but you need to be upfront with him if you decide that you just want to be friends. Us men don't do well with mixed signals," Gideon said.

"I know. I just did it without thinking and now I don't know what to think. He really is a charming rascal and hard not to like. I better go get some clothes on so that I can go do your dirty work for you."

Gideon studied Mary, thinking all the while that he'd give a month's pay to understand how the female mind worked before concluding that God made them that way to keep things interesting. "I'll see you after we are done," he said and gladly headed back to the alley before being interrogated any further.

He walked back to the jail and sat down on the bench out front to keep an eye on the Lucky Horse. Cal Simpson eventually appeared, unlocking the front door to the saloon and entering. Leo arrived a few minutes later. Gideon walked to the saloon and entered. Cal and Leo were behind the bar preparing for business. Looks of contempt lined their faces as they glanced up to see him.

"You gentlemen need to come with me to the jail. We have some things to discuss," Gideon said.

"Can't we talk here? I need to get ready for opening," Cal said.

"No, we need to go to the jail."

"If you want to talk to us, you can either do it here or get the hell out. Your choice," Cal said.

"Cal, I've never understood your dislike for me, but the feeling is now mutual. And the choice is yours not mine - either you can walk to the jail with me or I'm going to take this Colt Frontier and lay it upside your head and then drag you to the jail. Same goes for Leo," Gideon said as he worked the revolver up and down in its holster.

"You're going to get yours one of these days, and it's liable to be sooner than later if you don't watch your step," Cal said as he walked out from behind the bar with Leo closely following him.

"After you, gentlemen," Gideon said, motioning towards the door and ignoring the threat.

Mary watched from the front window of the Last Chance and headed towards the back of the building once she saw the men leave the Lucky Horse. She slipped into the back alley, walking a block out of her way before crossing the street and coming up the alley behind the other saloon. After entering through the back door, she began looking around until she found the side room. She opened the door to find the two girls sitting in it eating their breakfast. The two whores looked up at her with surprised expressions.

"Hi, I'm Mary. I own the Last Chance, and I was in your line of work until a few months ago. I want to talk to you. Cal and Leo are at the jail and will be there until I leave here so you don't have to worry about them finding out. May I have a seat?"

The two young women exchanged glances before the one on Mary's left said, "Sure, have a seat."

"What are your names?" Mary asked.

"I'm Constance and this is Sissy," the same girl answered.

"Girls, we all know what it feels like to be a whore. I've been beaten and had other vile things done to me that are too indecent to mention. It comes with the job, but Minnie lost her life. Mr. Druthers might have killed her, but there is a lot more going on here. Somebody killed Druthers because they were afraid of what he might say, and I know you girls know more than you're letting on. The sheriff or I will never give you away, but you need to help him end this. Any one of us could've been Minnie. Please help us," Mary pleaded.

The girls looked at each other again. Finally, Sissy nodded her head and Constance started talking. "If they find out that we talked to you, we're as good as dead. These people don't mess around."

"I'm going to sneak out of here and the only two people that will know what you said are me and the sheriff. You have my word and I'll stick to it. And if your information brings the Lucky Horse to the ground, you can come work for me if you want to stay in the whoring business or I will buy you a ticket to wherever you want to go to start over. I promise," Mary said.

"They will kill us without a second thought if they find out," Sissy reiterated.

"They will not find out. Was Minnie your friend?"

"Sure, she was good to both of us," Constance said.

"Then do it for Minnie and for yourselves," Mary said.

Constance hesitated and looked at the other whore again. Sissy again nodded her head.

"I'm not sure we know enough to help, but here it is. Sissy was bought from an orphanage up in Kansas. My pa sold me to the same man for a thousand dollars. Minnie's pa sold her too. Me and Sissy and some other girls were taken in a covered wagon to a cabin a couple days ride from here. That man and another man at the cabin made us strip off all our clothes and then they took a belt to all of us for three days. They got us to the point where we would do anything do avoid that belt. One girl wouldn't give in and they took a whip to her until she fell in line like all the rest of us. After they broke us, they put us back in the wagon. A couple of the girls were dropped off after a day's ride. Sissy and me ended up here. I don't know what happened to the others. They brought us in to town in the middle of the night. Cal isn't in charge. He just runs things here. He gets mean every once in a while and takes a belt to us just to make sure we don't forget how things are. We all knew better than to go to the law or we would've ended up just like Mr. Druthers. Cal gives us just enough money that we can buy a few things. We don't know who's in charge. We heard somebody threaten to kill Cal the other night if anybody talked. We were too afraid to get a look at them and Cal made sure we knew that we'd be killed if we talked. Mr. Druthers was in on it, too. He got to slip over here for all the free pokes he wanted. He liked to smack us around and choke us while he was poking. I think he got carried away on poor Minnie," Constance said.

Mary sat in stunned silence as tears welled in her eyes. She had been expecting a bad story, but this was so much worse than she ever could have imagined. Reaching across the table, she took hold of a hand of each girl. Still unable to speak, she closed her eyes and tried to bring comfort to the girls with her touch. After finally marshaling her voice, Mary said, "Thank you for your help. I'm truly sorry for what life has dealt both of you. When this is over, I promise that I will do whatever I can to help you get a new start. You have my word."

"Please be careful leaving here," Sissy said.

"I will be. One of you can stick your head out in the alley and have a look before I walk out of here. Thanks again. I'll be in touch when this is over," Mary said and arose from the chair.

Constance stepped out into the alley and slowly scouted in both directions until convinced that no one was in sight. She opened the door and waved Mary out into the alley. Mary retraced her steps back to the Last Chance, going so far as to enter through the back door and walk straight out the front door to head to the jail.

Mary burst through the jail door, interrupting the interrogation. "Gideon, that drunk you brought to town and talked me into hiring has got into my whiskey this morning. You need to do something about him," she ranted.

Gideon looked at Mary in surprise, not entirely sure whether she was acting or not. Turning his attention back to Cal and Leo, he said, "You two can get out of here. You're useless anyway."

Mary watched out the window until the two men were across the street before sitting down across the desk from Gideon. "Did you like my performance?" she asked.

"You should've been an actress. I wasn't even sure about it," Gideon said.

"What do you think being a whore is most of the time?"

Gideon chuckled. "I guess you have a point there. Did the girls tell you anything?"

Mary began retelling the information that she had learned. Tears trickled down her face before she finished, and Gideon had to pull a handkerchief from his pocket to give to her. Once she gained control of her emotions, she finished telling the girls' story.

Gideon sat back in his chair and rubbed his scar. He didn't know where to begin with the news he had just learned. The magnitude of the case sunk over him like an anchor. "We know a lot more now, but we still don't know a thing to help solve this. Cal and Leo would have to be tortured to get anything out of them."

"Druthers had to be the key to finding out more. He surely had to be the one that took care of the money and books. Why else would you have a small town banker involved? I wouldn't think that he would've had the money to be buying the girls or owning saloons. He had to be of some use and I would think that a banker would come in handy for quietly paying people," Mary said.

"That's a good point. I think I'll search the house and then talk to Mr. Fredrick," Gideon said.

"What about the girls?"

"I think we have to leave them where they are until we have something. They're safer that way. If we yank them out of there, Cal is the only one that we could charge, and I fear that they all would be killed even if the girls can't name anybody else. It would be hard to hide the girls around here without somebody knowing where they are and telling somebody else. The last time I tried that I about got my wife and daughter killed," Gideon said.

"I know. It's one thing to be a whore, but another thing entirely to be sold into it. We had better get out of here in case Cal is watching. You can walk me back to the saloon and then leave with Finnie. It's time for him to get off anyway," Mary said.

After leaving the jail with Mary and returning with Finnie to complete the ruse, Gideon walked to the bank. Mr. Fredrick stood at the teller counter and gave Gideon a warmer greeting than he ever had experienced in the bank before now.

"You're certainly in a fine mood," Gideon remarked.

"I've been appointed bank president and I get to hire my replacement. Mr. Druthers never liked me getting too friendly with the customers. He treated me and everybody else like redheaded stepchildren and that's going to change. People won't have to come in here dreading talking to their banker any longer," Mr. Fredrick said.

"That's very commendable. I need to ask you some questions. Has anybody been in here quizzing you about Mr. Druthers?"

"No. Everybody just seems glad not having to deal with him."

"Did Druthers have an account here, and if he did, could you please tell me how much money he had in it?" Gideon inquired.

"He did. It has a little over two thousand dollars in it. I guess the court will decide what to do with it if no will is found," the banker said.

"Mr. Fredrick, I suspect there may be a ledger around here somewhere that is of a personal nature and not bank business. I'd like you to keep your eyes open for it and let me know as soon as you find it. For everyone's safety, including your own, I suggest that you not tell a soul about this conversation. If there is a ledger, I can assure you that somebody will kill to keep it out of my hands," Gideon warned.

"I will keep it under my hat. Druthers didn't let me near a lot of things and I'm still making my way through them. If I find something, you'll be the first to know."

Gideon headed to Mr. Druthers' house. He searched the small house and found nothing. The place looked to be in order, but he had a suspicion that somebody had beaten him to the search. Drawers in the wardrobe looked as if maybe clothes were shoved back in place. As he closed the door behind him, doubts of his ability to solve the crime began to creep back into his mind and he felt as if the town would suffocate him. His shoulders sagged as he slowly walked back to the jail.

By the afternoon, Gideon had all of the town that he could stand. He had been anxiously pacing in the jail waiting for Doc to return from checking on Ethan. The fidgeting had gotten so bad that Finnie had made himself scarce. With his concern growing, he decided to ride on out to check on Ethan himself.

Gideon put Snuggles in a lope all the way to the cabin and found the doctor's buggy still in the yard as he arrived. Not bothering to knock, he entered the cabin and hurried to the bedroom. As Gideon entered the room, Ethan sat up and coughed violently into a handkerchief. Gideon could see nasty looking green phlegm on the cloth as Ethan moved it away from his mouth and collapsed back into the bed. Sarah picked up the rag that had fell from Ethan's head and dipped it into a pan of water before wringing it and placing it back on his forehead. Ethan did not acknowledge Gideon's entrance.

"His fever is worse. I might as well head back to town. There's nothing that I can do here," Doc said as he arose from the chair and walked past Gideon into the front room.

Gideon followed at the doctor's heels. "Doc, he's going to pull through this isn't he?" he asked.

The doctor pulled off his glasses and looked Gideon in the eyes. "It's bad, Gideon. That fever is high and his lungs are full of infected phlegm. I tell you that I just don't know," he said and rubbed his chin.

"Isn't there something that you can do?"

"I wish there was, but I'm afraid Ethan is pretty much on his own. A cool rag on his head is about it. We've come a long way in medicine during my years of practicing and I suspect we have a long way to go," Doc said.

Gideon took off his hat and ran his hand through his mop of hair before puffing up his cheeks and exhaling slowly while rubbing his scar. "Life's not fair. I should've died a dozen times with all the scrapes I've been in, and poor Ethan has lived a good clean life and now might die because some cowboy felt mean when Ethan was out doing nothing more than checking his herd."

"Gideon, life has never been fair and never will be. That's just the way it is and we all have to just keep moving forward one step at a time. I'm going back to town."

The doctor returned to the bedroom to say his goodbyes and then walked outside to find Benjamin and Zack sitting on the swing with the boy's dog, Chance, lying squeezed in between them. They had just returned from checking the herd.

"Benjamin, say an extra good prayer for your pa. He needs it. He's mighty sick," Doc said.

"Oh, I will. Don't worry about that or Pa. He's going to get better. I know it. When I prayed last night for him, I felt as if God told me that everything was going to be fine," Benjamin said.

"That's good. I admire your faith and I guess it wouldn't hurt me to have a little more of it myself. I'll see you two tomorrow," Doc said before climbing into his buggy and popping the reins to get his horse moving.

Benjamin looked at Zack and in a voice as earnest as a preacher, said, "I'm going to marry Winnie when I grow up."

"That's good to know. I like a man that knows what he wants in life. Winnie is a lot like her sister. They are both not meek creatures," Zack said.

"I asked Momma and she said that me and you would be brother-in-laws if I married Winnie and you married Joann. We would be related then," Benjamin said proudly.

"I don't think that's going to happen. I'm pretty sure that Joann has her a new man up in the Wyoming Territory, but you are sort of like my little brother anyway so that sort of makes us related."

"I could pray for you and Joann to get back together like I pray for Pa to get well."

"I think God probably has bigger things to take care of than me and Joann getting together, but thanks. You'd best use all of your sway with God to pray for your pa."

Gideon walked out onto the porch. "Benjamin, your momma asked me to remind you to get the chickens fed," he said.

"Those darn chickens. I'm not going to have any on my ranch when I grow up," Benjamin said as he slid off the swing.

Gideon didn't say anything else. He turned, walked back into the house and into the bedroom.

Ethan opened his eyes and studied Gideon. "Gideon, you're back. I always knew you'd return. What's it been – close to twenty years? They must think I'm going to die if they sent for you," he said.

As Gideon cleared his throat, he could hear Sarah begin to sob. Deciding not to confuse the situation by telling Ethan that he'd been back a year, he said, "I didn't come back to watch you die. I came back so that we can go hunting and fishing like we did in the old days. You need to get well."

Ethan nodded his head before drifting back off to sleep. Sarah bolted from the room, her sobs echoing down the hall as Gideon pursued her into the kitchen. He took Sarah in his arms and patted her back.

"Don't give up - never give up. It's not the way that you and me are made, Sis. We fight until the end," Gideon said.

"I'm so tired of the struggles. Life shouldn't be this hard and I'm not sure I've got much fight left in me. I don't know what I will do if I lose him," Sarah said.

"Ethan is strong and he has a lot to live for. Don't give up on him. It doesn't do either of you any good."

"It's so hard seeing him that way. He's always been my rock. And I'm so tired. I can't sleep and there are moments where I feel I can't go on."

"You have to keep your faith in Ethan. You just have to do it."

"I'll try. You had better get home. Abby never came over as she promised. I expect she is not feeling well."

Up until that point, it had not occurred to Gideon that Abby would have been there if she could have. "I expect you're right. I'll see you tomorrow," he said and kissed her on the forehead.

With his concern for Abby, Gideon rode home as quickly as possible. He found Winnie in the kitchen buttering a biscuit.

"What's going on?" Gideon asked.

"Momma don't feel good. I'm fixing her a biscuit and a glass of milk," Winnie said.

Gideon jogged to the bedroom to find Abby curled up in the fetal position. "What's wrong?" he asked.

"I had morning sickness that decided to last all day. I'm all right. I'm just sick to my stomach is all, but don't worry. I think it must be a boy. The girls never felt like this. He'll probably be as ornery as you," Abby said.

"Do you want me to go get Doc?" he asked, ignoring her attempt at humor.

"No, just come sit by me and pet me a little. I just need some attention. Everything is fine. Really."

Gideon sat down beside Abby and rubbed her shoulder. "I'm going to need a drink tonight with the way this day has gone," he muttered.

Chapter 14

Abby felt like her normal self a couple days after her sickness. She got up in the morning with Gideon to make their breakfast while he did the chores. The bacon, eggs, and biscuits were waiting on him when he returned.

"Breakfast smells as good as you look," Gideon said.

"Thank you, I guess. That's not the most flattering compliment you've ever made, but I'll take it anyway after the way I felt the last couple of days," Abby said as Winnie joined them at the table.

"I hope I don't catch what you had," Winnie said.

Gideon and Abby burst into laughter.

"I certainly hope you don't either," Abby said.

"Why is that funny?" Winnie asked.

Abby mouthed to Gideon, "Let's tell her."

"Go ahead. I think it's time," Gideon said.

"Winnie, I'm going to have a baby. You're going to be a big sister," Abby said.

Winnie sat in silence. Gideon and Abby could both see her trying to sort out the news as if her senses were overwhelmed.

Finally, Winnie asked, "Will you love it more than you love me since Gideon will be the daddy?"

"No, Winnie. I could never love anyone more than I love you. Just like I don't love Joann any more or less than I love you. It will be the same with the baby. It will take a lot of my time, and you might feel neglected, but you can help me. You will be just like a little momma," Abby said.

"I can do that," Winnie said, seemingly convinced. "Do I get to name it?"

Gideon chuckled. "How about we all name it together? We can make it a family decision."

"We could do that," Winnie said approvingly.

"Get to eating or you will be late for school," Abby said to end the conversation.

After Winnie had headed out the door for school, Gideon took his last sip of coffee and said, "Well, that went better than I feared it might."

"Me too. I think as long as we keep Winnie involved, she will be fine," Abby said as she began to clear the table.

"I'm going to run by and see Ethan before I head to town. Doc didn't say it, but I could see that he's about given up hope. If Ethan's not better today, I don't think he's going to have enough strength to get better."

"Don't say that. There's always hope. I can't bear to think otherwise."

"You haven't seen him since you've been sick. He's mighty weak," Gideon said as he placed his hat on his head.

Abby walked to Gideon and gave him a kiss. "I'm going to try to get over there and see if I can be of any help to Sarah. Things around here can wait another day. Maybe I'll see you over there this afternoon if you get a chance to get away from town."

"We'll see. I'll see you sometime," Gideon said before walking out the door.

Gideon saddled up Buck. He pulled off his jacket before mounting. The temperature was already warming up. The day would be a hot one for May. As he rode, he wondered how many times he had made the trip to Ethan's place since he had started going there at about ten years old. He and Ethan had practically been inseparable until the allure of Abby had begun occupying his time before he joined the army. As Gideon rode into Ethan's yard, he continued reminiscing about the old days to keep his mind off what he might find.

He saw no one outside and let himself into the house. "Is anyone home?" he hollered.

"I'm back in the bedroom," Sarah answered.

Walking into the bedroom, Gideon found Ethan sitting up and Sarah spoon-feeding him broth.

Ethan smiled at Gideon and said, "Hello, buddy."

Gideon sat down in a chair. His legs felt limp and he was so overcome with a sense of relief that he had to check himself from getting emotional. "Well, hello to you, too."

"I hear that I gave everybody a scare," Ethan said just before Sarah shoved the spoon into his mouth.

"That you did, my friend. That you did. I wasn't scared of losing you, just how much work I would have to do around here helping Sarah," Gideon joked.

"That's about the way I figured it," Ethan said.

Sarah fed the last spoonful of broth before standing. "I'll leave you two be. I've got things to do around here since I haven't been able to get much done. Ethan has been as much trouble to nursemaid as you were last year. You men are a bothersome lot of trouble," she said as she left the room still smiling.

"I guess she told us," Ethan said.

"I always thought that you had married yourself a mean one."

"It changes you, doesn't it?"

"What's that?" Gideon asked in confusion.

"Almost dying," Ethan said.

"Yes, it does. It makes life sweeter and the mountains a little prettier. It's sad that it works that way, but it beats the hell out of dying."

"Amen to that."

"I need to get to town. The city council is going to fire me if I'm not around there more. I'll try to stop by tonight if I can. You scared the hell out of me. You get well," Gideon said as he stood and shook Ethan's hand.

"Thanks for getting Pie back for me and being here."

"I'll see you later," Gideon said as he walked out of the room.

Sarah stood washing dishes as he entered the kitchen. "Looks like you won't have to be searching for a new man after all," Gideon said.

"No, but Abby might if I lay this frying pan upside your head. You shouldn't say things like that," Sarah chided.

"I'll be able to concentrate now and not worry all day. He scared me, Sarah."

"You and me both. Thank you for all you've done."

Gideon smiled at her. "I think I still owe you. I'll see you later."

After riding to town, Gideon started catching up on paperwork. His concentration had been so bad since returning with Ethan's horse that he had not bothered to attempt it and needed to get caught up. He never needed much of an excuse to neglect the deskwork anyway. The only break he took was to walk over and tell Doc that Ethan was much improved.

Finnie walked in just before noon. Gideon had not yet seen him that day as the Irishman had already left for the Last Chance by the time he got to town.

"Top of the morning to you. How is Ethan?" Finnie said.

"He's much better. I think he's turned a corner," Gideon answered.

"Good to hear. I need to ride out to see him and to keep my word to Zack on teaching him how to fight."

"You seem awfully cheery," Gideon remarked.

"That I am. I was torturing myself about what do over Mary. I thought what the hell, her turning me down couldn't be any worse than what I was putting myself through. She said yes. We're having dinner tonight."

"Good for you."

Finnie tossed Gideon a twenty-dollar gold piece. "Don't say that Finnegan Ford doesn't pay his debts."

"I didn't say it. I never was worried about it."

"I know. Do you think that I'm foolish to pursue Mary?"

"No. She showed interest in you, and you're both adults that can say no whenever you want. You both deserve to enjoy some companionship," Gideon said.

"You still can't really imagine us together though, can you?" Finnie asked.

"I never said that either."

"I didn't say that you said it. I said that you couldn't imagine it," Finnie responded.

"It surprised me, I must say, but it's not like I go around trying to match couples up in my head. That's something women do," Gideon said defensively.

Finnie let out a belly laugh. "I love riling you. It's just like the old days. I must admit that I can't imagine us together either, but there's a lot worse things than having a pleasant dinner with a fine looking woman."

Putting on his hat, Gideon stood and said, "I haven't done my morning walk of the town. Townsfolk like to see their sheriff out and about. They don't pay me to talk about your love life." He walked out the door to the sound of Finnie's roaring laughter.

Gideon had not walked twenty feet down the sidewalk when he felt a bullet tear into the inside of his upper left arm before the sound of the shot had even reached him. He dove behind a water trough and checked his arm. The bullet had torn through muscle, missing the bone. His arm still worked, but it hurt like hell to move it. As he tried to peek above the trough to find the shooter, another shot slammed into the water.

Finnie heard the commotion and ran to the door. He saw Gideon pinned down. As the third shot rang out, he located the shooter in the second story window of the hotel.

"Stay down until I get a gun," Finnie hollered to Gideon.

Finnie ran to the gun rack and pulled two Winchester 73s out before running back to the door. After leaning one gun against the wall, Finnie braced himself in the doorframe and started shooting at the window as rapidly as he could cock the lever-action rifle, making it impossible for the shooter to return fire. "He's in the hotel," he yelled.

Gideon drew his revolver and sprinted across the street and down the sidewalk towards the hotel. As he burst into the hotel, he kept his eyes on the stairs. A bloody man staggered down them. The shooter tried to cock his rifle using one hand with the butt of the gun shoved against his pelvis. Gideon crouched for a better angle and fired three shots in rapid succession into the man's chest, sending the shooter falling down the staircase in a slow macabre tumble while leaving a trail of blood on the carpeted steps.

After slamming his Colt into the holster, Gideon wanted to smash something and he knew what that something was. He marched two doors down the street and into the Lucky Horse. Several patrons were still standing at the window peering out. Cal had remained behind the bar during the gunfire. As Gideon hopped over the bar, he could see the fear in the bar owner's face. Cal backed himself into the corner as Gideon preyed upon him. A fit of rage banished the pain from Gideon's mind as he willed his wounded limb to grab Cal's arm and then grasp the back of the man's head with his other hand. He slammed Cal's face onto the top of the bar causing the bar owner to scream. With a grab of Cal's shirt collar, Gideon slung the saloonkeeper into the bottles of alcohol behind the bar, sending glass crashing and breaking to the floor. An overpowering smell of whiskey wafted through the air. Gideon drew his revolver and stuck it against the bleeding, broken nose of the bar owner.

"You ran your mouth to whomever had Druthers killed that I'm still snooping around," Gideon said as he cocked the Colt. "You tell them that I'm coming after them and the next time they better send a better shot. Do you understand?" Gideon yelled.

Cal nodded his head before Gideon holstered his gun and walked out from behind the bar. The saloon was deathly quiet. The patrons were still standing by the windows, their backs now pressed against the glass as they watched Gideon.

Finnie stood in the doorway. "Let's get you to the doctor," he said and took Gideon by his good arm.

"You saved me this time," Gideon said as they walked down the street and were joined by Mary.

"How bad are you hurt?" she asked.

"I think I'll be fine. The bullet missed the bone, but it aches like all get out," Gideon said. His anger had subsided and he became very aware of the pain shooting through his arm clear to his fingers.

Doc stood outside his office as the three of them walked towards him. While holding the door open as the others entered, Doc didn't say anything, deciding that any attempt to run off Finnie and Mary would be useless.

"Take your shirt off and have a seat on the table," Doc commanded as he scrubbed his hands.

Mary helped pull the shirt off Gideon after he unbuttoned it. He hopped onto the table as if he were there for a chat.

"Abby didn't need this kind of excitement," Gideon said.

Doc peered at the wound. "She would have been a lot more excited if that bullet had been three more inches to the left. You would be a dead man right now. Your shooter didn't miss by much. Do you know who he was?" he asked as he examined the entrance and exit wounds.

"I think it's Ike Todd. He's a hired gun out of New Mexico. Somebody is worried that I'm still digging into Druthers' murder. Cal Simpson will probably be in here to get his broken nose fixed. I'm going to take him down with the rest of them when I get to the bottom of this," Gideon said.

Doc Abram squeezed the muscles around the wound, making Gideon wince.

Mary asked, "How bad is it?"

"He should heal up just fine. Mary, can you hand me his shirt?" Doc asked.

"Damn, Doc, it hurts enough without you grabbing it," Gideon said.

"Quit your whining. You don't want to lose that arm do you? Now lay down," Doc said.

The doctor laid the shirtsleeve flat on the washstand and examined the entrance hole. "Gideon, I'm going to have to dig around for cloth in the wound. There's no way of knowing whether it's in your arm or came out with the bullet," he said as he retrieved his forceps.

Doc Abram instructed Finnie to hold a lamp near the wound as he began probing. Gideon grimaced in pain, but made no sounds. The doctor pulled out a small piece of material. Smiling in satisfaction at his handiwork, he said, "Thank goodness I found it. I would have worried about that until your arm rotted off or you got well."

"That's certainly reassuring," Gideon said sarcastically.

The doctor doused the wound liberally with iodine and proceeded to bandage the arm. "I'm not going to put your arm in a sling. I want you to keep moving it so that your arm doesn't get so stiff. Just don't do anything strenuous. And please try to stay alive."

"That I intend to do. Thank you once again for patching me up. I think I'll go sit for a while," Gideon said as he hopped down from the examining table.

Chapter 15

The morning after Gideon had been wounded, Abby sat at the table nervously rubbing her hands. She had barely slept throughout the night and had managed to wake Gideon up every time the pain of the injury had subsided enough for him to doze. They were both tired and in ill moods at breakfast. Abby's eyes were puffy and dark underneath them. Gideon looked pale. His arm throbbed and the stiffness made it difficult to move it. Winnie sized up the situation as she ate a piece of bacon, and decided it best to eat in silence.

"I don't see how you can continue being sheriff with the risk involved when you know that you have a child on the way that is going to need a father," Abby said, breaking the silence.

"Nobody has killed me yet. You told me before we ever married that you would support me in whatever I wanted to do, including being sheriff. It's what I'm good at, and you knew full well what you were getting into. Yes, it is a dangerous job, but Ethan about got killed riding in his pasture. People die in unexpected ways every day. It is just how life works. You just need to calm yourself. Everything will be fine," Gideon said.

"You were ambushed, and I'm smart enough to know that the bullet missed its target by a couple of inches. I just as easily could have been a widow. I don't know how you think that is all right," Abby said and started to sniffle.

"But it didn't hit its mark. Nothing is going to happen to me, I promise. There's way too much to live for these days to get killed now after all the years of misery that I went through. Trust me."

The sniffles turned into crying. "I'm so scared of losing you. I don't know what I would do with myself if I did."

Gideon got up from his chair and walked around the table to behind Abby, putting his hands on her shoulders. He leaned down and kissed her cheek. "I didn't wait eighteen years to marry a bossy woman just to get killed off and miss out on that fun," he teased.

Abby let out a little laugh between her sobs. "I must not be very good at bossing. It doesn't look like I had much luck at it this time."

"But I love you anyway."

"You think you're so charming, but Finnie, now that's a charming man. Compared to him, you're just a dried up old cowboy," Abby retorted.

Gideon let out a cackle. "Mary must think so, too. You women love a foreign accent, but he saved my bacon yesterday, that's for sure."

"Get over there and eat your breakfast, Sheriff. Your foods going to get cold," Abby said.

Winnie had listened to the conversation with keen interest. Since the time that her mother had begun seeing Gideon, she had come to realize how lacking her parents' relationship had been. The affection that Gideon and her mother showed each other had been a revelation. She still mourned the breakup of her family and not seeing her father every day, but understood more and more why her mother had divorced her father.

After breakfast, Gideon found that his injury made saddling his horse and pulling himself up into the saddle an ordeal. He could barely raise his stiff arm high enough to get the saddle onto the horse's back and had to use his right arm to awkwardly pull himself into the saddle. On the ride into town, he worked his arm in every manner that he could think of with considerable pain until it limbered up and gave him some hope that the limb would heal properly. He found Finnie in the jail making coffee and acting as giddy as he had after his first dinner with Mary.

"How's the arm?" Finnie asked.

"It hurts, but it works," Gideon said.

"Mary and I had a bully time last evening."

"Glad to hear that somebody did. My getting shot had Abby rattled all last night and this morning still."

"Did you know that she is twenty-seven?" Finnie asked, ignoring Gideon's comment.

"Can't say that I did. I didn't think you were supposed to ask a woman her age."

"I didn't. She just up and told me. I'm thirty-six now. Do you think that makes me too old?"

"Too old for what? You saved my life yesterday and you're killing me today. I'm sure Abby would agree that I'm about the last person in the world that should be giving you romantic advice. Get a grip on yourself. You sound like a chucklehead."

Finnie handed Gideon a cup of coffee. "I guess I do. I want to pinch myself to make sure it's real. I'm still having a hard time believing somebody like Mary would want to dine with me."

"Well, believe it. I know Mary and she wouldn't have accepted your invitation unless she wanted to go. How is your drinking going? That should be your big concern."

"I'm doing good enough for now. I must admit that it still has a powerful hold on me though. I had two drinks yesterday. It surely is a struggle."

"Keep it up. I know you can do it."

"I best be getting over to the saloon. I plan to get the old nag out today and go see Ethan and start teaching Zack to box if he's around. I need to keep my word to that poor boy before he gets worked over again," Finnie said before grabbing his hat and heading out the door.

Later in the morning, Gideon walked over to see Doc Abram to have his arm checked and the bandage changed. The doctor, satisfied with the condition of the wound, gave him another lecture on the need to be more careful before sending Gideon on his way.

Gideon walked to the bank and found Mr. Fredrick sitting at the desk formerly used by Mr. Druthers. The banker appeared busy, going over a ledger, and seemed to take a moment to become cognizant that Gideon had entered the bank. After walking into the little office, Gideon sat down across the desk from the banker.

"Good morning, Mr. Fredrick. I thought I would stop in and see if you have made any discoveries since we last talked," Gideon said.

"Sheriff, I've been so busy learning my new job that I haven't had much time to nose around, but to answer your question, no I haven't found anything," the banker said.

"I've been thinking about another possibility. Did Mr. Druthers or any other bank patron receive regular bank drafts or cash payments from out of town?" Gideon asked.

"I was only the teller. Mr. Druthers never let me near any business that came through the mail or stagecoach. Obviously, you are looking for some kind of money trail. I assure you that Druthers was too smart to put it in the bank ledgers. I may find a separate ledger with what you are looking for, but I believe that will be the only way it happens. I truly plan to look as time allows. I want you to know that you can count on me and you will be the first to know if I do find something," Mr. Fredrick said.

"Thank you for your time and I appreciate the help. You have a good day," Gideon said before leaving.

Walking back to the jail, Gideon's spirit started to sag. He was keenly aware that if Mr. Fredrick never found any evidence, it would be unlikely that Druthers' murder would ever be solved, and God knew how many girls would be left in forced prostitution. The two girls in the Lucky Horse also lay heavy on his conscience. If he got to the point that he gave up on solving the murder, he would have to come up with a plan to whisk the girls away to begin a new life. He had no idea how he would go about doing that or find the funds to make it happen. He dropped into his chair, clueless on what to do.

An hour later, Mayor Hiram Howard strolled into the jail. "How is the arm doing?" he asked.

"It hurts considerably, but Doc thinks I'm going to be fine. It's no fun getting shot," Gideon said.

"I would say not. The city council had a meeting this morning and wanted me to talk to you. Mr. Thomas raised a ruckus yesterday about his hotel getting shot all up. He's a big man in this town and carries weight. They wanted me to have you talk to your friend about being more careful with his shooting if such a situation were to arise again."

Sitting up straight in his chair, Gideon said, "I was pinned down and shot. Would you have rather had Finnie stand there and watch me get my head blown off instead of the hotel shot up? He saved my life."

"No. No. No. They just felt that he was a little zealous with his gunfire. It's going to cost the city some money to fix the hotel and quiet Mr. Thomas down," Hiram said.

"Well, considering that Ike Todd is dead and I'm alive, I think it was a pretty fair tradeoff," Gideon shot back.

Ignoring Gideon's reasoning, Hiram said, "The other thing that they are not pleased with is that they don't think it looks good for this Finnie fellow to be living in the jail. It reflects poorly that you let friends stay here."

"Hiram, would you and the city council like me to resign?" Gideon asked.

"No. No. No. We all think that you are doing a fine job and are the right man for being sheriff. Everybody on the council is happy with the job that you are doing."

Gideon ran his hand through his hair and then rubbed his scar. "Good. Now get the hell out of here. If I ever hear this nonsense again, I will resign on the spot and take up ranching full time," he said, staring at Hiram until the mayor got up and left without saying another word.

Lunchtime came and passed while Gideon remained sitting behind his desk. He hadn't accomplished a thing and couldn't get the mayor's visit or the unsolved murder of Druthers out of his head. It had been a long time since his spirit had sunk this low. Failure was not something that he had much experience dealing with or had ever learned to accept gracefully.

Finnie strolled into the office and immediately noticed the disposition of his friend. "You look about as sour as an old maid in a room full of beautiful virgins," he said.

Gideon chuckled in spite of his mood. "Yeah, I guess I am. It has to be a better day than yesterday. At least nobody has shot me yet."

"Why don't you ride with me to see Ethan? It'd do you good to get out of here," Finnie said.

"I think you are right. Let's go," Gideon said as he stood and picked his hat up off the desk.

On the ride to Ethan's cabin, the two men made small talk about guns and the weather. The wind had picked up out of the north, making for a chilly day in May. Both men lamented not wearing a jacket. Gideon never mentioned the visit from the mayor and Finnie avoided pestering him with questions about Mary.

They found Ethan sitting out on the swing covered in a couple of blankets. He looked thinner in the face and pale with dark circles under his eyes, but he smiled warmly at seeing his two friends arrive.

Gideon hollered, "Well, look there. You must be feeling more alive than dead."

"Barely. Walking out here just about tuckered me out, but it's a start I guess. I had to suffer a lecture from Sarah on how I didn't need to be breathing cool air, but I won. She insisted on the blankets and now that I'm out here, I'm glad she did," Ethan said.

"Glad to see that you are doing better," Finnie said.

"I'm glad that you came, Finnie. I've wanted to thank you for helping get Pie back for me. I'm much obliged," Ethan said.

"Just glad that I could help. It was good for me to find out that I still got a little grit in me," Finnie said.

Sarah walked out onto the porch. "I thought that I heard voices out here. Good to see you two. You're welcome to come in if you can get my hard-headed husband inside."

Finnie took off his hat and held it to his chest. "Good to see you again, Sarah. You look as lovely as the last time that I saw you. Ethan is a lucky man."

Ethan glanced at Finnie and then at Gideon, his expression revealing that he couldn't believe the Irishman capable of such flattering talk. All the while, his wife giggled like a schoolgirl. In his younger days, Ethan probably would have punched Finnie, but he now found the flirting downright amusing. "Well aren't you a silver-tongued devil. I'm telling you now that flattery doesn't take you very far with Sarah."

"How would you know? I don't remember the last time you tried it," Sarah teased.

"That's the problem. You don't remember," Ethan said and then grinned impishly, proud of his retort.

Sarah started to respond, but seeing the smile on Ethan's face and knowing all that he had been through, she decided to let him have the last word.

Turning her attention back to Gideon and Finnie, Sarah said, "Well get down from your horses. We do have chairs."

"I was hoping to see Zack and give him a lesson in the fine art of pugilism if you have no objections," Finnie said

"By all means. That pretty face of his can't stand much more thumping before he ends up with a crooked nose or missing teeth. Then we might never find him a woman. You should be able to find him straight north of here with the herd," Ethan said.

Finnie found Zack riding amongst the herd taking count of the calves. The Irishman watched patiently until the young man completed his task before hailing him. As Zack rode leisurely towards him, Finnie smiled at the realization of his fondness for the young man.

"By golly, your face is all healed up and you're back to being as pretty as one of those Greek gods that Homer was so fond of," Finnie said.

"I don't know no Homer, but it's nice to know that you think I'm pretty. I would prefer it be a female and considerably younger than you that would take notice though," Zack replied.

Finnie let out a snort. "I'm sure you would, but until you start getting out and about and stop looking so down in the mouth, that won't happen. Changing the subject, I came out here to begin teaching you how to box."

"Are we really going to do this?" Zack asked.

"We most certainly are. I gave you my word, and God knows you need to learn. Boxing is not quite the same as a brawl, but it will serve you well," Finnie said as he climbed down from his horse.

Zack dismounted and walked towards Finnie. The young man stood a good nine inches taller than the Irishman, towering over him in near childlike fashion. "You would think that I would be able to fight as big as I am."

"There's a lot more of you to hit, especially when you stand there with your arms so far apart like you're getting ready to wrap them around a gal for a big old smooch," Finnie chided.

Zack smiled. "At least a girl wouldn't have to bend near double over to get low enough to reach my lips."

"That may be, but I don't think either one of us has been kissed in a coon's age. Now get your fist up. I want your right hand up in front of your ear and your left about six inches out from your cheek," Finnie said as he watched Zack follow his instructions. "All right, good. Now bring your elbows down under your fist - there you go. Good."

Finnie proceeded to teach Zack how to stand properly and to drop his hips. Zack grew tense with all the instructions and it took a good while before he made even a semblance of doing the drop correctly. The fiery Irishman was extremely patient, never once raising his voice, but only offering encouragement.

"Now I'm going to throw some slow slap punches at you. You need to concentrate on your stance, hand location, keeping your hips dropped and tightening them as you block the punch, and of course, actually blocking the punch. Just relax. You're too nervous and it's making you stiff," Finnie said.

"I never knew there was so much to fighting."

"That, my dear boy, is painfully obvious," Finnie said before taking a boxing pose.

Finnie began slapping at Zack, using a variety of punches and charging in to force his pupil to move while trying to keep a correct stance. Zack did a good job of blocking the punches, but his footwork and hip dropping had a long way to go. He move clumsily and stood stiff and too upright. Finally, Finnie called a halt to the session.

"Not bad for your first time. I want you to practice a couple of times a day at what I've taught you. Just pretend to block the punches, but work on your footwork and your hips. And please don't get yourself into any fights until I teach you some more. All the girls in these here parts want to keep you pretty at least until you pick one of them. The rest might have a different opinion then," Finnie said.

Chapter 16

Two weeks went by with no breakthrough on Druthers' murder. Gideon visited the bank a couple more times and learned that Mr. Fredrick had begun inspecting various ledgers, but as of yet had not found anything. On each visit, the banker assured Gideon that he was diligently looking, but Gideon would leave dejected and feeling that the murder would go unsolved.

After leaving the bank on his last visit, Gideon decided to go talk to Mary. He hadn't been in the Last Chance much lately and he missed his talks with her. She had a way of getting to the heart of the matter better than anyone he knew and that's what he needed now. He sat down at his usual table while scanning the room for Mary without success, but saw Delta slip into the back room. Somewhere along the way, it became understood that only Mary served Gideon.

Henry Starks stood at the bar. Starks owned one of the largest ranches in the area. He was well liked in town and regarded as a pillar of the community. Folks could always count on him to donate money to civic projects, and he was known to contribute heavily to the town's Methodist Church. In his mid-fifties, he had a head full of dark hair. His regal bearing and expensive clothing made him appear much larger than his actual height. Henry ordered two beers and walked over to Gideon. He sat down at the table and pushed a drink towards the sheriff.

Gideon had known the Starks family since childhood when his father would play dances at the Starks ranch. Henry was several years older than Gideon, and they didn't know each other well, but the rancher always made a point of talking to him since his appointment as sheriff.

"How are you doing, Sheriff?" Starks asked.

"Nobody has tried to kill me yet today. Thanks for the beer," Gideon answered and took a sip.

"I heard about that. I'm glad you survived."

"It was close."

"Druthers surprised me. He wasn't the most personable man that I ever met, but I never figured him to be a murderer. Are you having any luck solving his murder?" Henry asked.

"Not much. There's not much to go on," Gideon said, intent on not divulging any information.

"I'm guessing that the whore had her a boyfriend that decided to settle the score."

"I doubt a boyfriend of that girl would have the means to hire Ike Todd to kill me."

"Are you sure Todd has anything to do with the murders? He wouldn't be the first man to show up here to settle a score with you since people learned that you are back in Last Stand," Henry said in reference to a mysterious man that came to town to harm Gideon and his family. Gideon had killed the man and to this day did not know his name.

"I guess that's a possibility," Gideon said.

"Enough about all that. I wanted to talk to you about something else. I know a lot of important people, and I wanted to see what you thought about me trying to get you appointed U.S. Marshal. It would be good for you and good for Last Stand. Businesses like to come to a town that has a strong law presence. What do you think?" Henry said.

"I've never thought about it. If I don't get Mr. Druthers' murder solved, I doubt anybody would want me for a marshal."

"I wouldn't worry about that. Nobody solves all the crimes. You think about it and I'll talk to you again the next time that I see you," Henry said. "I got to go. I'll be seeing you."

Mary had walked out of the back and waited behind the bar for Starks to leave. She poured Gideon another beer and brought it to the table.

"You're hobnobbing with the well-to-do," Mary said.

"I guess. Henry always makes a point of talking to me. What do you think of him?" Gideon said.

"I like him and he's always been respectful to me. He does a lot of good around town."

Gideon decided not to discuss his conversation with Starks. "How did you know that I didn't want whiskey?" Gideon asked and took a drink of beer.

Mary gave him a look as if it were a silly question and rolled her eyes. "Because you want to talk and you always prefer to sip a beer when you need to talk."

"Sometimes I forget how annoying you can be. Do you do the same thing to Finnie and does he know that you practically can read minds?" Gideon said before taking another drink of the beer.

"I can figure him out most of the time, but I haven't given myself away. I figure it might come in handy while I try to decide about me and him," Mary said.

"I thought that you always knew what you wanted."

"You give me too much credit. Finnie is a hard one for me to know what to do. You and him are different in so many ways, but you're alike in that neither one of you are like anybody else around this town. I just don't know," Mary said.

"So how are me and Finnie alike and how are we different?" Gideon asked.

"You are a leader and Finnie is a follower, and you are driven while Finnie is not, but he will kill himself to keep his promise to somebody. You're both good men with a strong sense of right and wrong, and you both used drinking to drown your sorrows, but Finnie has gone a lot farther down that road than you ever did. You are funny when the mood fits the occasion where Finnie sees humor in just about everything, including the crazy turns of life. I guess that about covers it," she said.

"I didn't know that you had made such a study of us, but Finnie sounds like a keeper. What has got you on the fence?"

"I don't know – a couple of things I guess. I'm not sure I'm wife material anymore, and I know Finnie wants to sober up, but I think it will always be a struggle."

"Questioning yourself about being wife material is just an excuse. You said that Finnie will kill himself to keep a promise. Maybe if you got him to give his word to give up drinking for you, that would be the key that unlocked the door," Gideon said.

Mary gazed at Gideon, digesting what he had said. "Since when did I ever start taking advice from you? It's always been the other way around. Why did you come to see me?"

Gideon grinned at her, knowing that he had hit a nerve. As he looked around to make sure that nobody sat within hearing distance, he said, "It's driving me crazy that I can't solve Druthers' murder and I constantly worry about those girls at the Lucky Horse. I feel guilty for leaving them over there and doing nothing about it. I'm at my wits end and don't know what to do. Mr. Fredrick says that he is looking for a ledger, and I believe him, but I'm beginning to have my doubts that there is anything over there. I don't take failure well."

"I know you don't. Have you ever thought about asking Mr. Fredrick if you could have a look? He certainly is a much friendlier man now that Druthers is gone. Maybe it needs a fresh set of eyes. That's about all that I can tell you. The girls don't have any more information and Cal is surely not talking, especially now that you broke his nose," Mary said.

Gideon chuckled. "I haven't seen him since that day. I hear that he has two black eyes. Doc said that when he set his nose that he carried on like he was having a baby. I hadn't thought about looking for the ledger myself. I'm not sure that I'd know what to look for, but I certainly don't have any better ideas," he said before draining the last of his beer.

"The glass is empty, so I guess that means the conversation is finished. I know that you're frustrated, but don't give up. I still think you'll get it figured out and we'll help the girls then. By the way, how is the arm healing up?" Mary asked as Gideon stood.

"Oh, it's about good as new. I don't have all my strength back, but that's about it," he answered before leaving.

Mary returned to the back room and sat down at the table. She hadn't intended on having a conversation about Finnie with Gideon. It had just sort of happened much like her impromptu invitation to Finnie for dinner. There were moments where she regretted having ever asked him. Once she had headed down that trail, she knew that it would either have to be ended or carried on to see where it would lead – there could be no in-between. She had loved two men in her life. Eugene had been her first love and her husband. He died way too young at the hands of Hank Sligo. Gideon had been her second and she had had to stand quietly to the side as he rekindled his romance with Abby. Mary wondered if she was cursed when it came to men or if the third time could be the charm. Finnie was a fine man, but she did not intend to endure a life with a drunk. She also worried that once the new wore off the relationship that he would resent that she had been a whore. Considering all the men that she had bedded as a prostitute, she wondered why she had ever dropped her guard and started the whole mess with Finnie.

∞

Mr. Fredrick had gotten into the habit of working into the evening since his promotion to bank president in the hope of mastering the new job that he proudly had achieved. His wife, happy with his new salary and status, had adjusted to his unpredictable arrival time by not beginning dinner until he walked in the door. They spent most of their evenings excitedly talking about plans for improvements to their home that the additional money would now allow.

Dusk had fallen upon the town as he locked the bank and headed home. He was walking down an alley when two men with flour sacks over their heads jumped out of the bushes.

The banker froze in his tracks, too panicked to run. The masked men moved toward him. One of the men punched Fredrick in the stomach, and as the banker doubled over in pain, the assailant hit him again with a haymaker to the jaw that sent him crashing flat onto his back. The masked man squatted over Mr. Fredrick's stomach before grabbing him by the shirt and lifting his head off the ground.

"We hear tell that the sheriff has been visiting you a lot. What does he want to know? You best speak up if you don't want more of the same," the masked man threatened.

Mr. Fredrick tried to catch his breath and focus through the fog the punches had brought upon him. Finally, after being shaken by the man, he stammered, "Sometimes he is just doing his banking. Other times he's asked me questions about Mr. Druthers, but I haven't been able to help because I don't know anything."

"What has he asked?' the man demanded.

"Things like whether anybody visited Druthers regularly and did I see his mail," Mr. Fredrick answered.

"What did you tell him?" the second man asked.

"I told him that nobody came to mind and that Mr. Druthers never let me handle the mail or stagecoach deposits," the banker said.

"So you've been no help?" the first man asked.

"No. None whatsoever."

The man released the banker and stood. "Good. You make sure that you keep it that way unless you want a lot more of the same," the man said before giving the banker a swift kick in the ribs that caused a cry of pain.

The two men disappeared back into the bushes as quickly as they had appeared while the banker rolled onto his stomach and managed to get on all fours. He stayed that way, sucking in air, until his head cleared some and the pain subsided. After getting to his feet, he started walking slowly back in the direction he had come, stopping occasionally to catch his breath. He needed to try to get to Doc Abram.

The doctor stood outside locking his door to walk down to the Last Chance. He heard footsteps on the board sidewalk and turned to see Mr. Fredrick holding his side and walking towards him.

"Doc, I got waylaid on the way home. I'm hurting," Mr. Fredrick called out.

Doc had the door unlocked and opened by the time the banker walked up. The doctor turned the wick up on the oil lamp, bathing the room in light. Doc then led Mr. Fredrick to the exam table. The banker grimaced as he raised himself onto the table and his face turned pale.

"Where are you hurt?" Doc asked.

"They punched me in the stomach and jaw and then kicked me in the ribs. I got a sharp pain where he kicked me," the banker said.

The doctor put his hand on Mr. Fredrick's jaw, instructing him to open and close his mouth as he manipulated it. The banker groaned in pain and squinted his eyes shut.

"Your jaw isn't broken. It's just bruised and is going to be sore," Doc announced and began unbuttoning the banker's shirt.

Doc began pressing his hand into various locations on the banker's stomach before moving onto the ribs. Mr. Fredrick let out a yelp.

"So what was this all about? Did they rob you?" Doc inquired in hopes of diverting the patient's attention.

"Two men with flour sacks on their head wanted to know what the sheriff had been asking me and what I'd told him," Mr. Fredrick said.

"I see. Did you tell them anything?"

"No, I did not."

"Mr. Fredrick, I don't think you have any internal injuries, but you have a couple of cracked ribs. I'm going to bandage you up and you need to take it easy until they heal, but you're going to be fine."

"Doc, I can't hit the broad side of a barn with a gun and I don't know a thing about fighting, but I'm no coward either.

If some ruffians think that they can scare William Fredrick into keeping his mouth shut, well then, they are sadly mistaken. If you would, please tell the sheriff that I think that it best he not come to the bank any longer, but I will get word to him if I find something. He can also send word to me if need be. They have only made me more determined than ever to help Gideon," Mr. Fredrick said.

Chapter 17

Gideon walked into the jail to find Finnie sitting at the desk, bleary eyed and slurping coffee. The room and the Irishman reeked of whiskey.

"What the hell happened?" Gideon asked with disgust in his voice.

"I'm just a drunk, Gideon. You can clean and dress me up, but you can't change what's underneath the skin. I'm sorry I let you down. I'm headed out after I tell Mary," Finnie said.

"You were doing so well. I don't understand."

"I got to thinking about Mary last night and I came to the realization that I'm not worthy of her. Why would some young, pretty thing that owns her own saloon want to be with an old drunk like me? It's pure folly, I tell you."

"You two are killing me. First off, you are not old. You're younger than I am, and I'll be damn if I'm going to think of myself as old. I have a baby on the way. A lot of men are a few years older than their wife. And second, I don't know where you come up with the idea that you are not worthy. Mary came from an orphanage. She's had some hard blows in life and made some questionable decisions. The only reason that she owns a saloon is because of the kindness of Mr. Vander leaving it to her when he died. Both of you are survivors of the hand that life has dealt. She doesn't know if she is capable of being a wife again, and you don't think you are worthy. She's afraid you won't quit drinking and you say you're a drunk. The parts about her not being capable of being a wife and you not being worthy are nothing more than excuses of two people afraid of the unknown. It seems to me the only real problem is your drinking and you've just proved everyone's fear. You're better than this," Gideon ranted.

"You can lecture all you want, but I'm leaving."

"You can't," Gideon stated with authority.

"I'd like to see your skinny ass try and stop me," Finnie hollered.

"I'm not going to try, but you promised Zack that you would teach him to fight. I've never known you to go back on your word."

"I'll have you know that in the last two weeks I've taught him how to defend himself against every kind of punch that I can throw at him. He's got it figured out and doing better than I ever would've imagined."

"It won't do him much good if he doesn't know how to punch back. That's not what I call teaching someone how to fight. It's not good enough," Gideon said smugly.

"Damn you, Gideon Johann. You're a haughty son of a bitch when you think that you've pulled one. Playing on my conscience is just plain mean and I intend to make you regret forcing me to stay here," Finnie bellowed before storming out of the jail.

Gideon walked over to the coffee pot and poured a cup. A few minutes later Doc came into the jail.

"You're out and about early," Gideon said.

"Mr. Fredrick got roughed up last night walking home. They were trying to find out what he has been telling you. He has a couple of cracked ribs, but he should be fine. I'll give the man credit, they didn't scare him, and he's more determined than ever to help you. He wants you to stay away, but promised he would send word if he found anything and said you could send word if you needed something," Doc said.

Gideon sat down in his chair and took a sip of coffee. "That poor man. I really hate that for him. Thank goodness they didn't scare him off because I think he is my only chance at solving this whole mess. I guess Cal keeps a close eye out from across the street. Nobody would have a better view."

"There are some people mighty worried about keeping secrets."

"Yes, there are and it proves that Druthers had the information that they are worried about us finding," Gideon said.

"I told Mr. Fredrick to stop by the office today so that I can check on him. Is there anything that you want me to tell him?"

"See if he would be willing to let me slip into the bank after dark. He could have all the shades pulled and we could look around together. I'm beginning to think there's a secret hiding place."

"I'll tell him and see what he says," Doc said.

Just then, Mary stormed into the jail, slamming the door. "Gideon Johann, I don't go jawing about the things that you talk to me about and I expect the same from you," she said in a raised voice.

Doc stood up and said, "I think I best be going."

"You stay right here. I may need medical attention by the time that this is all over," Gideon said.

"You just might. I didn't realize that it killed you to talk to me about Finnie, and I don't appreciate you telling him that I didn't know if I could be a wife again. I've never even kissed the man and now it sounds like I'm sizing him up to be my husband."

"You two are killing me. He thinks he is not worthy of you and you don't know if you can be a wife again. And you are sizing him up as a husband or you would've never mentioned it. You two are acting like nine year olds. I'll probably have to start passing notes back and forth between the two of you," Gideon said.

"He is worried that he is not worthy of me? Why would a war veteran feel that way about somebody that until a few months ago was a whore?" Mary asked.

"I don't know," Gideon yelled. "If I were one of those mind-readers, I would guess that you two really like each other and are scared to death over it. Like I told him, I think that your only problem is his drinking. You should be giving him hell for getting drunk again instead of taking it out on me."

"You are a smug man," Mary said and marched out of the jail.

Gideon looked up at Doc. "I think that went well. How about you?"

"Mary must be really conflicted over Finnie because I've sure never seen her behave that way before. I think that little leprechaun friend of yours just might have stolen her heart. And I fear that you are in a losing battle trying to navigate those two. Next time tell them that they are adults and can figure it out for themselves," Doc said.

"I think that is sage advice," Gideon said before the doctor took his leave.

Gideon never saw Finnie or Mary for the rest of the day, and he had no desire to head to the Last Chance to check on them. He figured it best to let things calm down before trying to have a conversation with either of them. Regardless of either of their feelings about the subject, he felt pretty confident that he had done nothing wrong, but was dealing with two normally rational people that had let fear of commitment turn them irrational.

Late in the afternoon, Doc returned to inform Gideon that Mr. Fredrick had agreed to let the sheriff come to the bank after dark in a couple days once the banker felt better. After the doctor left, Gideon decided to ride out to see Ethan. A couple of days had gone by since his last visit and he wanted to check on his friend's condition.

Seeing Ethan's barn doors open, Gideon rode up to the building and found Ethan inside brushing Pie.

"I see that Sarah has let you out of the house," Gideon said as he dismounted.

"I'm not sure that she let me out so much as it was that I just plain drove her crazy enough that she wanted to get me out of her sight," Ethan said.

Gideon chuckled at the remark. As he walked up to Ethan, he was pleased to see that his friend looked the best he had since the shooting. The loss of probably a good fifteen pounds remained a reminder of Ethan's ordeal.

"That's a good sign. How are you feeling?" Gideon asked.

"A little weak and a little short of breath, but it gets better every day. It won't be long until I'm good as new. How is your arm?"

"Kind of like you. It's a little weak and stiff, but getting better all the time. Do you think that you can ride?"

Ethan looked towards the house as he contemplated an answer. "Oh, why not. Sarah will put the blame on you anyway," he said with a laugh.

"You know what they say – it's easier to ask for forgiveness than receive permission," Gideon joked.

"The person that came up with that has never met Sarah Oakes. I can assure you of that."

"Nor, Abby Johann. Let's quit talking like we're scared of our wives and ride," Gideon said.

They rode at a leisurely pace to the top of Pint Ridge, Ethan's favorite spot on his property. The mountains to the north had always seemed godlike and humbling in their majesticness. The peaks were still snow covered and the robin egg blue sky made them stand out as if he could almost reach out and touch them.

"It sure is good to be alive," Ethan said.

"Yes, it is."

Ethan let out a war-whoop and nudged Pie into a gallop down the other side of the ridge towards Sweet Valley. Gideon sat surprised as Ethan raced away. Sarah would throw a fit if she knew what her husband was doing. Gideon wondered if nearly dying had changed Ethan. With a tap of his legs against Buck's sides, Gideon chased after his friend.

Ethan stopped in Sweet Valley to check his cattle. Zack had done a fine job of looking after the herd and Ethan was proud of him. The spring calves looked healthy as they ran around chasing each other. Gideon caught up to him as he watched them play.

Turning his head away from the cattle to look at Gideon, Ethan said, "The herd looks good. Zack is a keeper if I ever saw one."

"That he is. You shouldn't have ridden that hard. You could tear something open," Gideon cautioned.

"I'm fine. I think the wound's all healed now. You know you're starting to sound like me. I'm supposed to be the cautious one and you're the fun one," Ethan teased.

"There hasn't been much to feel funny about lately. If you think you feel fine, I'm going to go ahead and ride home from here," Gideon said.

"Sure, head on home. You're just scared that Sarah is going to fly out of that cabin and lay into you," Ethan said.

Smiling, Gideon pulled his hat down low over his eyes. "I'm also the smart one between the two of us," he said and took off riding.

Gideon rode west towards his homestead. About a quarter of a mile from home, he started getting a bad feeling. He never had believed in premonitions, but something didn't feel right. He put Buck into a hard lope and rode straight to the cabin instead of his normal routine of putting the horse in the barn. Rushing inside, Abby and Winnie were not in the kitchen fixing supper like usual. He ran to their bedroom and found Abby in bed with Winnie sitting beside her.

"What's the matter?" Gideon asked, trying to conceal his panic.

"Winnie, would you please go get me a glass of water?" Abby asked her daughter.

"Tell me," Gideon said anxiously as Winnie left the room.

Abby waited a moment until Winnie's footsteps faded down the hall. "I'm cramping bad and I'm spotting some blood. I think you better go get Doc."

"How badly are you bleeding?" Gideon asked as he sat down on the bed beside her.

"It's not that bad, but I'm scared I'm going to lose the baby," Abby said and began crying.

Gideon took Abby's hands into his own and leaned over, kissing her on the forehead. "I'm sorry I wasn't here sooner. I stopped to see Ethan. We're not going to lose the baby – we just can't. We've come too far for that to happen. I better get going. I'll be back as quickly as I can."

"Gideon, don't run Buck into the ground to get to Doc. I'll be fine until you get back. I love you."

"I love you too. I'll see you soon."

As Gideon walked to the front of the cabin, he found Winnie sitting at the table crying.

"What's the matter?" he asked.

"Is Momma dying?" Winnie asked.

Gideon pulled a chair over beside her and sat down. Winnie's arms were resting on the table, clutching the glass of water. He gently patted them. "No, don't you worry about that. The baby is just upsetting her belly. It happens sometimes. I'm going to go get Doc and he will make her feel better. Now stop your worrying. I promise everything is going to be fine."

"Are you sure?"

"Yes, I am. Go take care of your momma. I'll be back as soon as I can. I've got to go," Gideon said before leaning over and kissing Winnie's cheek.

Gideon loped Buck the five miles into town. The horse was lathered and winded, but still lively as Gideon pulled up in front of the doctor's office. Doc sat on a bench in front of the office, having just finished his supper at the hotel. He stood up and walked towards Gideon as he dismounted, knowing that something was wrong from the lathered horse.

"What's wrong?" Doc asked.

"Abby is cramping and bleeding a little. She's scared she is losing the baby," Gideon said.

"Oh, good gracious. Go have Blackie get my buggy ready and I'll go inside and get my bag and such."

The doctor stood waiting as Gideon drove the buggy back to the office. "Are you going to tie your horse behind and ride with me? You might as well. By the time you rest him there won't be that much difference in beating me there," Doc said.

"Yeah, I guess I might as well."

The two men talked little on the ride except for the doctor reassuring Gideon that he had seen episodes like Abby's many times before and not to assume the worst. He assured him that usually everything was fine. Dusk was setting in as they rode up to the cabin.

Doc Abram walked into the bedroom and ran Gideon and Winnie out, telling them to go fix something to eat. He sat down on the bed, taking Abby's arm and checking her pulse. "Have you gotten any worse since you sent Gideon for me?"

"No, the cramps have actually eased a little, but I'm so scared I'm losing the baby," Abby said.

"What all have you been doing?"

"All the usual things. Cooking and cleaning and such."

"Are you still riding?" Doc asked.

"Yes, but only at a walk. Nothing jarring," Abby answered.

Doc proceeded to check her over, using his stethoscope to listen to her heart and then moving it all over her abdomen. He used his fingers to press on different points on her belly, asking each time if it hurt and finding no tender spots. Next, he checked her bleeding before finishing and placing his stethoscope back in his bag.

"Have you felt the baby kick yet?" Doc asked.

"I thought I did yesterday, but I wasn't sure. Nothing today."

"I can't find a heartbeat, but it is rare that I do at this stage. We are probably a couple of weeks away from that. I'm pretty sure the baby is fine."

"Do you mean it? You wouldn't just say that, would you?" Abby said and grabbed his hand.

"Abby, you know me better than that. I would never lie to you. I think nature just gave you a wakeup call, and you're not going to like it," he said before calling out for Gideon.

After Gideon entered the bedroom, Doc stood and rubbed his chin before pulling off his spectacles. "I was just telling

Abby that I think that the baby is fine. I can't say for sure just yet, but that is what I truly believe, and I wouldn't give you false hope if I felt otherwise. Here is the part that you both need to listen to and Gideon needs to make sure that it happens. From now until the baby is born, Abby is to be in bed or sitting in a chair. I don't want her on her feet for more than ten to fifteen minutes at a time. She is to do no work - no cooking, no washing, and certainly no horse riding."

Abby spoke up first, her voice betraying her annoyance at the doctor. "Doc, if that is what you think needs to happen for me to have this baby, that is what I will do. I won't need Gideon to make sure that it happens."

"That's good. I shouldn't have said that. I know how much you want this baby," Doc said to smooth over his gaff.

Gideon started pacing. "I'm greatly relieved that the baby is fine, but what are we going to do? I don't know how I can be sheriff, run this ranch, and do all the other things that need doing," Gideon said more to himself than the others.

Doc rubbed his cheek and smiled. "Seems to me that you need to send a telegraph to Joann and tell her that she is needed. I can't imagine that she would turn you down, and from what I hear, it sounds like we need to get her out of the Wyoming Territory anyway. You never know what could happen with a boy and a girl hanging around."

Abby shook her finger at the doctor. "I have no intention of getting in the middle of Zack and Joann, no matter what I may want to happen, but yes, of course, we should telegraph her tomorrow."

"It makes a good excuse to get her down here for sure," Gideon said.

The doctor picked up his bag and turned towards Abby. "And you are not to get out of this bed until all your symptoms are gone. That's all there is to it. I'll be back out tomorrow to check on you."

Chapter 18

Abby was much improved on the morning after Doc had ordered bed rest. So much so, that Gideon felt comfortable riding to town. He waited anxiously at the telegraph office. The operator jumped back in surprise after opening the window and finding the sheriff standing there. Once the message for Joann was sent to Cheyenne, Gideon gave the worker unequivocal instructions to find him when a reply came.

After leaving the telegraph office, Gideon walked towards the general store owned by the mayor, Hiram Howard. His limbs felt heavy and he walked slowly. Sleep the night before had been hard in coming. He had laid in bed worrying about his wife and the baby while nestling up next to Abby and listening to her breathe.

The mayor had just unlocked the store for business and stood out front busily sweeping the dust off the sidewalk. He was still miffed at Gideon for throwing him out of the jail and offered up a cool greeting.

"Hiram, I need a favor. Doc has put Abby on bed rest until the baby is born. I'm going to have to be home a lot in the next week while I wait for Joann to get here, or if she can't come, hire one of widow ladies in town to come help. I want to make Finnie a fulltime deputy until I have someone to help me," Gideon said.

"So now you want me to do you a favor after you so rudely threw me out of your office. That's a fine way to do business," Hiram said as he leaned his broom up against the building.

"Hiram, answer me one question. Was it wrong for the city council to complain about a shot up building when it saved my life? Which is more important, me or that damn hotel? Actually that's two questions."

The mayor looked down at the sidewalk and kicked a pebble off it. "You are right, but I was just the messenger. I never said that I agreed with them. I've known you since you were a little boy that I used to give a piece of candy to every time you came in this store with your ma or pa. You could have been a little more respectful."

"You are right and you have my apology. You could've let me know that you didn't necessarily agree with them."

The mayor grinned for the first time. "I don't recollect getting much of a chance. Do what you need to do and I'll smooth it over with the council. Nobody but you and I know what happened in your office anyway. You're going to keep maneuvering until you get a full time deputy."

"The town needs one. I can't be here all the time, and to tell the truth, I don't spend enough evenings here as it is, but thank you. I appreciate your help," Gideon said and offered his hand.

The mayor shook hands and said, "Tell Abby to take care of herself. This town needs another Johann hellion running around."

Deciding to visit Mary, Gideon walked down the alley and through the back door of the Last Chance. He found her as he expected, sitting at the table in her housecoat and drinking coffee while looking at a ledger. She glanced up at him, smiling impishly.

"You don't have that shotgun of yours handy, do you?' Gideon inquired.

"I would have shot you yesterday if I wanted to do any killing. Today I feel like a silly schoolgirl for making such a spectacle of myself. I don't normally do that," Mary said.

"No, you don't, but I shouldn't have mentioned the wife thing to Finnie. I didn't mean to do it. It just came out in my frustration in dealing with him and for that I am sorry."

"We have too much history for it to matter. Finnie and I need to figure this thing out for ourselves anyway. We are adults after all. What brings you over so early?"

"Abby is not feeling well and Doc has ordered her to stay off her feet until the baby is born. I thought I'd let you know that I'm going to be making Finnie a fulltime deputy for a week or so until Joann gets here or I hire somebody. I expect he should be able to still help you."

"Gideon, I'm so sorry. Does Doc think everything is going to be all right?"

Gideon sat down beside her. "He thinks so, but it worries me to death. I wouldn't trade my life for anything, but there were some things about being a loner for all those years that were a lot easier."

Mary patted his arm. "I'm going to believe that everything will be all right and you should do the same. It's just as easy to believe in the good as it is the bad. And you know that if I can do anything to help, I will be there."

"Life is a whole lot harder than it needs to be," Gideon mused.

"Yes, it is. I guess it makes the victories that much sweeter," Mary said.

"Thank you. I better go to talk to Finnie."

"He's cleaning behind the bar. I have to tell you something that should make you smile. Yesterday, when Finnie and I were together raging against you, we decided that we'd go on a picnic today just to show you," she said and laughed.

"Show me what? I never said anything about you two not seeing each other."

"I know. That's the funny part. I don't have a clue either," she said.

"Like I told both of you yesterday – you guys are killing me," Gideon said with a smile.

Finnie was singing "Whiskey in a Jar" and dusting bottles as Gideon walked into the bar.

"You're certainly in a better mood than yesterday," Gideon said.

"Yesterday is over with and I don't want to talk about it," Finnie said.

"I bet not. I wouldn't either if I were you," Gideon said before explaining the situation concerning Abby and his need for a deputy.

"I can do that. Gideon, for whatever it's worth, you know that I'll put Abby in my prayers," Finnie said.

"Thank you, Finn. There's one condition on being the deputy. You have to promise me that you won't touch a drop of whiskey from now until I don't need you."

"Not a drop?" Finnie asked with alarm.

"None."

"Could I have a beer if I got parched?"

Gideon let out a chuckle. "Yes, I wouldn't want a parched deputy, but you have to stop at one."

"It's a deal. I always stop at one beer," Finnie said.

"Watch out for bees on your picnic. They love nectar from sweet things like you," Gideon teased.

"I'll say it again. Gideon Johann, you are a haughty man," Finnie said as Gideon walked out the door.

Once Gideon returned to the jail, he tried to get a handle on feeling overwhelmed. In the eighteen years that he had been away from Last Stand, he had gotten very good at going through life without feeling anything and living one day at a time. In the last year, he had gained a wife, daughter, stepdaughter, and now had a baby on the way. At times the responsibilities overpowered him. The changes in his life had happened so fast that at times he wondered if he were capable of keeping up with them. He despised feeling weak and that is what he felt now. His mind wandered to all the scrapes that he had been in during the war and the years that followed. The realization slowly sank in that somehow, someway, he always got through them, and he would do that now. He would not worry until he needed to and he would meet head-on the things that needed his attention.

Gideon had never had much of an opportunity to think over his conversation with Henry Starks concerning the rancher's offer to help him secure a U.S. Marshal position. The additional salary and prestige that came with the job was enticing. He would also undoubtedly be able to offer Finnie a job as a deputy marshal. Additional travel was the only downside that he could see. He decided that the next time that he saw Starks, he would tell him that he was interested.

Doc stopped into the jail at ten o'clock to let Gideon know that he was leaving to go check on Abby. Gideon told him of her improved condition. He also asked Doc to pass word to Mr. Fredrick that it would be necessary to wait another week before searching the bank.

The doctor noticed the weariness in Gideon's eyes and the furrow etched into his forehead. Doc walked over to Gideon and placed his hand on his shoulder. "I assure you that everything is going to be fine."

"I know. I'm just a little rundown right now," Gideon said.

"Get you some rest tonight. I'll see you later," Doc said before leaving.

Gideon planned to stay in town until evening in hopes of receiving a telegram back from Joann. He decided to go see if Sarah could spend time with Abby in the afternoon. On the ride, the sky clouded over and the wind kicked up, but the rain never appeared. He found Sarah sitting in the yard scrubbing clothes.

Sarah looked up at Gideon. "I didn't think I'd see you for a while after you snuck off after riding with Ethan."

Gideon grinned at her. "Now, Sis, I couldn't stay away from you for long."

"You're lucky I'm speaking to either of you. I planned to give Ethan the what for when he got back yesterday, but as he walked back from the barn, his walk had some spring to it. The ride did him good. So I guess I'll let you live another day."

"That's good to know. I would imagine death at your hands would be a tortuous affair," Gideon said.

"Ethan is out with Zack now. I did let him know that if I saw that horse in a lather again that he would never hear the end of it."

"You don't miss anything, do you?" Gideon asked.

"Not much."

"Abby was cramping and spotting blood yesterday. Doc has told her to stay off her feet until the baby is born. I want to stay in town to see if I get word back on whether Joann can come help. I wondered if you could go check on her this afternoon?"

Sarah stood up and walked towards Gideon, still sitting in the saddle. "Oh, Gideon, you must be worried to death. Of course, I'll head over and I'll make supper for you tonight. I had the same thing happen with Benjamin, and after three miscarriages, I just knew that I would lose him too, but I didn't, so don't give up hope."

"I'm not. Doc thinks everything is fine and that she just needs to take it easy. You know how Abby is. She doesn't want to admit that she is older this time and has been doing too much. I hope Joann can come and help. It sure would make things considerably easier," Gideon said.

"I'll head over as soon as I feed the men lunch."

"I'm going to head back to town. I appreciate your help, Sis. One of these days I hope that life will ease up a little."

"Don't count on that. This sure isn't a place for sissies. I'll see you later," Sarah said as Gideon turned his horse around.

As Gideon rode into town, he met Finnie coming down the street in a buggy. On first impulse, he wanted to give him a hard time, but thought better of it and nodded a greeting.

Finnie had talked Blackie into letting him use a buggy for the picnic in exchange for helping the blacksmith mend some tack. Mary couldn't help but be impressed when he pulled up in front of the Last Chance. He took the basket and blanket from her before helping her into the buggy. Finnie wore a string tie that he had bought that morning and Mary was wearing the only store bought dress that she owned.

"Where shall we go?" Mary asked as Finnie joined her on the seat.

"I don't have a clue. I really don't know my way around here yet. I've only been out to Gideon's place and to see Ethan. I'm open to any suggestions," Finnie said.

"I have an idea. If it doesn't bother you, we could go to where Eugene and I had our homestead. I haven't been there since I moved to town."

"Point me in the right direction. I would love to see it."

"Just head straight out of town," Mary said and pointed forward.

"Does anyone own it now?"

"I don't think so. It went back to being open range after I lost it. I think folks were too scared to buy it for fear that they would get murdered over it like Eugene did."

An uncomfortable silence fell upon them until Finnie said, "You look beautiful in that dress. You are the prettiest thing that I've ever seen."

"You're going to make an old whore blush and that isn't easy to do. You look pretty handsome in that tie yourself."

"Thank you, but you shouldn't call yourself that. That's in the past and it should be left there. You are now what they call a proprietor."

Mary let out a laugh. "Gideon tells me the same thing and it does sound a whole lot better I must admit."

Finnie began singing "Whiskey in the Jar" and other Irish songs and Mary joined in once she learned the words and melody. The Irishman had a strong clear voice and Mary's alto blended very well with his.

"We don't sound half bad," Mary said between songs.

"You have a lovely voice. I think you must have some Irish in you somewhere," Finnie remarked.

"That's one thing that I will never know. I think I was literally left at the doorstep of the orphanage. It makes me wonder," she said while pointing for Finnie to turn down a side road.

"It must have been hard."

"There weren't a lot of hugs, that's for sure, but they did make sure that I got an education. I could do numbers better than all the boys could. That sure didn't go over well," Mary said.

"I bet not. Us men folk don't take a shine to being out shone by a woman," he said, laughing.

They started singing again until Mary motioned to Finnie as they reached the remnants of a path heading off to the right of the road. The trail was overgrown in tall grass and small brush.

"This leads to the homestead," she said.

"From the looks of this path, it doesn't appear as if anybody has been back here in a long time," he said as he began maneuvering down the trail.

"Probably not. I think everybody has forgotten that I had a husband and started out as a homesteader."

The path wound around for a good quarter of a mile before the cabin came into view. Except for the overgrown yard, the structure looked as if it could still be occupied.

"I haven't laid eyes on this place in about four and a half years. The cabin looks like it has held up pretty well. We were only out here about a year and a half. We were going to build a barn the next year," she said as she studied the cabin.

"It's a fine place that you had here. I hope it doesn't bring back too many bad memories," Finnie said, noticing that Mary had become quiet and lost in herself.

"Memories are for when you get old. I'm fine. Under that tree over there would be a good place to spread the blanket," she said, pointing to a cottonwood away from the cabin.

Finnie drove the buggy up to the tree and climbed off before helping Mary down. She grabbed the blanket and spread it on the ground with childlike enthusiasm while Finnie retrieved the basket.

"I can't remember my last picnic," Mary said as she plopped down on the blanket.

"Me either, unless you count every meal during the war. Do you plan to go inside the cabin?"

"No, not today. Maybe some other time, but today is about us having fun and not the past," she said as she began pulling food from the basket.

They began eating the chicken, beans, and bread that Mary had prepared. Except for Finnie's bragging on her cooking, they talked very little as they ate. Finnie devoured three pieces of chicken, eating them as if he were starved.

"That food was fit for one's last meal," he said as he tossed a chicken bone into the grass. He stretched his legs out and leaned back, resting on his arms.

"So what do you want out of life before that last meal?" Mary asked.

"Oh, Mary, you are putting me on the spot. Until Gideon showed up, I was quite content to be a drunk. I don't know now. That whiskey is a powerful thing. I'm trying to keep it at arm's length, but I must admit that it still has hold of my sleeve. Besides beating the bottle, I don't know what I want."

Mary raised herself off the ground and sat back down in Finnie's lap. As she wrapped her arms around his neck, she asked, "Do you want me, Finnie?" Kissing his mouth before he could answer, his body felt so tense against her that she wondered if he might snap in two. She kept kissing until she could feel him relax.

"Mary, are you sure that you want to go down this road with a bloke like me?" he asked when the kiss ended.

"Finnie, after the life I've led the last few years, I would never ever do this again unless I wanted to," she said and kissed him again.

Her answer provided all the encouragement that Finnie needed. He returned her kisses with a desire that matched her own. Clothes started coming off at a frenzied pace, and they made love, both tender and desperate. Finnie rolled over onto his back and Mary snuggled against him, throwing a leg over his.

"Best picnic ever," Finnie said and let out a laugh.

"And you thought the chicken would be the best part," Mary teased.

They drifted off into a nap, still naked. Finnie woke later to find Mary still asleep with her head resting on his shoulder. He began kissing her forehead until she woke up. She looked up smiling at him. They made love again – this time long and slow.

While they were dressing, an awkward silence fell upon them. Neither of them dared say a word about how they felt about the other one. In fact, they both were confused and hesitant to admit to themselves how they really felt, and were scared to death to know how the other felt.

As Mary returned the plates to the basket, she nodded towards the spot where they made love. "Now that you are a deputy for the week, this here should make the points of your badge stand up and shine."

Finnie cackled and had to use his shirtsleeve to wipe his eyes. "Oh, Mary, you are a naughty girl. I'm not sure if they'll stand up or fall off," he said as they both burst into laughter.

∞

Doc walked over to the jail late in the day. He had been too busy with patients all afternoon to come see Gideon since his return from checking on Abby. He sat down in a chair across from Gideon.

"Abby is doing fine. In fact, she probably could start doing a few things around the house in a couple of days, but I'm not going to tell her that and neither are you. It's best to play it safe and not take a chance on her over doing things. Before it is over, you might have to tie her to a chair. That girl is the restless kind. You needed a good excuse for your daughter to visit anyway. Joann can keep Abby company," Doc said.

"You're the doctor, and you know I always do what you say," Gideon said lightheartedly.

Doc grunted and asked, "Have you got word back from Joann yet?"

"Not yet. I'm getting anxious. It sure would make life easier if she came, and it would be great to spend time with her again," Gideon said as he rubbed his hands together.

"By the way, I told Mr. Fredrick that you would be delayed in coming to the bank. He said to just send him word when you are ready."

The door to the jail swung open and the telegraph operator walked in carrying a telegram that he handed to Gideon. "It just came, Sheriff," he said.

"Thank you, I appreciate you promptness," Gideon said and then waited until the operator left before reading the telegraph.

"Well, hurry. What does it say?" Doc asked impatiently.

"She's leaving tomorrow and should be here next Thursday. Hot damn. That's a relief," Gideon said.

Chapter 19

One day before Joann's scheduled arrival to Last Stand, Gideon saddled Buck and began the ride to Ethan's place. He really needed to get out of the cabin for a while. Most of the last week had been spent at home doing the cooking, cleaning, and whatever else needed doing. Thankfully, Sarah had brought them meals when her time allowed her because Gideon's cooking left a lot to be desired. He tended to overcook everything, often to the point of burning the meat, and had to endure watching Abby and Winnie suffer through chewing food as tough as jerky while not complaining. Abby's restlessness since being put on bed rest proved as contagious as the plague. Winnie and he would both get as fidgety as a preacher in a whorehouse around her, and Abby's moods were all over the place. She would be euphoric over the baby one minute, the next moment crying that nature was telling her that she was too old for more children, and later on ask Gideon if he regretted marrying her. He had taken to praying each night that Joann would be the companion that Abby needed to make all their lives easier.

Gideon wanted to ask Zack to pick up Joann when she arrived on the stagecoach. He knew that he could do it himself, but he didn't want to stay in town any longer than necessary in case the stagecoach arrived late. The devilishness in him wanted to throw the two former sweethearts together right from the start. Figuring that Joann would probably do her best to avoid her former beau, and that Zack would lose his nerve and go down without a fight, Gideon would force them to meet right out of the gate and see how the winds blew. He had no intention of playing matchmaker, but wished to give Zack a fighting chance to win Joann back whether he liked it or not.

Gideon found Zack and Finnie sparring in the yard with Ethan and Benjamin watching intently. Sarah and Mary were sitting in the swing on the porch busily talking. Everything stopped when Buck nickered and everybody discovered Gideon.

"I guess I didn't get my invitation," Gideon said as he climbed down from his horse.

"How's Abby feeling?" Ethan asked.

"She must be feeling fine because she's about to wear me out," Gideon said.

"Serves you right," Sarah yelled from the porch.

Ignoring Sarah's taunt, and looking at Finnie, Gideon said, "I thought that you were supposed to be in town being my deputy. That's why the town is paying you."

"That's special coming from you. I've spent considerably more time this week being a lawman that you ever do," Finnie said.

"I'm surprised that you and Mary could come out here all by yourself without asking my opinion about it first," Gideon said to rile the Irishman further.

"You're in rare form today. Why don't you come down here and take Zack's place. I'll let you taste my haymaker."

"No thank you. If I were to hurt my hand I wouldn't be able to do the dishes or cook and such."

Mary shouted, "All that domestic work must be making you mouthy."

Deciding to aggravate some more, Gideon said, "Yes, I believe it is making me act like a woman."

Pointing her finger at Gideon, Sarah said, "Gideon Johann, you should be ashamed of yourself. Benjamin is going to think you are mean."

"Benjamin and Ethan are the only two smiling. Everybody else seems to be taking things a little too seriously today. I thought Colorado winters made people a little more thick-skinned than this. I came here to talk to Zack anyway," Gideon said and smiled devilishly at Sarah.

Zack stepped a couple of steps closer to Gideon. "What do you need?"

"The stagecoach is supposed to come in at two o'clock tomorrow, and I don't want to wait around down all day if it's late. I hope that you can take Ethan's buckboard and bring Joann to the cabin for me," Gideon said.

"Why me? Ethan is feeling well enough to get her," Zack stammered.

"I just thought that you would be the logical choice. Won't you do it for me?" Gideon asked, sounding innocuous.

"You know I will, but I don't think I'm the best choice. What am I supposed to say to her – glad you found somebody else?"

"I don't know about that. You'll just have to figure that out for yourself. I just need somebody to pick her up, and you came to mind. I want to see some of this boxing that Finnie has been bragging about you," Gideon said. Everybody except for Zack was glancing at each other and smiling at Gideon's scheming.

Realizing that Gideon had backed him into a corner, Zack returned to Finnie and the two men resumed their sparring. Finnie still had a hard time believing how far Zack had come with his boxing. His original intent had been to get the young man adequate in a fight, but Zack had picked things up better than expected. Zack had naturally fast hands. It had gotten to the point that Finnie had to stay on his toes to thwart his punches.

Irritated at Gideon, Zack punched harder than normal and stayed the aggressor. Finnie blocked his punches easily enough and countered with his own. The two men carried on this way for a couple of minutes before Zack threw a straight uppercut that Finnie missed defending. The blow caught the Irishman square on the jaw and dropped him to the ground.

Zack rushed to Finnie and dropped to his knees. "Finnie, I'm sorry. I'm so sorry. Are you hurt?"

Finnie held his jaw and shook his head. "I'm fine, my boy. I'm fine. I just slipped. It takes a lot more than that to hurt a square-jawed, hardheaded Irishman, but I must admit that was one whale of a punch. I've taught you well."

The entire group hurried over to Finnie while Mary kneeled down beside him.

"Are you sure that you're fine?" Mary asked.

"My dear, I have taken many a shot worse than that one and kept right on fighting, but I believe that I'm finished for this day," Finnie said before wobbling to his feet. He walked unsteadily to the porch with Mary by his side and sat down on the swing, still rubbing his jaw.

Gideon followed them up to the porch. "Are you going to be all right?"

"I will be fine. I just need to sit and clear my head is all," Finnie answered.

"Looks like maybe you taught your pupil a little too well," Gideon said.

"Aye, it surely feels that way," Finnie said.

∞

Zack hitched the horse to the buckboard wagon to go pick up Joann. Nerves had gotten the best of him and his hands shook as he adjusted the harness. He had made a point to bathe the night before in the stream behind his cabin, and he had shaved that morning before heading to work wearing his best shirt. As he worked, he berated himself for letting Joann upset him so badly and wondered if he should take a vow to remain a bachelor.

Sarah walked out to the barn, startling Zack out of his ruminations. "Zack, I wanted to talk to you before you left. Gideon kind of put you on the spot, but he was really trying to help you get that first meeting over with and out of the way. Otherwise, you would have stewed about it until it did happen. I know it is easy for me to say, but getting all nervous and worrying won't change anything. Just be yourself. I don't have a clue on how Joann will behave, but just make the best of it. She's going to be here for a while so don't try to win her back in a day."

"Thank you, Sarah. I know you care and I'll do my best, but women are just not my best subject. I guess I wasn't around them enough growing up," Zack said.

"Well, you won Abby and me over right from the start, and you won Joann over too until she headed back to Wyoming. You are better around us than you think, but Joann is such a spirited girl. The one thing with her is to not to let her get the best of you. You'll look weak otherwise. Just try to be yourself and don't act as if the world is ending because she moved on. I really think that she will come around in time."

"I best be going. Thanks again for the talk. In case I don't show it enough, I really do appreciate the way everyone has taken me in."

"We appreciate you, too. I don't know what I would have done when Ethan was hurt if you hadn't been around. Now get going," Sarah said and turned to walk back to the cabin.

Sarah's talk helped to calm Zack's nerves as he rode to town. Trying to think of anything but Joann, he planned the ranch that he dreamed of owning someday. Ethan had taught him so much about ranching, and even though he still had much to learn, he realized that he was a natural at it. He hoped to be as successful as Ethan was at ranching. The daydreaming worked, and it seemed as if he were in town in no time at all.

Parking the wagon in front of the hotel, he waited for Joann to arrive. He checked his pocket watch as the stagecoach approached from up the street. It arrived right on time. As the stage pulled to a stop in front of him, Zack could feel his heartbeat pounding in his chest and had to use his shirtsleeve to wipe the sweat from his brow. Joann stepped out of the coach with the assistance of another passenger, looking prettier than ever. Gone were remnants of childhood that had still shown in her face the previous fall. She appeared to be a young woman in all aspects now.

Upon seeing Zack, the first words out of Joann's mouth were, "Where is Daddy?"

"Well, hello to you too. He wanted to stay with Abby and asked me to bring you to the cabin," Zack answered.

"Is Abs worse?" Joann inquired, ignoring his sarcasm.

"I don't think so. When I saw Gideon yesterday he said that she was fine."

"Oh, all right. You scared me there for a moment."

The driver handed Joann's trunk down to Zack, and he carried it to the wagon. "You must have all your earthly possessions in this thing," he said as he heaved the box onto the buckboard.

"No, but I'm going to be here for a good while. I need some of my things," Joann said defensively.

Joann climbed into the wagon on her own before Zack could get over to help her. He decided that she didn't want him touching her so he climbed aboard and made sure he gave her plenty of space on the seat. They began the journey in silence, traveling a mile out of town with neither of them saying a word.

Finally, Joann broke the silence. "I hope that you're not upset with me for wanting to just be friends. I met somebody in Wyoming, and I didn't want to lead you on."

"I'm fine. It's a free country, and I think that you should do what makes you happy. Sarah tells me that there are a couple of the girls at church that are always talking about me. We can both move on and still be friends."

"That's good. I would like that."

"I always figured you'd end up with somebody with some status and money, and not some ranch hand like me anyway."

"Zack Barlow, are you accusing me of being shallow? I'm no such thing, and I don't appreciate that," Joann said with indignation in her voice.

"I never said anything of the kind, but I'll bet your new beau's daddy has money, doesn't he?"

Joann grew flustered and stammered in answering. "Why yes, yes he does, but that had nothing to do with it. We just hit it off one day."

"Just a coincidence then, I guess" Zack said with a smile.

"You can believe what you want, but I would never be interested in somebody just because of their wealth. And besides, I feel I have an obligation to stay close to the people that raised me. I love being down here with Abs and Daddy, and they might have brought me into this world, but Momma and Poppa raised me. It just makes sense to have a boyfriend from where I live," Joann said.

"You can tell yourself whatever you want to sleep easy at night. It's your life," Zack said.

The conversation ended for most of the trip until Joann began talking about her excitement over the baby. She had already come up with names that she planned on suggesting, most of them for a baby boy. Giggling, she wondered if her daddy had ever held a baby.

Gideon sat on the porch smoking a pipe as they arrived. Joann jumped down from the wagon like a man. She ran to Gideon and hugged him as he stood.

"Daddy, I've missed you so much. I love the looks of the cabin, and I know that it is a dream come true for you and Abs. You must be so happy. I can't believe I'm going to be a sister again after all this time," Joann said excitedly.

"I've missed you, too. Don't dare say anything about thinking Abby is too old. She's a bit sensitive about the subject."

"Oh, I won't. I'm going in to see her. We can catch up later," she said and kissed him on the cheek before dashing inside the cabin.

Gideon turned towards Zack. "Well, how did it go? Looks as if you lived through it."

"I don't know. It wasn't as bad as I feared, and I made my point. So I guess it went fine. Sarah always calls her spirited, but I think she's just a brat," Zack said.

Gideon grinned at him. "But you want her to be your brat nonetheless."

Chapter 20

The entire Johann household overslept. Gideon, Abby, and Winnie had spent the evening chatting away with Joann while catching up with all that had been happening in their lives. Winnie had been the first to retire when her bedtime came around, and Abby soon followed. Gideon and Joann continued talking until close to midnight. He was still getting to know his daughter and found it both amusing and charming to listen to her talk endlessly about any subject that caught her fancy.

Gideon quickly roused the family, asking Joann to fix breakfast while he rushed Winnie into getting ready for school. Breakfast proved a grumpy affair with little conversation. Nobody appreciated being hurried into action. Once everyone finished their meal, Gideon kissed Abby and Joann goodbye before heading to the barn. He saddled Buck to take Winnie to school to get her there on time. They arrived at the school just as the teacher came out and started ringing the bell. Gideon waved goodbye to Winnie, taking a deep breath and relaxing for the first time that morning. He began the trek into town to resume his job as sheriff.

Finnie sat in the jail looking glum as Gideon walked into the office. The Irishman had already returned his badge to the drawer.

"You need to get me on as a full-time deputy. It's a heap more respectful line of work than being Mary's maid," Finnie said.

Gideon hung his hat on the peg in the wall. "Trouble in paradise?"

"Oh no, nothing like that. It's just hard to be a self-respecting man when I get by on odd jobs. I barely make enough to make ends meet and I live here for free."

"I keep nagging the mayor for a deputy. Maybe it'll happen one of these days."

"If it doesn't, I need to find me something else."

"How's the drinking going?"

"I kept my word and never touched a drop of whiskey this week. In fact, I only had two beers. The lady on that glorious whiskey bottle keeps singing my name, but I try to ignore her," Finnie answered.

"Keep it up, I'm sure that I can get you a job as a ranch hand after I know that you've kicked the bottle."

"I best be going. Mary is a mean taskmaster," Finnie said as he arose from his seat and put on his hat. He gave Gideon a wink as he walked out the door.

Finnie spent the entire morning working at the Last Chance. A shipment of whiskey came in, and after finishing his cleaning, Mary had him unload the crates into the back room and inventory the bottles. Finnie had promised Blackie that he would help shoe a string of horses that one of the ranchers had brought to town, and once he finished counting bottles, he started walking to the blacksmith shop. He saw four men riding into town. They were a rough and scraggily looking bunch - the kind that bystanders would avoid looking at directly, but would watch from the corner of their eye. Tying their horses in front of the Lucky Horse, they disappeared into the saloon. Finnie spun around and headed straight to the jail, finding Gideon cleaning his rifle.

"I think we have a problem. Four men just rode into town and walked into the Lucky Horse. They certainly weren't a congregation of preachers," Finnie said.

Gideon cocked the rifle, satisfied that the oil had done the trick so that the gun operated smoothly. He squeezed the trigger and gently returned the hammer. "Maybe they're just passing through here. There's no law against coming to town and hitting the saloon."

"Gideon, I wasn't born yesterday. These men are either outlaws or hired guns or probably both. They didn't just show up to have a drink. I expect that since the last attempt to kill you failed, somebody has hired a whole slew to do it this time. What are we going to do?"

"You aren't going to do anything, and I'll just have to keep an eye on them and see what happens."

"Gideon Johann, you'll go this alone over my dead body. Now hand me my badge back. I won't take no for an answer. You need me."

Gideon eyed Finnie for a moment before smiling. He reached into the drawer and tossed the badge onto the desk. "One of these days we are going to have to figure out if an Irishman or a German is more hardheaded."

"That makes for an interesting conversation. I believe the difference between you American born types comes down to an individual's nature and such, but us Irish that first suckled the teat back in the homeland, well, there is no one more hardheaded than us. You Germans might come in a close second though," Finnie said.

"I think I'm sorry I mentioned it. I may need a beer to get that thought out of my head. You'd better get a rifle off the rack and grab those two shotguns. We best have them ready. We'll take turns walking the town until we figure out what those men are doing here. Hopefully, it's nothing," Gideon said as he retrieved a second revolver and shoved it under his belt.

For the next three hours, Gideon and Finnie took turns every half-hour walking the main street of Last Stand. The day had turned hot, and with no rain in the last week, little whirlwind dust clouds kicked up in the street. Nothing looked out of the ordinary and all was quiet outside of the Lucky Horse.

Finnie was walking back from the far side of town, down by the dry goods store. He saw the four men leave the Lucky Horse and cross the street. They entered the Last Chance. He had not taken another ten steps before patrons hurriedly started exiting the saloon. A chill ran up his spine and he shuddered as he realized that Mary was not among the crowd. He quickened his pace back to the jail, finding a cowboy named Larry Rogers in the office.

"What's happening?" Finnie asked.

"Those men took over the Last Chance and ran everybody out but Mary. They told Larry to tell me that I have a half-hour to show up or Mary would pay for it," Gideon said.

Finnie dropped into a chair. "Oh, damn. Oh, damn. What are we going to do?"

"Larry, thank you for coming. You can go now," Gideon said.

Gideon waited until the cowboy had gone before speaking. "I don't know how to play this. I wish we knew where they have Mary. If they have her tied to a chair or something like that, I don't see any way to surprise them without getting her killed. I guess I'll have to go through the front door and hope for the best."

"Gideon, that would be suicide and you know it. You would never have a chance with four men spaced out and shooting at you. Mary would never stand for you doing that. She would rather die than let you sacrifice yourself. Maybe we can go in the back way and I can take the back steps. There's bound to be one of them at the top of the front stairs. I can shoot him and then take his spot. You can come through the side door and we can shoot it out. Let's hope they left Mary behind the bar and she can dive behind it."

"Finnie, one of them might be in the back room. It's too much to chance and we could all three end up dead. This is on me."

"Gideon Johann, don't even go there. We have gone through too many battles together to even think that I would let you go it alone. I think my idea is our best chance for everyone. If we find someone in the back, we'll kill them and charge through the side together."

Gideon rubbed his scar before blowing up his cheeks and exhaling slowly. "I never thought being the sheriff of Last Stand would be so dangerous. I should have gone into ranching. Let's do this," he said and got up and retrieved the two shotguns. "No need in missing the target."

They walked out of the jail and away from the Last Chance before taking a side street to the alley and going the block and a half to the back door of the saloon. Gideon took a position with the shotgun pointed at the door as Finnie attempted to open it.

"They must have locked it," Finnie whispered.

"Damn it," Gideon cursed.

Reaching into his pocket, Finnie said, "I have a key."

Gideon smiled and whispered, "Now why would you need a key to get into here?"

"Let's just say that while I was deputy I did night inspections," Finnie said with a grin as he unlocked the door.

"I'll bet you did," Gideon said as Finnie opened the door.

The room was empty and they entered quietly. The saloon was eerily silent in contrast to its normal hustle and bustle. Finnie pulled off his boots before opening the door to the backstairs. He paused, looking Gideon in the eyes and holding out his hand. They shook before he headed up the stairs. Taking each step as lightly as possible, he made it to the top with only a couple of creaks. Finnie peeked his head around the corner and saw a man sitting on the floor at the end of the hall with his rifle trained on the downstairs.

Not wanting to waste his shotgun shells, Finnie pulled out his revolver. He swung his arm and head out into the hall, taking aim at a spot under the man's left armpit. Gently squeezing the trigger, the sound of the shot echoed down the hallway as the man jumped up as if he had just startled a bumblebee's nest. As the gunman turned towards Finnie, he dropped his rifle and swung his arms wildly in the air before falling backward and down the stairs. Finnie could hear outlaw tumbling as the Irishman ran to take his place at the top of the stairs.

Gideon waited until he heard Finnie running down the hall before he yanked the door open. One of the men stood at the end of the bar so close to Gideon that he did not have room to raise the shotgun to his shoulder or time to drop it and draw his revolver. Gideon jammed the butt of the scattergun into his pelvis and squeezed one of the triggers as the gunman lunged at him. The shot caught the tall man in the chest at an upward angle, sending him flying through the air like a bird.

As Gideon rapidly scanned the room, he saw no one. An overturned table was the only sign of anything out of place. "Finnie, where are they?" Gideon shouted.

"One's behind the overturned table and the other one is on the other side of the bar next to you. He's crouched down in the corner with Mary as a shield," Finnie answered back.

Gideon dropped the shotgun and headed towards the table, shooting into it as he walked. On the third shot, a scream rang out from behind it. The gunman stood up and came charging towards Gideon. Finnie's shotgun roared, and Gideon fired two more shots before the man dropped at Gideon's feet.

Gideon called out to the man hiding behind the bar. "You're the only one left. Give yourself up and live for another day."

"I don't think so. If you want to see this pretty little thing serve you another beer then you best do what I say. I want to see the one at the top of the stairs throw that scattergun and his pistol down the stairs as well as my partner's rifle. Right now," the gunman ordered.

"Do it, Finnie," Gideon said.

Finnie tossed the three guns down the steps. The gunman hollered, "All right, Sheriff, I want to hear that pistol of yours hit the floor."

Gideon used his left hand to pull the extra revolver from his belt and tossed it. He had already cocked his Colt after firing his last shot into the gunman at his feet. Raising the gun towards the bar from where the voice came, he waited. "Just don't hurt Mary and you can get the hell out of here," he yelled.

The man stood up with an arm around Mary's neck and his gun pointed at her head. Gideon did not pause to think or aim, but fired his last shot at the gunman's head with a reflex as assured as taking a breath. Mary let out an ear-piercing scream as blood spattered on her face and the man dropped away from her. She ran out from behind the bar as Finnie bolted down the steps to meet her.

Finnie pulled a handkerchief from his back pocket and began wiping her face as he held her. She cried hysterically, unable to talk while he tried to comfort her. Holding her in his arms, Finnie wanted to protect her forever and realized that he loved her. A sense of relief began to settle over him to the point that his legs felt weak.

Gideon walked over and patted Mary on the back. "I'm sorry, Mary. I didn't see any way around shooting him. He could have killed any of us. I thought that killing him was our last hope for all of us getting out alive. I knew that I wouldn't miss."

"I know," she managed to stammer. "I'm just glad the son of a bitch is dead. I'm going to have to rebuild this place if you don't quit shooting it up." She laughed before burying her head against Finnie and crying some more.

"Finnie, I don't know what I would do without you. I'm sure glad that the fates threw us back together," Gideon said as he looked around the room at the carnage.

Finnie glanced up at him. "It's right handy to have the luck of the Irish by your side. That's for sure."

Chapter 21

Telling Abby about the shootout at the Last Chance proved a mistake. As Gideon broke the news to her, he realized that her isolation would have allowed him to avoid the subject. She more than likely would've never heard a word about it until after the birth of the baby. The news badly upset her. Joann's outburst of tears further agitated the situation. Two distraught women at the same time was just about more than Gideon could handle and had him thinking that gunfights were easier to deal with than women.

By the following morning, both of the women were in much better spirits, but far from being their normal selves. Abby was not thrilled that Gideon planned to stay in town late to go to the bank to search for the ledger. After the shootout, Gideon had asked Doc to arrange for a visit to the bank with Mr. Fredrick.

Gideon didn't want to spend the whole day in town and rode to see Ethan. He found him sitting on the porch smoking his pipe. As Gideon walked up onto the porch, he noticed that Ethan still showed signs that he had not fully recovered from his gunshot. He was still dark under the eyes and had not regained the weight that he had lost.

"Looks like you're hard at it," Gideon said.

"I'm sitting here waiting for an excuse not to get started," Ethan said.

"How are you feeling?"

"I still tire out at the drop of a hat and get short of breath. It's getting old, I tell you," Ethan answered.

"It's just going to take some time. Most men die from a shot to the lung. You'll get there. Just don't get discouraged."

"Tell me what you've been up to lately," Ethan said.

Gideon told him about the shootout and the reaction that he received at home before changing the subject to the baby.

"Can you believe that I'm going to have a baby? It just doesn't seem possible. I'm not sure that I've ever held one."

"You'll be fine – probably a lot better at it than if you were younger. Age does wonders for one's patience. You are going to love every minute of it. I sure did."

"I just can't imagine what it will be like. Babies are so darn helpless. It's a lot of responsibility."

"Do you want a boy or a girl?"

"I kind of hoped for a boy since I already have plenty of girls around, but it doesn't matter much. It'll all be new either way."

Out of the blue, Ethan said, "I'm thinking about giving up the preaching. I just don't know anymore. Look at all that's happened. You end up here near dead, Benjamin is kidnapped, you were shot again, and I almost died because some cowboy wanted my horse. I just don't know anymore."

Gideon glanced up at Ethan, surprised by his remarks. Ethan was not one to say such things and it conflicted with Gideon's view of him as a mighty oak that no winds could bend. "Ethan, my life would've never turned around if I had not ended up here near dead, and we all have lived through the misfortunes. It's just life. Life in the West is hard, but it's who we are. It's probably hard everywhere for that matter. It's what makes the good taste a little sweeter. You're just down because you're not back to your old self yet. You'll get there. Look how long it took me to recover, and I didn't have any injuries as bad as yours. You are the last person in the world that I need to hear has doubts. It's not you."

"I suppose, but I still don't know why it has to be this hard. I feel old and tired right now."

Sarah walked out onto the porch. "Hello, Gideon. How's Abby?"

Gideon again explained the events of the day before and Abby's condition. He could see that the news also unsettled Sarah, and he wondered if he should have just said that Abby felt fine and left it at that. Dealing with another upset woman was the last thing that he wanted. Ethan had already disturbed him enough for one day.

Sarah stepped off the porch. "I'm going to have Zack hitch the wagon and take me to see Abby. Sounds like she could use some cheering up."

"There is work to do around here. Can't you drive yourself?" Ethan asked.

"Well if there is, you sure wouldn't know it by watching you sit on that swing," Sarah said as she headed to the barn.

Ethan looked at Gideon. "I don't think that we trained our wives properly, and it's sure too late to start now."

"I don't think our wives are trainable, and we probably wouldn't want it that way either. I'd rather train a goat than Sarah or Abby," Gideon said.

Ethan laughed. "At least with a goat you could roast it if it failed at training."

A few minutes later, Zack quickly hitched a horse to the buckboard wagon. As Sarah and Zack rode past the cabin, she waved mischievously at Ethan and Gideon while Zack drove the wagon looking as solemn as an undertaker.

As they rode to see Abby, Zack said, "Sarah, I know what you are trying to do, and I don't think it's going to work. Joann wants a lot bigger gun than I'll ever be. I know my station in life and I accept it. She's too much of a brat for me anyway. I could never handle her."

"She may want somebody different than you, and if that is the case, there isn't much you can do about that, but don't sell yourself short. You are cut from the same cloth as Gideon and Ethan. I see a lot of both of them in you. It's not where you start in life, but where you finish. And I'd bet on you finishing on top. You're right, that girl is a handful, but so were Abby and I, and we turned out just fine. Girls with a lot of spirit are more fun anyway," Sarah said and elbowed Zack in the ribs.

Zack, unsure how to interpret Sarah's last statement, had no intention of asking for fear that she would tell him exactly what she meant. His mom had died when he was very young and he had spent very little time around women, but he felt certain that Sarah, Abby, and Joann were not typical. They were much more opinionated and fiery than most ladies. He still wasn't convinced that that was a good thing, but Gideon and Ethan sure seemed to think so, and he had to admit that things were seldom dull when they were around.

Sarah and Zack kept the conversations about the ranch and Benjamin for the rest of the trip and never mentioned Joann again. As they rode up to the Johann place, they found Joann sitting in the yard with a washtub scrubbing clothes. Sarah climbed down from the wagon and met Joann, giving her a big hug. Despite what the girl put Zack through, Sarah couldn't help but love her. The two spent a few minutes catching up on their lives before Sarah retreated into the cabin to see Abby.

Zack remained sitting on the wagon seat as Joann returned to scrubbing.

Joann called out, "What's the matter? Are you afraid I might bite?"

"No, I just have never seen you work. I kind of enjoy the view," Zack said.

"I know how to scrub clothes just fine and I know how to shoot a gun better than most men. You best not forget it," Joann said testily.

"If my memory serves me well, you missed Ted McClean and he rode straight at you," Zack said in reference to the time that the outlaw had ridden towards Joann and Winnie with intentions of raping her. Her shot had missed him, but startled his horse, allowing the girls to escape.

"Well, I wouldn't miss somebody as big as you. That head of yours would be like aiming at a big old pumpkin," Joann retorted.

Zack grinned at her. "I remember when you didn't mind kissing this big old pumpkin head."

"There's no law that says you have to marry the first pumpkin that you kiss."

"Marry? Who said anything about marriage? I just liked kissing you. I wouldn't marry an ill-tempered thing like you. Your offspring will probably be so mean that Gideon will have to arrest his own grandchildren."

"Shame on you. That is a terrible thing to say."

"I'm just getting you back for calling me pumpkin head. I didn't mean it."

"Can't we just be friends? I really like you, and we are going to be crossing paths too much to always be feuding. We were just kids last fall and now we're adults. Let's act like it," Joann said.

Zack climbed down from the wagon and walked over to Joann. "I suppose so. I still think you're a brat, but I like you anyway," he said.

∞

After leaving Ethan, Gideon rode to town and anxiously waited for the day to end so that he could look inside the bank for evidence. If he failed at the bank, he had considered arresting Cal Simpson for concealing the murder of Minnie Ware in the hopes that the bar owner might finally talk if facing prison time. Gideon felt certain that someone would come to kill Cal and he planned to be ready for him if they did.

Henry Starks walked into the jail late in the afternoon and sat down across from Gideon. He was dressed as usual, looking as if he were ready for a dance and smelled of hair tonic from a fresh barbering.

"I just heard about the shootout. Thank goodness you survived," Starks said.

"It wasn't any fun. That's for sure," Gideon said.

"Have you decided if you're interested in the U.S. Marshal job?"

"I would be interested."

"Excellent. That's what I wanted to hear. I'll start making inquiries."

"I'm much obliged."

"It's for the town as much as you. We'll all prosper. Any luck on solving Druthers' murder?" Starks asked.

"No, I haven't a clue," Gideon replied.

"You be careful. I have to get home. Good talking to you," Starks said and left.

Gideon, accompanied by Doc and Finnie, had a supper of steak and potatoes at the hotel. The hotel owner, Mr. Thomas, came over to apologize for complaining about Finnie shooting up the place and gave the three men their meals on the house, which put the doctor in a fine mood. Doc challenged Finnie to checkers and the two men headed back to the jail after finishing the meal while Gideon walked across the street and entered the Last Chance.

Mary brought him a beer and sat down beside him.

Gideon looked Mary in the eyes and asked, "Are you upset with me about yesterday?"

"No, not at all. Everything turned out just fine. If you would've missed and hit me, well, then I would have been riled up," Mary said with a laugh.

"Me too, but I knew before he even stood up that I wasn't going to miss. Sometimes you just know."

"Somebodies going to kill you if you don't get this figured out."

"I know. I didn't think that they would try a second time, but I was wrong. I should have never waited to search the bank until after Joann got here. That was another mistake. Somebody is very determined to keep this quiet, but I hope to get it figured out tonight," Gideon said.

"I wish that you would. Every day I think about those poor girls over at the Lucky Horse," Mary said.

"Me too. Let's hope we can help them soon."

"Since you're blaming yourself for your mistakes, let's not forget that you're the cause of my romance with Finnie. What am I supposed to do with that little Irishman?"

Gideon chuckled. "Don't blame me for that. I would've never seen that one coming in a million years. I don't think me having a baby on the way is even as surprising as you two," he said before taking a sip of beer.

"You are the one that dragged him over here and got me to hire him. You should have known that I'd fall for that charm," Mary said.

"I didn't even know that he had a way with the ladies. We didn't see many of them in the war."

"Gideon, I'm head over heels in love with him. I can't believe I let myself do that. I need a man about as much as I need that hole that I thought you were going to put in my head yesterday. He better give up the whiskey for me or you might be arresting me for murder."

"You two will have to figure that out for yourselves. I know that he wants to give the bottle up, but he's not there yet. He needs a real job. No man can take pride in himself when he doesn't have a job that suits his calling."

"I know. I guess time will tell. You'd think I'd have my fill of men by now anyway," Mary said and let out a little sigh.

Doc and Finnie soon joined them at the table. The four of them drank beer and told stories. Finnie, limiting himself to one beer, commandeered most of the conversation. He kept the others in laughter with a seemingly endless barrage of anecdotes from his life. Gideon kept vigil with his pocket watch, excusing himself a little before eight o'clock.

Gideon mounted Buck and rode to the edge of town before he took the last side street. He rode two blocks, and then turned back towards town. After tying the horse on a hitching post, he quickly walked to the bank and slipped in unnoticed. Mr. Fredrick jumped up from his desk and rushed to the door, locking it. He checked it twice before satisfied of their security.

The oil lamp was turned down so low that Gideon could barely make out the features of the place. "How are we supposed to see?" he asked.

"We can turn the lamp up back in the room with the vault," Mr. Fredrick said as he picked up the lamp and scurried to the back room.

The banker turned the wick up on the lamp before deftly working the combination and turning the handle to open the vault. The vault's size surprised Gideon. Looking at the bags of coins, he realized the thrill that Jesse James must have experienced in his life of crime. A stack of ledgers sat on the right-side shelf.

"You can look around all you want, but I don't think you're going to find anything. I've gone through every one of those ledgers, page by page, and it's all bank accounts. I even looked for anything that looked out of place and couldn't find it," Mr. Fredrick said.

Gideon gazed inside the vault and realized that there was no place in it to conceal anything. "If you are sure that those ledgers are legitimate, then there is nothing else to see here. Go ahead and close it. There has to be evidence somewhere or they wouldn't keep trying to kill me and scare you. Can I look in your desk?"

"Help yourself, but I've gone through it, too."

Gideon carried the lamp into the banker's office and set it on the desk. He pulled open the deepest drawer, finding it filled with files. As he leafed through them, he came to a gap in the hanging folders and noticed that the bottom of the drawer barely sat below the files even though the drawer looked much deeper. In a rush of excitement, Gideon ripped the folders out of the drawer and dropped them haphazardly onto the floor. At the rear of the drawer bottom was a small hole. He stuck his finger in it and pulled up a fake bottom, finding a ledger.

He plopped the ledger onto the desk as Mr. Fredrick joined him and looked over his shoulder. Upon opening it, Gideon found a tab that said Lucky Horse and turned to it. There were journal entries for the purchase of the saloon, payments to Cal Simpson, and the purchase of the girls among others transactions.

"We got it. I should be able to find out all the names now. With your permission, I'm going to take this home and study it," Gideon said excitedly.

"By all means. I'm glad that I could do my part," Mr. Fredrick said.

"Make sure that you don't tell anyone or you might get us both killed. If I were you, I wouldn't cross the street to go home here by the saloons. I'd walk back a street and then go down a couple of blocks before coming back and crossing where nobody will be. It's best to be cautious."

"I'll do that. You go on and get out of here and I will follow shortly."

Gideon grabbed the ledger and slipped out the door. He walked briskly back to his horse. Gideon rode in such a state of elation that the trip back home seemed only to take a minute. As he walked noisily into the cabin, he discovered Joann still up and reading.

"I have found the buried treasure," he said and held the ledger up for her to see.

Chapter 22

Gideon and Joann worked into the early morning hours going through the ledger. Gideon poured over its content while Joann made notes for him. The journal entries revealed a ring of prostitution bigger than anything Gideon had ever imagined. Six saloons were involved, stocked with girls bought from orphanages and farms. The saloons were deeded to the men that ran each saloon, such as Cal Simpson, and the profits were funneled to Druthers for deposit into accounts in a Denver bank for each of the two owners. After Gideon finished scouring the last page, Joann handed him her notes, and he again read the names of the ringleaders. Learning that Mr. Druthers had been one of the actual owners was surprising enough, but Gideon was absolutely floored to find out that Henry Starks was the other one.

In the morning, Gideon stopped by the general store and told the mayor that he needed to talk to him at the jail. An hour later, Mayor Hiram Howard strolled into the sheriff's office.

"What's going on, Gideon?" Hiram asked nonchalantly.

Hiram was obviously in a good mood and Gideon hated to ruin it, but he had no doubt that he would. "You might as well sit," Gideon said and waited until the mayor took a seat. "I'm going to need Finnie as my deputy for a while. I'm shutting down the Lucky Horse today. Mary will let the two whores from there stay with her. They might need protection."

"What? Protection from whom? It doesn't look very good to shut down one saloon and move the whores to the other one. People will think you are helping your friend. What is going on?"

"I've known for a while that those girls are slaves bought from a farm and an orphanage, and that Druthers had a hand in it. I found his ledger last night. Henry Starks is his business partner. He killed Druthers and has tried to kill me twice. He might try to kill those girls. I'm arresting him today," Gideon said.

The color drained from Hiram's face as he rubbed his forehead. "Sweet Jesus. I think you must be bad luck. This town has had nothing but trouble ever since you took the job. This will get the town in an uproar."

The mayor's comments pissed off Gideon. "It's not the job I envisioned either, and I'm getting a little tired of people trying to kill me. Do you want a law abiding town or not?" he said tersely.

"Are you sure that Henry is mixed up with this? Where is this ledger?" the mayor asked.

"I can't prove he murdered Druthers, but that ledger sure is damning. I have it hid for safekeeping. This is a lot bigger than Last Stand. I'm going to talk to District Attorney Kile and see what he wants to do. They owned more saloons and had more slaves in other towns."

"Oh, sweet Jesus. We will be the talk of Colorado. Should you wait to see what Kile wants to do?"

"Probably, but those girls have waited for me to help them long enough. I'm going to do right by them," Gideon answered.

"Do what you have to do, but you better be right or we will all be out of a job," Hiram said and stood. "You certainly ruined my day."

Gideon watched the door shut behind the mayor. He stared at it and wondered about the mess into which he had gotten himself. Back when he had taken the job of sheriff, he had envisioned breaking up the occasional bar fight when the trail herds moved through, and resolving an occasional dispute. The job had proved to be much bigger.

Having not actually had a chance to hide the ledger, Gideon grabbed it out of his drawer and walked to the District Attorney's office. Gideon had not had the chance to get to know Stephen Kile well, but he liked him. Kile sat at his desk studying some papers when Gideon walked in the office.

"Sheriff, what brings you here?" Kile asked as he dropped his papers and stood to shake Gideon's hand.

Gideon handed Kile the ledger and began explaining everything that he knew about the crimes. The attorney perused the ledger as Gideon talked, glancing up upon hearing some of the more shocking details.

"That's quite a case that you have here. Since the other saloons are in other districts, I could refer it to the Attorney General or we could prosecute it here on what went on just at the Lucky Horse. I probably need to write the U.S. District Attorney since it involves buying girls out of state. It really should be theirs if they want it. I doubt we'll ever have enough evidence to prosecute for the murder of Mr. Druthers or the attempts on your life," Kile said.

"I doubt it too. I'm making the arrests today. Those girls have suffered long enough."

"I agree. The judge is still in town for today. Let me take the ledger and see if I can get a court order to freeze those accounts. Two accounts with twenty thousand dollars apiece is a lot of money. I'm afraid it might disappear if we don't."

"That sounds good, but I want the ledger back to hide after you are done. They've tried to kill me twice to keep me from finding it. I fear that they will try to get it now. I'll make sure that Starks understands that I have it and that you don't know where it is. That should keep you and your family safe. I'll tell someone where it is in the event that something happens to me," Gideon said.

"I appreciate that. Just come by later on and get it. You're an honor to your profession, Sheriff," Kile said.

After leaving the district attorney, Gideon walked into the Last Chance. No one occupied the bar so he opened the door to the back room. Mary and Finnie were sitting at the table eating eggs and giggling.

"Sorry to interrupt the party. I need to talk to both of you," Gideon said.

Looking over her shoulder, Mary said, "Don't be silly. Come join us. Can I make you some eggs?"

"No, I'm good, but I'll help myself to some of that coffee," Gideon said as he walked to the coffeepot and poured a cup before sitting down across from Finnie.

"What's going on?" Finnie asked.

"I found the ledger and I'm going to need you as a deputy for a while. We're going to arrest Cal and a rancher name Henry Starks," Gideon said.

Mary interrupted Gideon before he could continue. "Oh my, I wouldn't have guessed him in a million years."

"Yeah, you finally made a wrong judgement of a man. He's not the good guy that you thought he was," Gideon said.

"He certainly had me fooled," Mary said.

"I hope that the girls from the Lucky Horse can stay here until this gets sorted out. I don't know what else to do with them," Gideon said.

"Yes, of course. They can stay in my old room. It doesn't look like I have it in me to hire my replacement anyway. If I knew what to do with Delta, I would get out of the whoring business altogether," Mary said.

"That's what I thought. You'll have this place so respectable one of these days that it won't be fit for the likes of Finnie and me," Gideon said.

"Speak for yourself. I clean up just fine. There's an aristocrat waiting in me to spring on Last Stand," Finnie said to the amusement of Gideon and Mary.

"I didn't even know that you knew such big words. Come on over to the jail when you finish your job here, and we'll get started. It should make for an interesting day," Gideon said before taking a last sip of coffee and exiting through the back door.

Finnie ambled over to the jail a couple of hours later and was surprised to find Zack with Gideon. Gideon had just returned from Ethan's place. He had gone there to recruit Zack to help with the arrest of Starks. The rancher had a lot of hired hands that could present a problem if they so desired and Gideon wanted to even the odds a little.

"Come for a boxing lesson? I still owe you for that clip to the chin," Finnie teased.

"No, Gideon wants to see if he can get me shot along with you two. He only asks me to be his deputy these days when there's a chance to get killed," Zack said.

"I know that you have your hands full helping Ethan since he was shot, and besides, Finnie needed a job. I figured that we would go arrest Starks first. That way we won't have to worry about somebody running to tell him about the Lucky Horse. Let's go for a ride," Gideon said.

Starks' ranch sat an hour's ride south of town. It adjoined the land of Abby's ex-husband, Marcus Hanson. The country on this side of Last Stand trailed away from the mountains and provided some of the finest grazing. The abundant grass stood lush and tall, making a sea of green as it swayed in the breeze. The sky was a cloudless blue and the temperature would have been ideal for a day of pleasure riding.

Turning down the ranch road, Gideon said, "I don't know what to expect, but if this all goes to hell, make sure that we kill Starks before they get us. That bastard is going to pay now or later."

As they rode up to the ranch, three cowboys were working horses in the corral and a couple more men were mingling around the barn. They tied the horses to fancy brass hitching posts, and Gideon lead the way to the door of the massive house. A maid answered the door.

"Ma'am, I'm Sheriff Johann and I would like a word with Mr. Starks," Gideon said.

Henry Starks appeared from a side room. Dismissing the woman, he said, "Gideon, what brings you all the way out here? Looks like you thought you needed backup."

"Henry, you're under arrest for slave trafficking, and if I can prove it, the murder of Mr. Druthers and the attempts on my life," Gideon said.

Starks took a step back. "You have a lot of nerve riding out here to arrest me. Don't you know with whom you are dealing? You'll never be able to prove anything."

"Did you really think that you could try to kill me twice and also bribe me with the marshal's job? Neither of them worked," Gideon said.

Starks smiled. "You'll never be able to prove any of that, but you're a fool for not letting me help you become the marshal."

Drawing his revolver, Gideon said, "That will be for the court to decide. I'm warning you right now that if any of your cowboys try to stop us that you'll be the first to die. And when we get out there, you had better tell them to keep their noses out of things because I swear to you, if anybody comes to harm while you are in jail, I will kill you myself and suffer the consequences of having committed murder. Two attempts on my life or anybody else's is about my limit."

"You came back to Last Stand after all these years acting like you own the place. You'll get yours," Starks said as his wife entered the room.

Gideon pointed his Colt at Starks' nose. "That I may, but I swear to God so will you," he said and moved behind the rancher. He grabbed the back of Starks' jacket and shoved him towards the door.

"We got company," Zack said as he looked out the door.

"Ma'am, I'm sorry that you had to see this, but your husband is under arrest," Gideon said to Starks' wife. The woman had grown visibly pale and pressed her hands to her mouth.

Seven men were standing outside with rifles and blocked an exit to the horses. One of them was Starks' son, Henry Jr., that everybody called Hank. Finnie and Zack were carrying their rifles and both chambered a shell.

"I'll go out first with him and you two follow. Don't get trigger happy and I think that we can get through this," Gideon said as he pointed his revolver at Starks' head and shoved him out onto the porch. Seven rifles pointed back at them.

"Mr. Starks, I suggest that you talk to your men," Gideon said.

"Everybody needs to put their guns down and let us through. We will win this battle in the court of law and not out here. You'll just get me killed," Starks said.

The seven men lowered their guns, but still held them gripped with both hands. Gideon studied their faces, not convinced that the message had been received.

"You men best set your rifles and pistols on the ground. I swear to you that Mr. Starks will be the first to die if you try something. Now put them down and get him his horse," Gideon barked out at them.

The cowboys looked at each other until Hank complied with Gideon's orders and the others followed. Two of the ranch hands walked to the barn and soon returned with a saddled horse.

"Tell them the rest," Gideon said to Starks.

"Men, I want you all to stay out of this. Don't do anything that could jeopardize me. My lawyer will handle this and get me out of it. This sheriff seems to have it in for me and assures me that he will kill me if anybody comes to harm. Hank is in charge. Just do as you're told until I return."

The men parted as Gideon pushed Starks to the horses. Finnie and Zack followed closely and turned to keep an eye on things as Starks and Gideon mounted their horses. Gideon held the reins of Starks' horse and kept the horse beside his own with his Colt still pointed at the rancher as they began riding. The two deputies followed on their horses, sitting turned in the saddle as they rode away.

The four men rode back to town without incident. Starks never uttered a word on the journey. Gideon took a back street through town, not wishing to cause the spectacle that arresting Mr. Druthers had caused. Coming to the jail from the backside of town, Gideon had Henry Starks locked in a cell before anyone seemed to have noticed.

Gideon shut the door to the cell room as he came out. "Grab the shotguns, Finnie. I'd love to have an excuse to blow the hell out of the Lucky Horse. We can go shut the saloon down and arrest Cal. We'll then walk the girls over to the Last Chance before we have lunch there. We only have two shotguns, Zack, but maybe you'll get an opportunity to try out your new boxing skills."

"I'd just as soon not have to try them out," Zack said skeptically.

The men marched across the street and entered the Lucky Horse as if they owned the place. Cal Simpson stood behind the bar. His facial expression turned from mid-laugh to a grimace at the moment he glanced up at the men standing in the doorway. Gideon pointed the shotgun at him.

"Cal Simpson, you are under arrest for slave trafficking. This establishment is shut down until further notice," Gideon called out loud enough for everyone inside to hear.

"You never know when to quit. You're going to fool around and get yourself killed yet," Cal said.

"Is that a threat, Cal? If it is, well then you are going to force me to defend myself. How goes it?" Gideon asked.

Cal raised his hands in the air and did not speak.

One of the two whores sat at a table having drinks with a cowboy. Gideon looked at her and said, "Where is the other girl?"

"She is with a cowboy," she answered.

"Go fetch her, and if you have any trouble with her customer, holler down the stairs," Gideon commanded. The girl jumped up and ran up the stairs.

Finnie walked in amongst the tables and yelled, "Everybody get out of here right now."

The patrons wasted little time exiting the saloon. By the time that they had cleared the room, the two whores had returned with a cowboy still buttoning his shirt and looking perturbed on his way out the door.

"I'll walk Cal to the jail and you two can wait here with the girls until I get back," Gideon said.

"Where are the keys?" Finnie asked Cal.

Nodding his head toward the bottles of whiskey, Cal said, "Right there by the bottles."

Cal walked out behind the bar and towards the door with Gideon right behind him.

"Cal, I want you to think about something. Henry is going to hire a lawyer for the two of you that is going to try to talk you into going along with whatever is best for Henry. If I were you, I would go along with what they say until you get a chance to talk to the district attorney, and then I would make a deal with him to tell all you know in exchange for leniency. Otherwise, they will hang you out to dry," Gideon said as they walked towards the jail.

"I suppose that you care about my best interest. I guess you feel guilty for breaking my nose," Cal said sarcastically.

"No, not at all, but I damn sure well would like to see Henry pay for his crimes and not you. You are just a dog turd in the grand scheme of all this."

Cal shut up and remained silent as Gideon locked him in a cell across the aisle from Starks. Heading straight back to the Lucky Horse, Gideon found Finnie excitedly trying to explain to the two girls what they needed to do. Neither of them seemed to be buying the idea.

Gideon sized up the situation and decided that a little authoritarian persuasion was in order. "You two girls go get what you need to get by for a couple of days. We can get the rest later. Mary is going to take care of you. Hurry, we have to get on the move," he said sternly. The two whores exchanged glances before marching up the stairs to their rooms.

Finnie looked on in astonishment. "That's quite impressive. I've been arguing with them since you walked out the door. Does that work on Abby too?"

"Hell, no, that doesn't work on Abby. You try that on her or Mary, and you're liable to get your head blown off. These girls here are used to taking orders. I wouldn't have done it, but I wasn't in the mood to stand around all day debating the situation. It's for their own good anyway," Gideon said.

"What do we do now?" Zack asked.

"We'll help the ladies carry their belongings across the street and lock the place. I expect everyone will be running around like chickens with their heads cut off and spreading all the news," Gideon said.

By the end of the day, Last Stand buzzed with the news of the arrests and the shutdown of the Lucky Horse. Gideon had walked past the Last Chance as he returned from the D.A. with the ledger. He saw that Mary was doing a brisk business from the extra customers that had drifted in from the shuttered saloon. The editor of the local paper had stopped by the jail to get some quotes, but Gideon had disappointed him with only the briefest of facts. As the editor took his leave, Gideon concluded that the arrests were going to be a bigger story than he had even imagined.

Walking into the cell room, Gideon said, "Henry, I've hid the ledger until the trial. I've sent a couple of letters to other sheriffs with its whereabouts if something happens to me. The D.A. doesn't even know where it is. So I want to remind you one more time that if anything happens to my family or me, I promise you that you will die before there is a trial. I have enough friends to make sure of that." Gideon walked out of the room before Starks had a chance to reply.

Gideon felt confident that nothing would happen the first night after the arrests and planned to spend the evening at home. He left the jail and rode to see Ethan. Finding him in the barn feeding horses, Gideon explained the events of the day and the need to hide the ledger. He asked if he could conceal the book in the barn loft and Ethan consented. The two climbed into the loft of the barn where Gideon found a spot to hide the ledger beneath some hay with his spare revolver under it. Ethan would be the only other person knowing its whereabouts. The long day was wearing on Gideon as he thanked Ethan and said his goodbye. He mounted Buck and rode towards home, ready for a hot meal and the lively chatter of three females.

Chapter 23

Nearly two weeks had gone by since the arrests of Starks and Simpson. Mary was trying to make the best of the situation at the saloon. The two young women had nothing to do or any money to spend. They were bored and a nuisance. Finally, Mary reached her limit and put the women to work cleaning and serving drinks. With the extra business that she received from the demise of the Lucky Horse, she needed the extra help anyway. In return, she gave them some spending money and everybody appeared happier.

Gideon was sleeping in the jail every other night. Finnie stayed with Mary on those nights and at the jail on the nights that Gideon went home. There had been no signs of trouble so far and Gideon had little fear of a jailbreak. Starks had too big of a ranching empire to ever run from it. He also held little fear for the girls. Since arresting Starks, the whores had only been able to identify him as someone that occasionally came into the Lucky Horse for a drink. Cal was the only person that they could help convict and no one would bother to harm the girls for him.

Starks had received visits from his wife, son, and a prominent local lawyer named Billy Todd. The rancher proved to be a model prisoner and very little trouble.

The townsfolk had taken the news of the arrest of Henry Starks better than Gideon had imagined that they would have. He had expected a cool reception out on the street, but the residents seemed to give him the benefit of doubt on the arrest for the most part. Starks apparently had some enemies, too. A few people had come up to Gideon to congratulate him on finally standing up to the rancher.

The annual summer town hall dance was coming up on Saturday. The dance was the town's biggest event of the year, and all the cowboys from the local ranches would attend in search of single females. Gideon doubted any of Starks' ranch hands would cause any trouble before then and jeopardize a chance to socialize with some young women.

Sarah had visited Abby earlier in the week and the two had hatched a plan to try to encourage Joann and Zack to go to the dance. They had no misgivings that the two would go together, but held out hope that crossing paths there might rekindle some flames. Finding neither a willing participant, the two women had resorted to getting Winnie and Benjamin involved in the plot using both promises and threats. By Thursday, the two youngsters had begged and guilted both Joann and Zack into taking them. Gideon and Ethan were both aware of the scheme and found the lengths that their wives would go to in their matchmaking to be quite amusing.

Gideon had decided that he and Finnie would both stay in town on Saturday night. He would guard the jail while Finnie patrolled the dance. In the past, fights between cowboys had occasionally occurred when too much whiskey mixed with too few young women.

On Saturday, Zack and Benjamin rode towards town on their horses. The boy had come to love Zack like a brother and he talked non-stop on the ride, jumping from subjects as varied as frogs to dancing with Winnie. Zack seldom had an opportunity to add to the conversation, but instead nodded his head as required. He so dreaded the dance that he was grateful to Benjamin for helping keep his mind off the awkwardness he already felt.

Joann and Winnie headed to town on the buckboard wagon. Once Winnie had succeeded in wearing Joann down about the dance, Joann had found herself getting excited about the event. She wore her best dress and spent so much time fixing her hair that Abby had told her that she might brush it all out. Abby and Joann had also made sure that Winnie looked her best. She wore a new dress that Joann had sewn and Abby styled her hair in big ringlet curls.

The town bustled with people by the time that Zack and Benjamin arrived. The Last Chance was so packed that patrons had spilled out onto the sidewalk. They tied the horses up in front of the jail to avoid riding through the crowd in the street and walked to the town hall. By the time they got there, Zack felt so self-conscious that he would have turned around and left if not for Benjamin. Once inside, he found an empty spot along the wall and pressed his back up against it.

A few minutes later, Joann and Winnie made their entrance. Zack watched as all the cowboys spun their heads as if on a swivel to catch a view of Joann. He longed for her, too, but had come to accept that she would never be his. Winnie spotted Benjamin, and the two girls headed their way.

"Are you holding the wall up there, Zack?" Joann asked as a means of greeting.

"No, I'm just resting my back and picking out girls that I intend to ask to dance," Zack replied.

"Well, save one for me before you wear yourself out on all of them."

"I'd like that."

"I'm holding you to it," Joann said just before a cowboy came up and asked her to dance. She walked out onto the floor with the man, giving Zack a little wave as she went.

Benjamin and Winnie walked out onto the floor and started dancing to "Oh! Susanna" without the least bit of reservation. Zack watched them admiringly and wished that he possessed the self-assuredness to be so bold. Wanting to go home, he knew full well that he would not ask a girl to dance.

Zack remained leaning on the wall as an hour passed. He kept a watchful eye on Benjamin and Winnie, making sure that no harm came their way. A couple of girls seemed to have an eye for him, but he could not make himself ask them to dance. Finnie saw him standing there and sidled up to him.

"Aren't you going to ask any of these fine young lasses to dance?" Finnie asked.

"No, I can't do it, Finnie. I'm just no good around women. I'm hopeless and I know it. I'll probably die a lonely old bachelor," Zack said.

"Aye, God, you can be as backward as a breech born lamb. Could a rejection from one of these girls be any worse than standing here all miserable?"

"It would be for me," Zack answered.

"I don't know how somebody that is fearless in battle can be such a coward towards women. A woman telling you no don't hurt half as much as a bullet. You're a fine looking fellow and well-mannered, too. A lot of these girls would be more than happy to have you."

"Finnie, I know that you mean well, but please just let it go," Zack pleaded.

"Suit yourself, but you don't know what you're missing," Finnie said before walking away.

The hall was sweltering from the packed crowd and Zack felt as if he were suffocating. He made his way to the back door and out into the alley. A group of young bucks stood around passing a bottle while making catcalls and jokes as women came out to use the privy. Zack ignored the group and stood a few feet away, content to breathe some fresh air.

He had been standing there a few minutes when Joann came out with Benjamin and Winnie in tow. Joann led Winnie to the outhouse and waited by the door as the girl went inside of it. As she stood there, one of the young men reached over and pinched her on the butt.

Joann spun around. "Keep your hands to yourself," she warned.

The men all laughed and the offender held out both his arms and made pinching motions as if he were going to pinch her breasts. Joann tried to kick him, but he easily blocked her attempt.

"Ooh, a feisty one. I like them feisty," he said to a round of laughter.

Zack came charging towards the man. "Don't touch her again," he warned.

"You're that big lunk-head that deputies sometimes. I don't see no badge on you tonight. You best run home to your momma before you get a licking. No man has whipped me yet," the young man boasted as he made a move to pinch Joann again.

Zack stepped between Joann and the young man, putting his fists up as he did. The man threw a big right hook at Zack that he easily blocked. Dancing around the bully, Zack peppered his face with left jabs. Joann's tormentor had never fought anyone in such a manner before and it threw him off his game. He would swing wildly at Zack and be repaid with a punch to his body. In frustration, he bent over and charged. Zack stepped to the side, and the man lost his balance, landing on his face. Laughed at by his friends, he quickly jumped up and came running straight up at Zack. Zack caught him with a vicious right hook that sent the bully down in a heap. In vain, he tried to get on his feet.

Turning around, Zack saw Benjamin and Winnie huddled together beside Joann. Joann's face scrunched up in anger, and for a moment, he assumed the look was for her tormentor until she raised her hand and started shaking her finger at him.

"Zack Barlow, you are a lunk-head. You stand around here all night too scared to ask me or any other girl to dance, and then you come charging in like you're some kind of hero. I don't need your help or a washy man for that matter. I can take care of myself just fine. I should've known that first time that you asked to kiss me what kind of man you were. You're brave as they come when there is danger, but you're scared of life. Just leave me alone," Joann screamed.

Zack looked at her in stunned silence. He could hear the crowd behind him chortling. The longer he looked at her, the madder he got. Joann Minder had pushed him too far. In a move so quick and sudden that Joann never had time to react, Zack threw her over his shoulder.

"Come on, kids. Follow me," Zack said as he began walking down the alley and then between the town hall and the dry goods store toward the front of the buildings.

Joann pounded Zack's back with her fist. "Zack Barlow, you'd better put me down this instant. Daddy will have your head," she yelled.

Zack reached up and smacked her smartly on the butt. "Stop that, it hurts."

The pounding ceased, but the demands to be put down continued. As Zack emerged between the buildings, the crowd standing in front of the hall looked on in surprise as he marched towards them. Zack swung Joann around into his arms as if he were holding a baby. Joann let out a squeal just before he dropped her into the horse trough. The crowd burst into laughter as Joann's head popped out of the water spitting and sputtering.

"You said your piece and now I will say mine. You are a spoiled brat. I don't know why any man would want you or could put up with you for that matter," Zack said.

Joann climbed out of the trough as the crowd continued to cackle. Humiliated, she began trudging towards the jail. Zack and the children followed in close pursuit. As they walked, Benjamin and Winnie kept exchanging glances, but neither of them dared say anything.

As Joann burst through the jail door, she surprised Gideon. He jumped to his feet at the sight of his drenched daughter.

"Daddy, arrest Zack or shoot him or hang him, but do something with him. He threw me in a water trough. I'm the laughingstock of Last Stand," Joann cried.

Zack and the children entered the jail and Gideon started walking towards them.

"What is going on here?" Gideon yelled.

Zack held out his hands towards Gideon to fend him off if need be. "Gideon, you need to hear the whole story before you start jumping to conclusions. Let Benjamin tell you. He saw the whole thing and you know that he wouldn't color things one way or the other."

"Did you see everything?' Gideon asked Benjamin.

"I did," Benjamin replied.

"Daddy, he threw me in the trough and he also smacked me on the butt. What more do you need to hear?" Joann interjected.

Gaining a sense that there could be more to the story, Gideon ignored Joann. "Benjamin, you know that you are one of my best buddies and I know that I can count on you. Just tell it to me like you saw it." He then returned to his chair and leaned back in it, ready for the narration to begin.

Benjamin began recounting the events. Zack listened in amazement at the particulars that Benjamin could recall. The boy had an incredible memory and he left no part out in his telling.

After Benjamin finished, Gideon asked, "Does anybody have anything that they disagree on with Benjamin?"

The room fell silent until Zack said, "I think he got it all as it happened."

"Good job, Benjamin. I knew that I could count on you," Gideon said to the beaming boy.

"It sounds a lot different in telling it than it felt when while happening," Joann chimed in.

"I see," Gideon said while gazing at his daughter. "So if I have this straight, Zack defended you and then you got mad at him for it, whereupon he got mad at you and threw you over his shoulder, smacking your ass when you started pounding on him, and then he threw you in the water trough. Is that about the long and short of it?"

"Yes, Daddy, but he had no right to do that. The sheriff's daughter will be the joke of Last Stand. Aren't you going to arrest him or something?" Joann pleaded.

Turning toward Zack, Gideon said, "Zack, if I were you, I would throw her in that horse trough outside of the jail and I wouldn't let her out until she thanked you and apologized."

"Daddy," Joann protested.

Zack looked at Joann and she looked back warily at him.

"No, Gideon, she is your problem now. I'm done with her. At least tonight cured me of thinking that she was the one for me," Zack said.

Joann began shivering and Gideon instructed her to get blankets out of the cabinet. She huddled up in a couple of them and sat down in a chair, looking miserable.

"Zack, I have a favor to ask. I planned to ride home alongside of the girls, but since they are going to have to go back early, and I can't leave yet, I was hoping that you and Benjamin could ride with them. I'm asking you to do it for me and my peace of mind," Gideon said.

"I can get us home just fine," Joann said.

"Hush. You've said enough for one night," Gideon said sternly.

"Yes, sir, I would be glad to do that for you," Zack said.

Gideon waited until the four had left the jail and were down the street before he slapped his leg and let out a cackle. He thought the incident so hilarious that he decided to walk to the Last Chance to find Doc to tell him. There was no doubt in his mind that the doctor would love the story and would soon be spreading it to anyone that would listen.

The ride home proved a somber affair for the four. Winnie and Benjamin were at a loss for words, and Joann and Zack had no intention of talking to one another. They arrived back at the cabin and Joann darted inside, leaving Winnie to say her goodbyes alone.

Winnie rushed into the cabin and straight to her mother's room. She couldn't wait to see how her mother would react and did not want to miss any of the conversation.

Joann sat on the bed beside her mother. She sobbed as she recounted the events of the evening. Abby put her arm around her daughter as she listened in silence until Joann finished.

"Why did you get mad at Zack?" Abby asked.

"I don't know. Well, yes I do. I know everybody thinks that I dumped Zack because I met a rich rancher's son, but that wasn't it at all. I want a relationship like you and Daddy or Ethan and Sarah. You know, one with some give and take and some fire. Zack, God bless him, he wanted my opinion on everything before he would make a decision. He even asked permission to kiss me the first time. I don't want a man that bosses me around all the time, but I don't want one that I have to lead around like a puppy either. While he was beating the snot out of that man, it dawned on me that Zack was willing to stand up for me, but not to me. And it just made me mad. I guess it sounds crazy," Joann said.

"No, not really. We all have our moments where we react with emotion instead of logic. I've been mad at your father for sillier things, and him at me. There just wasn't a crowd around to see it. So you do care about Zack, don't you?"

"Yes, I guess I do - or did. He caused the whole town to laugh at me. I'll never be able to show my face in Last Stand again thanks to him."

Abby smiled as she imagined the scene play out. She pulled Joann's head next to her to comfort her daughter. Thinking back to when she had been Joann's age, she remembered being a bit impetuous herself. The apple certainly hadn't fallen far from the tree with either of her daughters and she wondered if the baby would be the same. "Yes, you will. You just have to be a good sport and go along with it if anybody teases you. I know you don't believe it now, but I'm pretty sure that there will come a day when you will look back on tonight and think of it as one of the funniest nights of your life. As you get older, you learn to laugh at yourself and not take everything so seriously."

"I better live to be a hundred then. I bet that you hope that the baby isn't as difficult as me," Joann said and managed a laugh.

"I love you and Winnie just the way that you both are and I will love the baby no matter how it is. Why don't you get yourself cleaned up and get to bed. I bet the sun will still come up tomorrow," Abby said and gave Joann a kiss on the forehead.

"I really made a mess of this," Joann said.

"But at least you found out that Zack will definitely stand up to you. You got want you wanted," Abby said.

Chapter 24

Finishing a walk of the town, Gideon returned to the jail to find D.A. Kile waiting for him.

Waving a letter in his hand, Kile said, "The U.S. District Attorney doesn't want the case. It's ours and I've decided to prosecute here. Judge Laurel is a fair judge and we should get convictions easily enough. I think he'll take a dim view of things and hand out stiff sentences. I'll go ahead and notify the D.A. offices that have jurisdiction over the cities with the other saloons so that they can shut them down."

"I'm surprised the Feds didn't want it," Gideon said.

"Me too. I guess their plate is full, but I think that it's a mistake. When the papers pick up on orphanages selling girls into prostitution, they'll have to do something. We will be the first domino in a bunch of dominoes."

"When will we get started?"

"The judge should be back around in two to three weeks. His dockets have been busy lately and he hasn't been coming around as quickly as the old days. We'll be ready when he does," Kile said.

"It can't be soon enough for me."

"Let's bring Cal out here. I want to make him a deal if he knows anything about the murder of Druthers or the attempts on your life," Kile said.'

Gideon stood up and pulled the cell keys from his drawer. "Good luck with that. He's not one for much cooperation," he said before heading to the cell room.

"Sit," Kile commanded as Cal Simpson walked into the room followed by Gideon. The prisoner took a seat beside the D.A. and Gideon returned to his seat.

"What do you want?" Cal asked.

"You know that we have the ledger that proves that you were involved in slave trafficking and falsifying documents since the saloon wasn't really yours. I suspect that with Judge Laurel's well-known fondness for women that you are looking at twenty to thirty years behind bars. If you have any information that I think I can use to get a conviction on the murder of Mr. Druthers or the attempted murder of Gideon, I will knock it down to assault and falsifying documents. Sissy and Constance told me how you beat them. You'd be looking at a year in prison at tops and maybe less. I'd make sure that you wouldn't end up in the same place as Starks. You would also have to agree to never set foot in Last Stand again. What's it going to be?" Kile asked.

Cal looked nervously at Kile and then Gideon. "Mr. Starks would have me killed if he found out."

"He won't find out until you testify and then it will be too late. If he asks anything, just tell him that you wouldn't talk. I don't have all day," Kile said.

"I went to the ranch and told Mr. Starks that Druthers got arrested and he told me that he would take care of it. And sure enough, Druthers ended up dead the next day. Mr. Starks came into the Lucky Horse a couple days later and told me that he killed Druthers but that he wanted to hire somebody to kill the sheriff. He asked me if I knew anybody. I told him about Ike Todd and how to reach him in New Mexico. That's how that came about. I don't know anything about how the other four showed up to kill the sheriff," Cal said.

Gideon had to resist the urge to pull out his revolver and give Simpson a good whack with it. Hearing Cal talk so matter-of-factly about helping locate someone to kill him was a bit much to listen to without retaliating.

"Will you testify to what you just told us?" Kile asked.

"I will," Cal said, looking at Gideon warily.

"I suggest that you stick to bartending. You don't strike me as the kind that would last long in prison. I'll reduce the charges then," Kile said.

Gideon arose from his chair and grabbed Simpson by his collar, yanking him to his feet as he did so. He shoved Cal towards the cell room. After opening the door, Gideon pushed him again. "You and Henry can rot in prison together for another thirty years if you don't want to talk," he said before locking the prisoner back in his cell.

"That should be enough to get a conviction on murder," Kile said when Gideon returned to the room.

"I'm not sure that I like Simpson getting off that easily. He would have danced on my grave. That bullet only missed its mark by about three inches," Gideon said.

"He's just a pawn. We are going after the king," Kile reminded him.

"I forgot to tell you that Starks raised hell with me the other day after he found out about his frozen account. I guess his wife or son must have tried to make a withdrawal. His knowing that the account is frozen is one more thing tying him to the ledger," Gideon said.

"Yes, it is. Keep that ledger safe. I have got to go," Kile said before shaking Gideon's hand and departing.

Gideon dropped into his chair and grumbled to himself about Cal Simpson getting off lightly. He heard the jail door open and looked up to see Sarah walk into the jail.

"Hey, Sis, what brings you to town?" Gideon asked.

Sarah sat down in a chair. "I had some things that I needed and I wanted to see you anyway."

"Well, here I am," he said lightheartedly.

"Ethan has got me worried. He's just not himself since he got shot. Physically, he is about back to good as new, but spirit wise he sure isn't. He's still talking about quitting preaching, and you've seen how lifeless his sermons have been since he returned. I've never seen him like this – not even when I had the miscarriages. I want my Ethan back."

"He'll bounce back. I just hope that he doesn't quit the preaching before he does. With all the turmoil that has happened since I've been back, he has lost some faith in mankind and had to deal with his own mortality. It takes some time to come to terms with all that, especially someone as sensitive as Ethan."

"Do you really think that he'll come back around?" Sarah skeptically asked.

"Of course. We are talking about Ethan. He's as steady as they come. Just be patient."

"I hope so," Sarah said wistfully.

"Changing the subject, I thought that Joann and Zack were going to bump into a pew yesterday - they were trying so hard not to look at each other," Gideon said with a chuckle.

Sarah smiled. "I know. It was kind of funny. Zack is as bad as you are about needing to talk things over with me. I really do feel like I have two brothers these days. I feel sorry for him, too. Women are not his strong suit and your daughter certainly doesn't make it any easier. He told me all about Saturday night. At least he finally stood up to her. For good or bad, I think he has her out of his system now."

"I wouldn't want to place a bet on that. Abby had to make Joann go to church. That girl did not want to show her face. She is scared to death that people will still be laughing at her, and she carried on about Zack like he is a dog, but I could tell that she was trying to convince herself and save face at the same time. I think she knows that she overplayed her hand and what she might have thrown away. It could get interesting," Gideon said.

"She gets that orneriness from you. If she had a lick of sense, she would have just appreciated Zack for what he is and not what he isn't. He would have learned to hold his own with her in time," Sarah said.

Gideon grinned at her. "I think that her mother is every bit as ornery as me, but you're not telling me anything that I don't know about Joann. She's still mad at me for not taking up for her at the jail. I think Saturday night will turn out to be good for both of them in the long run no matter how it all shakes out."

"Probably. And it sure gave us a good laugh, though I'm sure neither one of them will think it's funny for a while."

"I still think that Zack Barlow might be the daddy to my grandbabies one of these days," Gideon said, causing Sarah to let out such a laugh that it caught him by surprise.

"You are so funny. Here you have a baby on the way and are talking about grandbabies. A year ago, I couldn't even make you see your own worth. The times have changed."

Gideon turned red. "It just goes to show that people change," he said defensively.

"That you have. I'd better get home. Thanks for the talk on Ethan. I do feel better," Sarah said as she arose from her seat.

Gideon walked her to the door and gave her a kiss on the cheek. "I'll check on Ethan, but quit your worrying. I promise that he'll be fine," he said as she walked out the door.

Just before noon, Finnie and Doc came into the jail. The unlikely pair had become lunch companions, usually eating the free lunch at the Last Chance and washing it down with a beer.

"Come have lunch with us. You could use some fattening. I'm surprised Abby ever found you in the sheets," Finnie said.

"From the looks of her these days I don't think that there's any doubt that she found me just fine," Gideon said as he put on his hat.

The Irishman grinned. "Now you're bragging."

They walked to the Last Chance and were lucky to get their usual table. Mary's idea to offer free lunches with a one-drink minimum had been such a success that on some days the patrons were forced to eat standing with their drinks setting on the windowsills. The men were served plates of boiled ham and potatoes with their beers.

"I can't figure out what made Henry get involved in such an enterprise," Doc said. "He had more land and cattle than he knows what to do with and one of the finest houses around here. I don't know why he thought he needed that other money."

"It's like a disease with some men. I've seen it before," Finnie said.

"All I know is that it about got me killed," Gideon remarked.

"How is your arm these days?" Doc asked.

"I don't even think about it anymore unless I touch it. It still has a numb spot," Gideon said.

"Henry's daddy was on the committee that recruited me out of school to move to Last Stand. The town was growing and didn't have a doctor. Live long enough and things sure change," Doc reminisced.

Mary joined them at the table, sitting down between Gideon and Finnie. "I just couldn't resist sitting at a table with a doctor and two men with badges," she teased.

"I have to agree that Finnie does look better wearing a badge than pushing a broom," Gideon said. "After the trial, I'm going to keep him as a deputy until somebody has the nerve to tell me that I can't. We'll see what happens."

"I do like a man with a badge," Mary joked to a round of laughter and Finnie's embarrassment.

"I thought it was my accent," Finnie said.

"Did you ever come close to marrying?" Gideon asked Doc.

The question seemed to catch the doctor off-guard and for the briefest of moments, the others saw a wistful look betray him. "When I was younger, I was always looking for the perfect woman and never finding her, and now that I'm old, they all look perfect," he said.

The others laughed and Mary said, "If I had been around in those days, I guarantee that I would have made you think that I was perfect - one way or another."

"I think that you would have," Doc said.

The foursome continued their banter until the meal was finished and they took their leave. The doctor left for his office and Mary returned behind the bar. Gideon sent Finnie to check on a complaint of a pig rooting around in a neighbor's yard while he retrieved the key to the Lucky Horse and checked the saloon for any signs of vandalism.

By early afternoon, Gideon needed to get out of town. All the extra hours spent there since the arrests were beginning to wear on him. He decided to ride to see Ethan and have the talk that he had promised Sarah. The July sun warmed the air and he perspired just sitting in the saddle and riding. Occasionally, he would have to remove his hat and wipe his brow on his shirtsleeve. He found Ethan south of the cabin chopping up a tree that had blown over into his pasture. Ethan, shirt drenched in sweat, swung the axe in a steady rhythm that could have been mistaken for a metronome.

"You should be having Zack do that," Gideon said as he rode up.

"I need to build myself back up. I'm getting stronger every day and it's good for me," Ethan said as he set the axe down, picked up his canteen, and took a big swig of water.

"Are you feeling any better about life?"

"Not really. I'm thankful to be alive and such, but I just don't feel the call to preach anymore. I'm starting to feel like an imposter up there giving my sermon. I've never been a hypocrite and I don't plan on being one now."

"Give it a few more weeks before you decide. Do it for me if for no other reason. I'm not ready for the most steadfast person I've ever known to change on me."

Ethan pulled the front of his shirt up to his face and used it as a towel to dry the sweat. "Don't go getting all sentimental on me. It doesn't go with my image of you either. I won't make a rash decision."

Gideon grinned at Ethan. "That's all I ask. I've seen plenty of men in the war that were shot, and after they came back, it took a good while before they were themselves again. It just takes time."

Zack rode up to the two men. "I checked on both the herds and they were fine. The calves are really starting to grow."

"I wish somebody would check on mine. I've been in town so much lately that they probably have wandered off the place," Gideon said.

"I could check on them tomorrow if you want," Zack said as he climbed down from Chester.

"No, that's all right. You might cross paths with my daughter and try to drown her again," Gideon teased.

"That's not funny. I didn't try to drown her and you don't have to worry about me crossing paths with Joann. If I saw her coming, I would hightail it out of there."

"You're a bit sensitive. I'm just teasing. I would have thrown her in a trough, too. I've told you that I threw Abby into a stream one time. Of course, neither of us carried on like we were mortal enemies after we cooled down."

"I never said that she is my enemy. I'm just through trying with her. I don't have what it takes to make her happy and I know that now," Zack said.

Ethan looked at Zack and then over at Gideon and winked. "I thought he had a little more fire in him than that. You'd think that a man that is brave enough to take a bullet helping you catch some outlaws wouldn't be so skittish around a spirited girl."

Gideon rubbed his scar. "I know it. I'd think that now that he stood up to her and got her attention that he would go in for the kill instead of running away."

Zack pulled his hat off his head and threw it on the ground. "If I hear one more person call Joann spirited, I'm going to go crazy. She is just a big brat. Why would I want to deal with that? I'm not running. You two sound like a couple of old ladies trying your hand at matchmaking. I want no part of it. I'd rather go keep company with the herd than listen to you two," he said before scooping up his hat and mounting his horse. He took off in a gallop and soon disappeared over a hill.

"I've never seen him get riled. Maybe we overplayed our hand," Ethan said.

"I doubt it. Ain't love grand?" Gideon said with a grin. Picking up the axe, he started chopping. "I could use a little building up myself."

Gideon and Ethan took turns chopping and stacking the wood. Their shirts stayed drenched in sweat as they worked at a feverish pace. Competition between the two men kept them swinging the axe with ferocious blows in an unspoken contest. As the sun settled well to the west, they finished the tree.

"Pretty good work for a shot up rancher," Gideon said as he dropped the axe.

"I could say the same about a skinny sheriff. Thank you for the help. I'm glad we got to spend some time together," Ethan replied.

"We need to go fishing soon. We could take Benjamin and Winnie and whoever else wants to go and make a day of it."

"Maybe we should take Zack and Joann, and if they don't behave themselves, we could use them for bait."

"That's an idea. I'd better get home. It's about suppertime," Gideon said as he climbed up onto his horse.

"See you later," Ethan said as he picked up the axe and empty canteen.

Gideon rode home to find Joann and Winnie playing in the yard with the dog, Red. They were trying to teach him to retrieve a ball and the animal showed no inclination for the game. He would chase after it and then return to them without the ball.

"I thought that you would be busy fixing supper," Gideon said to Joann.

"I didn't realize that it's so late. I guess the time got away from me. Abs usually tells me when it's time to start. She must have fallen asleep," Joann answered.

"Winnie, would you please go check on your mother? Tell her that Joann and I will be in directly," Gideon said.

"What's up?" Joann asked as Winnie scurried to the cabin.

"Let's go sit under the tree," Gideon said as he climbed down from Buck, leaving the horse untied in the yard. He walked with Joann to the bench that he had constructed. "I'm wondering if you're still upset with me for how I handled things at the jail the other night?"

"No. The only person that I am mad at is myself. I'm not even mad at Zack anymore. I deserved it. I really made a fool of myself, didn't I?" Joann said.

"Kind of. It wasn't one of your finer moments. I just came from Ethan's place and Zack is still riled up about it."

"He'll probably never speak to me again for as long as I live. I guess I deserve that, but sometimes he is so clueless that I can't stand it. I think Sarah talked to him about it, but it never lasted. He would go right back to being his timid self. Sometimes I think that if I would have said boo that he would have taken off running."

"He's not the most confident man around women that I've ever seen, I'll give you that, but you probably ruined him for life. He'll probably end up a bachelor is my guess. I think a little encouragement would've gone a lot further. He's not really timid by nature and he's certainly brave. He's just backward with women. I think he would've been fine in time. You can catch more flies with honey than you can vinegar."

"You really know how to make me feel worse than I already do. How can I fix things?"

"I don't have a clue. You'll have to figure that one out for yourself. Let's go check on your mother. I'll help you with supper," Gideon said.

Chapter 25

On Friday night, Finnie found himself on his own. Gideon had gone home for the evening and Doc was out at a ranch delivering a baby. The Last Chance was so busy since the demise of the Lucky Horse that Mary had little time to flirt with him during the evening. He had drunk a beer in the saloon, wishing that he had recruited Zack to come to town for the evening. Deciding that it was too late to ride to Zack's cabin, and tired of the crowd, Finnie walked back to the jail. He had a bottle of whisky stashed there and he felt himself drawn to it like a bee to a blossom. Since becoming a fulltime deputy, he had not touched a drop of whiskey or gotten drunk. Beer did not hold a spell on him, and until tonight, he had been content with a mug of it in the evening.

Finnie walked to the ammunition cabinet and pulled the bottle out from behind the stacked boxes of cartridges. As he held the bottle up to the light, he gazed at it and tried to convince himself that he wouldn't open it even though he already knew that he would. He uncorked the bottle and took his first pull. He loved the taste of whiskey and the fuzzy warmth that came with it. After sitting down at Gideon's desk, he began sipping from the bottle in earnest. An hour later, the bottle was half-empty. He stared at the whiskey setting on the desk as self-loathing filled his drunken mind. Once again, he had let Gideon and Mary down, and they would be disappointed in him.

Finnie picked up the whiskey and staggered out of the jail. Hurling the bottle against the building, it exploded as shards of glass tingled down onto the sidewalk. He walked back inside, dropped onto the cot, and fell to sleep.

Waking before dawn, Finnie wanted nothing more than to run. He walked to the livery stable and retrieved his horse. Not having any destination in mind, he headed south out of town. The horse's rough gait jarred his aching head, but he didn't care. He wanted to pay the penance he deserved.

Gideon arrived at the jail early, surprised not to find Finnie. They had begun a ritual of Finnie having the coffee ready and they would sit around drinking a cup. Doc sometimes would join them. Finnie would then take a walk of the town, and once Mary arose, he would join her for more coffee.

Checking the cell room first, Gideon then walked outside and saw the broken bottle near the end of the building. He walked towards the glass and caught a whiff of the whiskey before halfway there.

Doc walked across the street. "Is the coffee ready?" he asked.

"I'm afraid not. Finnie is missing and there's a broken bottle of whiskey," Gideon said, pointing at the glass. "I have a hunch that he is passed out somewhere. I'll go check with Mary after she gets up. Come on in and I'll get a pot started."

"I thought that maybe this time he had kicked his demon for good," Doc said.

"Me too. Maybe it's too much to expect from him. I don't regret bringing him back. He's a whole lot better than when I found him, but maybe we have to accept that he's going to get soaked every now and then," Gideon said as they walked into the jail.

"You might be able to accept that, but I don't think Mary ever will. It's too bad for both of them. They are good for each other and God knows that girl deserves some happiness," Doc said as he took a seat.

"That she does," Gideon said as he poured the water for the coffee.

The two men continued talking until Doc had to leave for his first patient. Gideon needed to make a walk of the town and get breakfast for the prisoners. Once he had completed those tasks, he checked the back door of the Last Chance and found it unlocked. He entered to find Mary eating breakfast by herself.

"Good morning. You're up early," Gideon said.

"I couldn't sleep. I should be exhausted. The Lucky Horse closing has been the best thing that has ever happened to this saloon," Mary said.

"Have you seen Finnie?" Gideon asked.

"No, not yet."

"He's missing and I found a bottle of whisky smashed against the jail. I guess he must be sleeping it off, but I don't know where."

"I'm about down to my last straw with that man. He's as afraid of happiness as you used to be. I'm sure that he thinks he has a weakness for whiskey, but I know he has a fear of happiness. He makes sure that he sabotages things so that he can never commit to anything," Mary fumed.

"I don't know about that. I think he just has a weakness for whiskey, but whatever the reason, I'm pretty sure he slipped."

"I don't know why I ever got myself mixed up with Finnie in the first place. You'd think I'd know by now that men and me mix like oil and water," she said and pushed her half-eaten breakfast away.

"I'm sorry to have upset you. I just thought that he might be over here," Gideon said. "I'll see you later."

Gideon thought that Mary looked as if she were on the verge of tears. Crying was something that she just did not do. She might have been the strongest woman that he had ever known.

"Everything is fine. I'm a big girl, Gideon. You know that," Mary said before opening the door to the upstairs and disappearing.

As Gideon walked back to the jail, he wished that he had never stopped in to see Mary. He felt sure that she would have found out anyway, but he wouldn't have been the bearer of bad news. In the time that he had known her, she had very rarely complained about anything, and for her to do so now, betrayed her deep feelings for Finnie.

Gideon reminisced about the part that he had played in Mary's view of the men in her life. There was little doubt in his mind that Mary had been in love with him back before he became involved with Abby again. He also knew that he would have fallen in love with her if things had turned out differently. He had never regretted his decision, but he did regret that he had hurt her. It seemed to him that people like Mary or Doc always got the short end of the stick when it came to love. He dropped into his desk chair already depressed and the morning barely started.

∞

The farther that Finnie rode, the worse he felt about himself. He was willing to own the fact that he was a drunk and had let his friends down, but he now felt like a coward for running away and not having the courage to say goodbye. At the lowest point in his life, he had never considered himself a coward. More than once he had gone into a fight with the assumption that he would die, and had never been swayed, but here he was hightailing it rather than face the people for which he cared about.

He stopped at a creek to let his horse drink. Once the horse had its fill, he turned around and headed back towards Last Stand. Upon his return, he planned to say his goodbyes and take his leave without feeling like a coward provided Mary didn't blow his head off with the shotgun she kept behind the bar.

Finnie arrived back in town just before noon. He tied his horse in front of the jail and went inside the office. Doc and Gideon were inside getting ready to go to lunch.

"Where in the hell have you been? Blackie told me your horse was gone. After lunch, I planned to go look for you. I thought that maybe you were so drunk that you fell off your horse and broke your neck," Gideon said.

"I'm leaving. I decided that I couldn't do it without saying goodbye so I came back. I appreciate your and Doc's friendship, but it is time to move on," Finnie said.

Gideon popped up out of his seat and ran his hand through his hair. "You mean to tell me that you've come this far and are going to run off now. Even if you continue to get drunk every couple of weeks, you are still a lot better off than you were. At least you aren't sleeping in horseshit and getting wasted every day. Don't be foolish."

"It wouldn't be fair to Mary, and I couldn't bear to stay around and not see her. I know what I am and I won't disgrace my friends."

Doc began rubbing his chin. "Finnie, I lived a lot of years and hopefully gained some wisdom during my time. I'm telling you that running away is a mistake. You are one of us now. This community needs you and you need us. Just take a couple of days to think it through."

"Doc, I appreciate your kind words, I truly do, but my mind is made. I'm going to tell Mary goodbye and be on my way. Please tell Ethan, Sarah, and Abby that I said goodbye. It's been my pleasure to get to know them."

Gideon grabbed his hat. "I'm going with you. Maybe I can wrestle the gun away from Mary before she kills you."

The three men walked into the Last Chance and up to the bar to where Mary was bartending.

Before Finnie could say a word, Mary hollered, "Finnegan Ford, I've had about all the shenanigans from you that I'm going to put up with." She grabbed a beer mug and slammed it onto the bar in front of him. She then turned around, grabbed a bottle of her finest whiskey, and filled the glass to the top. Setting the bottle down, she wrapped her hands around Finnie's head and pulled him to her. She kissed him passionately to a chorus of catcalls from the bar's patrons. "You can have me or that glass of whiskey, but you can't have both. You need to figure out which one brings you the most pleasure."

Mary darted out from behind the bar and exited into the back room, leaving Finnie to endure the whistles and jeers from other customers. He would have bolted for the door, but stayed for fear that someone would see his aroused state.

Finnie eventually walked out of the saloon to a chorus of laughter. He holed up in the jail and stayed there all day. Late in the afternoon, his belly growled loudly from hunger. Gideon had offered to bring him supper before going home, but he refused. Anger and embarrassment had blocked out any need for food until now. He still wasn't ready to show his face around town, but if his hunger grew worse, he would have no choice.

He was well aware that he could have jumped on his horse and left as he had planned. Mary's anger had not surprised him, but the ultimatum certainly had. She had succeeded in grabbing his attention, and now that she had it, he wasn't sure what to do about it.

Doc walked into the jail and looked around. "I guess Gideon has gone home. Do you want to go get some dinner?"

"Doc, Mary made me look like a fool. I don't know if I can face people. I should have just left again," Finnie said.

"Oh, for crying out loud, you didn't leave because you didn't want to go. You stayed for Mary. Just admit it. I'm not going to offer to bring you food like Gideon did. You can either come with me or starve," Doc groused.

"You're in an ill mood."

"Why didn't you drink the whiskey that Mary poured?" Doc asked, ignoring Finnie's claim.

"I don't know. I just didn't want any."

"No, you didn't drink it because you didn't want to choose whiskey over Mary," Doc said. "You've already made your decision. Now decide if you can stick to it."

"You don't know that," Finnie protested.

"I wish that I was a young man, because you know what I would do? I would steal Joann away from Zack and Mary away from you and I would walk down the street with them on each arm. You two are both pathetic."

"That's pretty big talk for a lifelong bachelor," Finnie said, unable to keep from smiling at the doctor's boast.

"I'm going to go eat. You can come if you want," Doc said before heading to the door with Finnie following him.

The two men had dinner at the hotel. Neither of them brought up the subject of Mary, but instead talked about the upcoming trial. Doc grabbed the two tickets after they finished eating. "I'm buying today just in case this is your last meal," he said and smiled for the first time.

Doc and Finnie parted as they left the hotel. As Finnie watched Doc amble back to his office, he realized that the doctor had been right - he had already made his decision. The only thing left to do was to declare it. He walked to the back of the Last Chance and had to unlock the door to enter. The back room stood empty and he sat down at the table.

Finnie had no intention of going into the bar. He sat there and patiently waited. The door to the stairs opened and Mary entered. She jumped back and let out a shriek of surprise at seeing Finnie sitting in the room.

"You startled me. I wasn't expecting anyone to be in here. What do I owe this pleasure?" Mary asked.

Finnie waited for Mary to sit down. "I have something that I want to say to you."

"I'm listening. Go ahead and talk."

Finnie reached over and took her hand in his. "Mary Sawyer, I promise you that I'll never take another drink of whiskey as long as I live. You know that I'm a man of my word and I give you my word. I'm not saying that it'll be easy, but I'll manage."

Mary looked coyly at him. She stood up while still holding Finnie's hand. "I guess I better keep my end of the bargain up then," she said before leading him up the stairs.

"Don't you have business that you need to attend to in the bar? It's Friday night and time for all the ranch hands to get here," Finnie said.

"Oh, believe me, we have some business that we're going to attend to," Mary said.

Chapter 26

Gideon watched the clock, ready for the afternoon to end and to go home. Nights spent at the jail had grown old and he missed the time spent with the family. The trial couldn't begin soon enough in his book. Feeding and caring for the prisoners was a thankless job. Finnie did his part, but it all got tiresome.

He needed a break from Finnie also. His friend had been so giddy since swearing off the bottle and making up with Mary that he bordered on annoying. Finnie had been talking up a blue streak to both Doc and him. They had begun the habit of nodding their head in response since there was little opportunity to get a word in anyway. Gideon was happy that Mary's ultimatum seemed to have done the trick in forcing Finnie to come to the decision that the whiskey had to go and that he seemed totally at peace with himself for the first time since coming to Last Stand, but he had heard enough about it.

Walking into the jail, Finnie said, "I thought that you would have headed for home by now."

"I'm leaving. I'm tired and I don't sleep well without Abby anymore. As many nights as I have slept on the cold hard ground, you wouldn't think that anything would bother me," Gideon said.

"You've gotten spoiled. That's what a woman will do to you. I hope that I get there, too."

"I think it's safe to say that you are well on your way."

"I do thank you for what you've done for me. You've been a good friend," Finnie said.

"You'd have done the same for me. I'll see you in the morning," Gideon said as he grabbed his hat and headed out the door.

Gideon had retrieved Buck from the stable an hour earlier. He mounted the horse and rode out of town at an easy gait. Joann had promised to make fried chicken for that evening and he looked forward to the meal. He had not eaten that day and his belly growled loudly. Eating in town had grown monotonous. Some days he didn't bother with food or ate hardtack at his desk.

He had ridden a mile out of town to the area where the land turned brushy and covered in scrub trees. Oblivious to his surroundings, Gideon thought about baby names. Out of the brush, two men appeared in front of Gideon and two more behind him. All of the men had revolvers aimed at him. Gideon pulled his horse to a stop and rested his hands on the saddle horn. The men were some of the same crew from the day that he had arrested Starks at his ranch.

"Sheriff, we need you to take us to that ledger," Hank Starks said.

"You don't want to do this. That ledger is only one piece of the evidence. You can't get rid of all of it," Gideon said.

"Those two whores don't know anything except about Cal, and what Cal knows don't matter. He'll be dead, and probably your deputy too, before the night is through."

Swiveling his head to look at the other men, Gideon said. "Do you boys really want to turn to crime for Henry Starks? He doesn't give a damn about any of you and he wouldn't offer a hand if you were in trouble."

"Sheriff, this isn't about loyalty. It's about money. What these men are going to be paid for today buys a lot of goodwill," Hank said.

"And what if I refuse?" Gideon asked.

"I've already been by your place today. I saw your pregnant wife and those two pretty girls all outside. The young one had just gotten home from school. I can either take you to them, and you can watch them die before I kill you, or you can take me to the ledger before I kill you. Either way you are going to die today. You just need to decide on which is more important – your family or the ledger," Hank said.

"You are one lowdown son of a bitch. Let's go get the ledger," Gideon said.

"Eddie, get his guns and take hold of his reins," Hank ordered.

"Where are we headed, Sheriff?" Eddie asked.

"To Ethan Oakes' ranch," Gideon answered as the men led him away off the road.

Gideon realized that he had made a terrible mistake at placing the ledger in Ethan's barn. He had convinced himself that his threat to Henry Starks would be enough to prevent this from happening. His lack of planning could get the Oakes family killed, and he saw no chance to rectify the danger.

"Hank, let me go in there and get it. I can't endanger the Oakes family, and I won't pull anything and risk my own family," Gideon said.

"I'm afraid we can't do that."

"You have to promise me that we will sneak in there and not disturb Ethan and his family. They have nothing to do with this and can't come to harm," Gideon said.

"Fine by me. You have my word. I just want to save my daddy. I don't cherish killing anyone, not even you. You should've just left well enough alone. A few whores that never had a life beforehand anyway weren't worth dying for," Hank said.

"Who is going to kill Cal?"

"Eddie likes the money. I'm paying him extra. When we are done with you, he is going to slip into town and kill Cal. Maybe he'll get lucky and not have to kill your deputy, but I doubt it. That Irishman seems like a likeable fellow."

They rode cross-country, avoiding any roads until they reached Ethan's property. Gideon directed them to a tree line behind the barn. The double doors on each end of the barn were open to allow airflow and no one was in the structure.

"It's in the barn. Someone needs to check the yard to make sure no one is out there. They should be eating about now," Gideon said.

"Eddie, work your way down the trees and have a look. It's better for all of us that we not be seen. It could get one of us killed," Hank said.

Eddie returned in a few minutes. "No one's outside and there's smoke coming out the stovepipe. I'm guessing they're eating. There's a dog on the porch."

"Damn dogs," Hank said. "Maybe he won't notice us coming in from the back."

The five men walked from the trees through the open gate and entered the barn from the rear. The dog started barking as they did.

∞

As Ethan dried his hands before sitting down to the meal, he heard the dog. Glancing out the window, he saw nothing but the dog standing on the porch barking towards their big cottonwood tree and the barn. "Chase must be barking at the squirrels again. They like to taunt him. We need to have us squirrel some night and put an end to this."

"If you want squirrel you are going to have to cook it yourself. A squirrel isn't nothing more than a rat with a bushy tail. I had to eat them as a girl and I'm not about to do it now," Sarah said.

"I'll just do that. Benjamin and I can eat them and you can fix what you want," Ethan said.

∞

"Where is it?" Hank whispered.

"It's up in the loft," Gideon answered.

"Eddie, you go up there first and keep an eye on him," Hank said, motioning with his gun at the ladder.

Eddie climbed the ladder and then Gideon followed. As Gideon climbed the stairs, his mind raced to decide what to do. He was torn between trying to save his own life at the cost of endangering Ethan and his family or accepting his fate of sure death. As Gideon reached the loft, he realized that his nature would not allow him to die without putting up a fight. Otherwise, his life would have ended a long time ago.

"Get it and make sure that I can see what you are doing," Eddie said.

Gideon began raking hay away, making sure that Eddie could see as the ledger came into view. He picked the book up with both hands, wrapping his fingers around the butt of the concealed gun as he did. Keeping the gun shielded, Gideon moved to hand the ledger to Eddie. "Here it is," he said, cocking the gun at the same time and firing. The bullet tore into Eddie stomach. Eddie was still screaming when Gideon dropped the ledger and shot him in the heart.

Hank shouted for Eddie as Gideon tried tiptoeing away from where the body had crashed to the floor. Gideon kept his eyes on the floor opening, ready to shoot if a head appeared while he tried to figure out what he would do. He knew that sticking his head through the opening and shooting it out with the other three would be suicide.

∞

Ethan was giving the dinner blessing when the two shots rang out, startling them all badly and causing Benjamin to bump his plate and spill his glass of water.

Instinctively, Ethan knew that Gideon needed him. He shouted, "Benjamin, hide in your room. Sarah, get the shotgun and if anybody comes through the door shoot them with one barrel and save the other for more."

After grabbing his rifle, Ethan dashed into the yard. He saw the three men standing in the barn hallway forty yards away. One of the men spotted him and the three began firing their guns. Ethan did not flinch but raised his rifle. He took careful aim and squeezed the trigger. One of the men flopped backward. From the time that he and Gideon had first started shooting, he had always been the better rifle shot. He had no doubts in his ability with a rifle. Unmindful of the shots fired upon him, he took aim on a second man and fired. Another one dropped.

Gideon realized that Ethan was involved and made a run for the loft entrance. Making a dive, he slid across the hay covered floor and stuck his head and arm through the hole ready to fire. As he did, he saw Hank Starks fall on top of the other two men.

"Ethan, it's me," Gideon shouted before bounding down the stairs.

Two of the men were already dead as Hank Starks took his last gasp of breath. Ethan walked into the barn and looked at the carnage he had committed.

"I've never shot anyone before," Ethan said as he viewed the enormity of his actions.

"Ethan, I'm so sorry I caused this. I should have never hid the ledger here," Gideon said.

"I better go tell Sarah that we're all right," Ethan said, oblivious to Gideon's remarks. He walked trancelike towards the house.

As he neared the cabin, Sarah flung the door open and came running out into Ethan's arms. "Are you hurt?" she cried.

"No, I'm fine. I think I killed three men."

"What happened?"

"Gideon was in trouble. I think I killed three men," Ethan repeated. "But I'll explain later. We'd better check on Benjamin. He's probably scared to death."

Sarah took a step back and looked at her husband. His face had a blank expression and she realized that he was in shock. She then saw bullet holes on either side of his shirt where the material bunched at the waist. "You have bullet holes in your shirt," she whimpered.

Ethan looked down and found one of the holes, sticking his finger in it. "At least it missed me this time," he said before taking Sarah's hand and walking into the cabin.

"Benjamin, everything is fine. You can come out," Sarah shouted.

The boy came running out of his bedroom and wedged himself between his two parents. "I thought that you were dead," he mumbled into his father's leg.

Ethan realized that Benjamin needed him and snapped out of his lethargy. Patting his son on the shoulder, he said, "Everything is fine. I just had to help Gideon. Bad men were trying to hurt him, but it's all over now. You just need to stay in the house with your momma. There are things out there that you don't need to see."

Gideon appeared in the doorway. His face looked ashen and he seemed unsure of whether he should enter the cabin. "I'm so sorry that I brought you into this. I should have never done it."

Sarah spun around and glared at him. "Gideon, for God's sake, what have you done? Ethan has bullet holes in his shirt. He could have been killed," she yelled.

"I hid the ledger for the trial here and told Ethan where it was in case something happened to me. I didn't think about the danger it could put you all in."

"You didn't think about it? How in the hell could you not? You should have known that this could happen," Sarah shouted.

Ethan held his hand up to bring a stop to the yelling. "Sarah, it all turned out all right. Everything is fine."

"No, it is not. Benjamin and I are still shaking. We've all been through enough before this and now you have to live with killing three men. You are not the type of man that can do that easily."

"No, you are wrong. I defended my family and my friend and I did nothing wrong in the eyes of the Lord. I didn't stand there and let someone try to kill me this time. I fought back," Ethan said.

Sarah collapsed into a chair and covered her face. Great sobs escaped her as she mumbled, "I don't know how much more I can take. Things have to get easier."

Ethan squatted down to Benjamin's level. "Benjamin, I know that you are upset, but there's nothing to be scared of now. It's a terrible thing to have to kill men, but I had no choice. It was either kill or be killed, and they would have killed Gideon, you, and your momma, too. You are safe now and I will keep you safe."

Benjamin nodded his head, but watched his mother as he did so. He moved to her, patting her on the back and reassuring her.

Gideon walked into the cabin and dropped into a chair beside Sarah. Doubts about his abilities as sheriff were filling his mind and he was devastated that he had failed to comprehend the risk to the family by hiding the ledger in the barn. He had badly overestimated the weight his threat upon Henry Starks' life would carry. His was a profession where glaring mistakes could result in tragic results. This one almost had.

Sarah popped up from her seat. The spilled water still dripped from the table to the floor. She grabbed a towel and began drying the mess. As she neared Gideon, she put her hand on his shoulder. "Go do what you need to do. I forgive you."

Her words brought some sense of relief to Gideon. He didn't feel absolved of his mistake by any means, but was grateful that he had not destroyed his friendship with Sarah. With such a small circle of friends, he couldn't imagine not having her in his life.

"Ethan, do you think that you could come outside to help me?" Gideon asked.

Ethan seemed eerily self-composed now. His change in demeanor had been decisive as if his sense of being the head of the family had overridden any emotional turmoil that he felt. "Let's get it over with," he said.

Gideon retrieved the horses from behind the trees and walked them to the barn. Feeling the need to apologize again, he said, "Ethan, I'm so sorry to have brought this upon your family."

"I could have told you no. We underestimated Henry's desperation. He is the one that will suffer the most once he learns that he cost his son his life. Benjamin and Sarah will both be fine in a couple of days. This isn't anywhere near as bad as Benjamin's kidnapping and we all got through that."

"What about you?" Gideon asked. Ethan had never had the temperament for violence. He was much calmer than Gideon could imagine.

"I'm at peace with myself. They gave me no choice but to shoot them. I hope I never have to do it again, but I don't feel powerless anymore. I defended us. Let's get the bodies loaded."

Once they had the bodies tied across the saddles, Gideon strung the horses together. "I better get back to town. So much for that fried chicken I was promised tonight," he said.

"I'll harness up the wagon and take the family to tell Abby what happened. It will probably be good for all of them to be together anyway," Ethan said.

Dusk was settling in as Gideon rode into town. After tying the horses to the rail in front of the jail, he walked into the building and grabbed the cell keys. As Gideon unlocked the cell that housed Starks, he said, "You need to come with me."

Starks looked up suspiciously at Gideon, but rose to his feet and left the cell.

Gideon walked Starks outside and said, "See what you've done."

Starks ran to his son and lifted Hank's head before falling to his knees. "My God, what have I done?" he cried.

Chapter 27

A voice called out to Finnie. It sounded muffled as if coming through a wall and he thought he was dreaming. As he slumbered in the jail, he tried to ignore the shouting until he jumped with a start, realizing that the voice was real. Finnie opened his eyes to see the first gray light of day barely illuminating the room. He ran to the cell room door and threw it open. Cal Simpson was the source of the disturbance.

"Henry hung himself," Cal yelled. "He was hanging there when I woke up."

Finnie saw the body hanging at the window and ran to grab the cell keys. He opened the door and walked cautiously up to the body, half expecting the prisoner to yell boo. The color and appearance of the face told him otherwise. He touched the skin on Starks' arm and found it cool to the touch.

Cal hollered, "Get him out of here."

"Oh, shut up. He's not going to do you any harm now," Finnie said before walking out of the room and shutting the door.

Ignoring his inclination to wait for Gideon, Finnie walked over to the doctor's office and pounded on the door. Doc, in his housecoat, eventually trooped to the entrance.

"What is it?" Doc grumbled.

"Henry Starks hung himself," Finnie said.

"Is he dead?"

"He's already cool to the touch."

"Well then, what do you want me to do about it? I'm a doctor, not an undertaker. If he is already cool to the touch, only God is going to revive him, and I think He has better things to do than waste his time on Henry Starks. He can hang there until Gideon gets in. I'm going back to bed," Doc said and shut the door.

In spite of the situation, Finnie burst out laughing. "I hope that I don't get that crotchety in my old age," he said aloud to no one.

Walking back to the jail, Finnie decided to go back to bed. Gideon would not be in for at least another hour and there was nothing else that could be done. He wasn't keen on sleeping with a dead body in the next room, but he soon dozed off. Doc revenged his awakening by doing the same to Finnie a little over an hour later.

Gideon arrived at the jail later than usual. The aftermath of the evening before had taken most of the night to resolve. Abby had still been upset when he got home despite Ethan and Sarah doing their best to reassure her that everything was fine. Calming her had taken what seemed like forever and then he had had trouble going to sleep. He lay in bed listening to Abby breathe for hours before drifting off to sleep.

Hanging his hat on a peg by the door, Gideon said, "Good morning. I sure hope today is better than yesterday."

Finnie looked at Doc in hopes that the doctor would break the news, but Doc strategically sipped his coffee and refused making eye contact.

Clearing his throat before speaking, Finnie said, "Starks hung himself last night."

"Oh, Christ. That's just what we needed – more deaths. I guess the guilt over getting Hank killed proved too much for him. That might make me do the same thing. I don't cherish riding out to tell Mrs. Starks that her husband and son are both dead," Gideon said.

"He's still hanging back there. I thought that you should see him first before we moved him," Finnie said.

Gideon walked into the cell room with Doc and Finnie in tow. "You lift him and I'll unfasten his belt," Gideon said to Finnie.

"Nothing like hugging a dead man first thing in the morning. I'll probably be seeing his ghost in my sleep tonight," Finnie said as he bear-hugged the body and lifted.

They laid the body on the bed.

"Finnie, will you go get the cabinetmaker and have him get the body out of here," Gideon asked.

After Finnie had left, Doc said, "Greed is a funny thing. It can turn a successful, well-respected man into a raving lunatic. Henry Starks had everything and now the only thing he'll have is a pine box. It's hard to understand."

"And it about got me killed on three different occasions. I would like to see my baby born," Gideon said.

"You will. You've got more lives than a cat," Doc said. "I have to go."

Gideon waited until the cabinetmaker removed the body before retrieving the ledger from his saddlebag and walking to see District Attorney Kile. He walked into the office and sat the ledger on the desk.

"Hank Starks, Henry's son, was killed last night trying to get the ledger. Henry Starks hung himself in his cell sometime during the night. Apparently he was overcome with guilt for causing his son's death," Gideon said.

Kile gazed up at Gideon with disappointment etched on his face. "I really wanted to prosecute this one. It would've been high profile and could've launched my political career. I guess he just ended up hung a little earlier than he would have anyway. We can go after Cal Simpson now. I won't have to honor the deal I made with him."

"I would've liked to have seen Starks convicted too. He caused me enough grief."

"I would say so. I'm still going to try to get the money from those accounts and the sale of the Lucky Horse for those girls. I don't know if the judge will go for it, but I'll try."

"That would be a good thing. Those girls were robbed of their lives and it would help give them a new start."

"You did good work, Sheriff. I'll talk with you before the trial," Kile said.

Gideon walked to the jail and mounted his horse to ride to see Mrs. Starks. He found himself holding Buck back to as slow of a pace as possible. The thought of telling the woman that her husband and son were dead filled him with dread. Imagining his own grief if presented with such news, he wondered if he could find the strength to carry on in such a circumstance.

As Gideon rode into the yard of the ranch, he noticed that the ranch hands were doing their best to ignore him. He suspected that they were well aware of Hank's death. Tying the horse, he walked up to the door and knocked. The same maid as before answered the door.

"I need to see Mrs. Starks," Gideon said.

Mrs. Starks entered the room before Gideon had finished his sentence. The maid made a hasty retreat.

"What do you want, Sheriff?' Mrs. Starks asked.

"Mrs. Starks, I'm afraid that I have some bad news. Your son was killed last night trying to take a ledger that was to be used for evidence. Henry was told of this last evening, and sometime during the night, he hung himself. They're both gone, ma'am," Gideon said.

Mrs. Starks stepped backwards until she collapsed onto a couch. The color drained from her face and she looked as if she might faint. She mumbled, "My sweet Hank is gone."

"Ma'am, I'm truly sorry things had to turn out this way."

"Oh, shut up. Nobody cares what you think. That stupid son of a bitch talked my son into doing his dirty work for him and got him killed. I hope you both end up in hell," Mrs. Starks screamed, her finger pointing at Gideon with her hand trembling as if inflicted with palsy.

Gideon stood stoic with his back straight and his arms to his side. "I had to uphold the law. I take no pleasure in killing a man."

"I said shut up. You could have left well enough alone. It was just some whores that nobody gave a damn about anyway. I'll have to tell my daughter that her brother and father are gone. I'm going to pray every night for the rest of my life that you rot in hell. I hope that you know this feeling before you die," Mrs. Starks yelled at the top of her lungs.

Gideon walked out of the house and jumped onto Buck. He rode the horse at a lope all the way back to town.

Chapter 28

Abby sat on the porch swing knitting a baby blanket. Making things for the baby and reading kept her from going stir-crazy. She rested her hands on her bulging belly as she worked. The baby kicked her, letting her know that it was alive and active. All the bed rest and sitting had been hard to take, but she had enjoyed everything else about being pregnant. Her pregnancy with Joann had been too stressful of a time in her life to take pleasure in it. She had enjoyed being pregnant with Winnie, but this time getting to share it with the love of her life and her two daughters had made it extra special.

Joann came out of the cabin and sat down beside her mother. "Abs, you look beautiful today. The blanket looks good too," she said.

"Thank you. I do feel good today. I'm not tired at all," Abby said.

"Have you and Daddy came up with names for the baby yet?"

"No, Gideon wants to have a family meeting where we all come to an agreement on a name. I keep telling him to be careful for what he wishes. You and Winnie are liable to never agree to something sensible," Abby said with a smile.

"I wouldn't ever do that. It just needs to be a good strong name. It's going to be a boy, isn't it?"

"I think so. The baby feels different from you and Winnie. God help us if we have another little Gideon running around," Abby joked.

"Life is hard to predict. Who would've ever thought that you and Daddy would be together again or that I would get to know him? Sometimes I have a hard time believing it," Joann said.

"You are not the only one. Sometimes life has a way of surprising us. Thank God for second chances."

"I was wondering if I could take Snuggles for a ride?"

"Sure. It's a nice day for that. I wish that I could go with you. Are you taking Winnie? She loves being with you," Abby said.

"I don't think so this time. This might take a little while," Joann said.

"You are going to go see Zack, aren't you?"

"Yes, I can't leave things the way that they are. Daddy may end up arresting me or Zack, but it'll be better than avoiding each other forever."

"What are you going to say to him?"

"I'm going to apologize, and besides that, I don't have a clue. I guess I'll just see what happens."

"You'll figure it out. Just remember that Zack is a fine young man whether or not he is the right one for you," Abby said.

Leaning over, Joann kissed her mother on the cheek before walking to the barn and saddling the feisty horse. Letting the horse have free rein, they loped almost all the way to the Oakes' cabin. She found Ethan and Sarah setting on the swing together, and Benjamin whittling a boat on the steps.

Joann greeted the family from the saddle and then asked, "Is Zack around somewhere?"

Ethan took a puff from his pipe and exhaled. "I decided that we would take the day off. I expect that you will find him at his cabin."

"I'm going to go see him."

"I see that you're unarmed. Would you like me to loan you a gun?" Ethan asked.

Sarah elbowed her husband. "Ethan, be good," she said.

Joann smiled. "No, I prefer a frying pan. I hear that's better for knocking some sense into a man."

"I hear a cold bath does the same for a woman," Ethan said with a grin.

"Ethan Oakes, keep your nose out of things," Sarah warned.

"You are bad today. I'm going to let Sarah straighten you out," Joann said.

"I'm just joking with you. Gideon and I were teasing Zack the other day. That boy is still riled. He might not be in much of a listening mood, but good luck," Ethan said.

"I'll see you all later," Joann said and rode away.

Zack stood in front of the cabin, splitting kindling, as Joann rode into the yard. He worked shirtless and his sweat-drenched muscles shined in the sunlight. Surprised at seeing Joann, he set the axe down, grabbed his shirt, and hastily slipping it on.

"What do you want?" Zack asked warily.

"Well, hello to you, too," Joann said as she climbed down from her horse.

"Joann, why are you here?"

"Zack, we can't go on for the rest of our lives avoiding each other. I came here to apologize. I know that I was wrong and that it was all my fault. I should've been thanking you instead of chewing you out. I'm asking for your forgiveness."

Zack looked at her for a moment before saying, "I forgive you and I'll speak when we see each other. You can go ahead and ride out of here with a clear conscience. I promise that I won't get in your way again."

"Zack, please stop. This is a lot more than riding out here to clear my conscience. I want to make things right between us. I truly am sorry. I wanted you to be something that you are not and it wasn't fair."

"You drive me crazy. You act as if I'm some scared little boy. I killed a man helping your daddy catch some outlaws, and I got shot in the bargain, but I wasn't ever scared. Maybe I wasn't around women much growing up, but I was taught to have some manners. You get mad at me for being polite, and then you get mad at me for standing up to you and throwing you in the water trough. I don't think you know what you want unless maybe you just like being mad at me," Zack yelled.

Zack's face had turned red with anger. Joann reminded herself to stay composed. She didn't want things to turn into a shouting match. Speaking in a calm voice, she said, "I never said that I didn't want you to be polite. I just want you to be yourself around me. You always act so timid as if you have to tiptoe around me. I don't want some bossy man, but I don't want a puppy that I have to lead around either. I don't know. Maybe there is no pleasing me. I just thought that you always tried too hard. I'll just go home."

"You don't want me timid and you want me to be myself. Well, I think what I want is to get me a switch and wear you out. See who's tiptoeing when I give you a good switching. I still think you are a brat that is impossible to deal with," he shouted.

Joann didn't know what to make of the threat, but was relieved to see that he made no attempt to carry out his plan. "Zack Barlow, you wouldn't dare hit a woman. You're not that kind of a man, and if you did, I would blow your head off."

Zack snickered and walked up to Joann until they were standing toe to toe as he towered over her. "That's mighty big talk for such a little lady," he said, the anger no longer in his voice.

"If you remember, the last man that tried to have his way with me got shot at, and if I hadn't missed, I would have blown off his head," Joann said.

"Do you want to blow off my head?"

"You haven't given me a reason to yet."

Zack looked down into her unbelievably blue eyes. His heart thumped like a dog's tail on a porch, and he still had no clue what she really wanted from him, but he did not intend on being accused of being timid. He had no doubt that Joann was feisty enough that she could blow his head off if provoked, but he wanted to kiss her and was willing to see if she really wanted him to be himself or if she was just impossible to please. As Zack bent over, he wrapped his arms around Joann and kissed her for all that he was worth. He half expected to get a knee in the groin, but found her ardently returning the kiss.

Chapter 29

With the arrival of Judge Laurel, the trial was finally ready to begin. After the death of Henry Starks, much of the town lost interest in the case, and few spectators were in attendance as court was called into session. Cal Simpson looked nervous sitting with his lawyer, Billy Todd. During his time in jail, the bartender had lost weight and his skin had taken on an ashen tone from lack of sun. District Attorney Kile brimmed with confidence and seemed eager to begin. Well-groomed and dressed in a tailored suit, he looked the part of a future politician. Gideon sat with the two whores, Constance and Sissy. Mary had sewn each of the women a dress to make their appearance presentable in court. Judge Laurel, a well know ladies' man, took a keen interest in the young women as soon as he entered the court.

D.A. Kile presented the evidence and called his witnesses. Attorney Todd had nothing to refute in any of the testimony and no witnesses to call. The trial came off as a one-sided affair with no chance for Simpson to win an acquittal. By mid-afternoon, both sides made their closing arguments. The judge gave his instructions to the jury and sent them to deliberate. Barely a half-hour later, the jury reached a verdict and Cal Simpson was pronounced guilty of all charges.

Judge Laurel pounded his gavel, letting the reverberation die out before speaking. "Cal Simpson, I sentence you to twenty years in the Colorado State Penitentiary. Your treatment of women disgusts me. May you find yourself in the same position in prison as you put these women – a sex slave."

The judge paused as if he had lost his train of thought before continuing. "Mr. Kile, based on the ledger, how many women do you believe are in forced prostitution from this operation?"

"Counting these two women, I believe there to be a total of thirteen, Your Honor," Kile answered.

The judge rapped his gavel again for no other reason than he liked the noise. "I hereby declare that the Lucky Horse Saloon and the assets from the two accounts listed in the ledger will be forfeited to the State of Colorado. These two women will receive all the proceeds from the sale of the Lucky Horse Saloon and each will be entitled to one-thirteenth of the assets of the aforementioned accounts. Court is adjourned," the judge said and once again sounded his gavel.

Gideon could feel all the stress melt away. The case had been the most challenging one of his career on so many levels and he felt elated to see it end. He suppressed the urge to throw his hat in the air and let out a holler.

The two women were still sitting beside Gideon as the courtroom emptied. They seemed dazed and confused as D.A. Kile walked up and congratulated them.

"What does it mean?" Sissy asked.

Kile smiled. "It means that in a month or so, you girls are going to have more money than you ever imagined. You'll be able to start a new life."

The two women looked at each other before squealing and hugging. In unison they said, "Thank you, Mr. Kile."

"Don't thank me. I had the easy part. You need to thank the sheriff. He is the one that wouldn't let the case die even when it nearly cost him his life and looked for all the world that things were hopeless," Kile said.

Gideon said, "There were a lot of people that played a part in justice being served. I have to get my prisoner back to the jail." Gideon abruptly walked over to Simpson and Todd before the girls had a chance to make him uncomfortable with their gratitude.

Gideon locked Simpson in his cell before walking across the street and found Doc asleep at his desk. Banging the door for orneriness, Gideon cackled when the doctor jumped.

"The trial is over. He got twenty years and I'm buying the first beer if you want to meet me at the saloon. I have to go find Finnie," Gideon said and flew back outside before the doctor had a chance to start cussing him.

Finnie stood outside the livery stable talking to Blackie when Gideon walked up behind him. The Irishman was carrying on an animated debate on the merits of black horses and did not see him approach. Gideon could not contain himself. He reached over and goosed his friend. Finnie jumped straight up in the air and began cussing before his feet landed on the ground.

"My God, Finnie, I didn't know that you could jump that high," Gideon said between fits of laughter.

"I'll give you an uppercut that lifts you higher than that if you ever play with my arse again," Finnie threatened.

"Meet me at the Last Chance if you think that Mary will give you permission," Gideon said before walking away.

Doc and Mary were sitting at the usual table drinking beer by the time Gideon walked into the saloon. The beer and Mary's company seemed to have revived the old doctor. He was laughing as Gideon took a seat.

Pointing his finger at Gideon, Doc said, "If you ever startle me like that again, I'll castrate you the next time I have you on that table."

"You and Finnie are awfully disrespectful to the sheriff. I just got Cal Simpson put away for twenty years and you want to fuss on me," Gideon said as he motioned for Delta to bring two beers.

Mary patted Gideon's arm. "We all still love you. The girls were just in here telling me that they were going to be rich. Thank God for that. I'm ready for them to move out of here. I owe you for that if nothing else," she said.

"That's what I like to hear. Appreciation for the sheriff," Gideon joked.

"I thought that's why we paid you. I didn't know that flattery came with the deal," Doc said.

Finnie walked in and sat down. "I hear the trial is over. I guess that is why we are given the pleasure of your fine company and rowdy mood," he said as Delta delivered the beers.

Gideon shoved one of the mugs at Finnie. "Have a drink and smile. Neither of us will have to sleep in that damn jail much longer."

Mary held up her hand. "Hold it there a minute. You need to speak for yourself. I only agreed to let Finnie stay over when you stayed in town. Nobody said anything about him taking up residence here."

Finnie appeared crestfallen. "I'm destined to die a lonely old Irishman. I'll be called the leprechaun of Last Stand," he said, causing a chorus of laughter.

Mary leaned over and kissed Finnie's cheek. "You never know what might happen if you are a good boy," she said.

The four friends continued their light-hearted banter until Gideon realized that he needed to go home. He paid his tab and said his goodbyes before riding out of town. The ride gave him a chance to absorb all that had happened. He still felt jubilant as if a heavy burden had been lifted. The last couple of months had been a trying time and he looked forward to happier days.

Joann stood at the stove frying steaks when Gideon walked into the cabin. The mouthwatering smell of the cooking meat filled the air. Abby sat at the table with Winnie, helping her with homework. Gideon greeted the family and eagerly told them the verdict. Abby, grasping the importance of the completion of the trial, beckoned him to sit with them until suppertime.

During the meal, Gideon said, "I think that it's time that we come up with a couple of names for this baby. If we don't get started, it will be a year old and we'll still be calling it baby."

Abby rolled her eyes at her husband. She still had doubts about how successful it would be to let the whole family in on the naming. Winnie never swayed away from an idea once she struck upon it, and Abby feared that they would never get her to agree to a reasonable name.

Winnie chimed in immediately. "I think we should name it Buddy if it's a boy. We could call him Buddy Boy. If it's a girl, we could name her Sissy. I would never forget her name that way."

"I would hope that you could remember your sister's name," Abby said.

"That's it. We could name her Hope," Joann said.

"I like that," Gideon said.

"Me too," Abby added.

Everyone turned to see Winnie's response. She looked around the room at each member of the family, wishing that she had thought of the name for the baby.

"Sure, I like Hope too," Winnie said.

"Hope it is," Gideon said.

A lively debate broke out in choosing a boy's name. Winnie kept spurting out names that were rejected. She began sulking. The others continued listing names, but nobody came up with a name that satisfied everyone and the search began to grow old.

Finally, Gideon said, "How about we name him Chance? It was quite a chance that we would all ever be together."

"That's it," Winnie said.

"I believe you are right. I love it," Abby said.

"Chance it will be," Joann added.

Chapter 30

Two months had passed since Zack and Joann had made up. The couple continued playing cat and mouse with each other. Zack, having learned his lesson well, found the less that he talked about their futures and the more he acted self-assured, the better things went. Joann would be coquettish one time that they met and cool and distant the next time. Somehow though, before a night would end, they would manage to be alone together and the petting would begin as if there were no tomorrow.

At church, Zack had asked Joann to go riding later that day and she had accepted. In preparation, she sat in her room brushing her hair, having changed into her favorite blouse and Abby's riding pants. Her blue eyes would always link her to her daddy, but otherwise, she appeared very much her mother's daughter.

Abby waddled into the room. A month remained before the baby's birth and she looked as if she had swallowed a large pumpkin. Her weight gain had been all baby, throwing her out of balance and forcing her to walk with her back arched and with steps that were more side-to-side than forward.

As Abby pulled her daughter's hair off her shoulders and down her back, she teased, "Here you go off consorting with a man. They all lead to no good, I tell you that."

"I think it took more than consorting to get you wearing the bustle wrong," Joann replied.

Abby let out a laugh. "Yes, but it begins with consorting. That's for sure."

"Is this one of those talks where you are trying to remind me to be a good girl?"

"Maybe. I'm not sure that I meant anything by it, but lugging this belly around all this time makes me very aware of what got it started," Abby said with a laugh.

"You've been the happiest that I've ever seen you," Joann reminded her.

"That I have, except for your father's job worrying me to death. Having you here with Winnie and the baby on the way has been special - more than I ever dreamed. And I would have gone crazy if I hadn't had you here to talk to."

"I wouldn't have missed it," Joann said.

"So has Zack won you back or is he just a diversion until you get back to Wyoming?" Abby asked as she took the brush from Joann and began brushing the back of her daughter's hair.

Joann smiled. "He's won if he strikes while the iron is hot. He has gotten a lot better at not be washy, but I fear this could go on forever just like it is."

"I see how you are around him. You need to quit playing games and sending him mixed signals. That's fine for a while, but if you know that he's the one then you need to stop. Men aren't good at deciphering those things. If you love him, you had better start showing it. Time is running out before this baby gets here and you have to decide whether to go back."

"I do love him. I already have names picked out for our babies."

Abby gazed at their reflections in the mirror and tried to hide her surprise at what her daughter had just said. Joann looked like her more all the time and she realized that they were a lot alike. Her daughter was more impetuous than she had ever thought about being, but they were cut from the same cloth. "Zack's right, you are a brat. On one hand, you're planning a life with him, and on the other, you are keeping him at bay. You're the one being washy. And no matter how this turns out, don't you be thinking about having babies. I'm too young to be having my baby on one hip and a grandbaby on the other."

Joann let out a laugh. "I know. Abs, I think about you and Marcus, and then I get scared and start worrying that the same thing could happen to me."

"I knew that I loved Gideon. I convinced myself that I loved Marcus. That's the difference. Listen to your heart and not your mind and you won't go wrong."

The voices of Gideon and Zack carried from the front of the cabin. The two were engaged in a lively conversation and laughing as they talked.

"Sounds like Zack is here. Thanks for the talk," Joann said and gave her mother a peck on the cheek before the two women walked to the front of the cabin.

Zack saw them coming. "Abby, you should just lie on the floor and let somebody roll you around."

Abby was surprised by the tease from the usually reticent Zack and when the laughter quieted down, she said, "Zack, I grew up on a ranch. You need to ask Gideon sometime about what I know how to do to steers."

Pausing while deciphering her meaning, Zack's face lit up at recognizing that she meant castration. "Oh, that wouldn't be good. You women grow up mean down here in Colorado," he said.

Deciding to join in on the fun, Joann said, "How would you know? I think we are the first women that you have ever talked to."

"No, but you are the first one that I ever dropped into a horse trough. Gideon and I were just debating on which one of us did a better job. He thought that he had since it was cold water that he threw Abby into and I said that it had to be me because of the crowd. Gideon ended up agreeing with me," Zack said.

Joann snickered. "You may have done it to me once, but if there is ever a second time, you'll never live to boast of it again. Did you come here to go riding or talk all day?" she said as she walked past the men and out the door.

Gideon said, "You held your own against her that time. You're learning."

"I never know with that girl," Zack said in resignation.

Abby wobbled over to the young man. "You're doing fine. She likes it. Believe me, she likes it," she said.

"I better get out there. I'll see you later," Zack said before hustling out the door.

Joann had the bridle and saddle blanket on Snuggles. She stretched to grasp the saddle off the stall wall when Zack reached over her and grabbed it. He dropped the saddle onto her horse and tied the cinch. Joann didn't say anything, but smiled mischievously before mounting and riding away, leaving Zack in her dust.

He knew her destination and didn't bother hurrying to his horse. His plans for the day seemed to be going up in the cloud of dust Joann had stirred. He had hoped that for just one afternoon that they could have a nice time together without their usual games. As he watched her crest a hill, he wondered if he was doomed to chase her forever.

After climbing up on Chester, Zack set out at an easy pace towards the aspen grove that Joann liked. Gideon and Abby used to ride to the spot for picnics in their youth. Zack suspected that Joann was drawn to the place now because it made her feel connected to a childhood that she never got to have with them. On one of their visits there, Joann had shown him a tree where Gideon had carved his and Abby's initials. She had talked as if it were one of the most romantic things that she had ever seen. Truth be told, he imagined that Joann had probably been conceived there.

He found Joann's horse tied at the bottom of the hill of aspens, but she was nowhere to be found. His shoulders sagged as he looked around to try to see her from atop his horse. Undoubtedly, she was hiding behind one of the huge trees and was not ready to stop playing games.

"Joann Minder, either come out or I'm riding for home. I didn't ask you to go riding so that I could spend the whole day chasing you across half of Colorado. I'm tired of the games," he hollered.

Joann did not answer or appear. Zack pursed his lips and shook his head. He scanned the trees one more time, letting out a sigh, before turning the horse around and riding.

He had not ridden twenty yards when Joann hollered, "I'm right here. Don't be such a spoilsport. I was only having a little fun with you."

Zack reined the horse to a stop, going against his first inclination to keep riding. Closing his eyes, he gathered himself. The only things stopping him from leaving were his desire to tell Joann how he felt and not to appear defeated by riding away. He turned the horse around and climbed down to wait for her as she pranced down the hill.

Joann walked to within a few feet of him and stood with her hands on her hips. He wasn't sure if it was a pose of defiance or if she was bracing herself for a disagreement. Either way, she looked beautiful and a pang of love welled up in him. He was hopelessly in love with her and figured in a few minutes he would be regretting it.

"Joann, I can't do this anymore. One day you act as if you're crazy for me, the next you're cool, and today you're running. And I have to pretend like I can take it or leave it and not care either way. I think this is all just a big game to you and I'm tired of it. The baby will be born shortly and you'll be running back to Wyoming. I'm not even sure that you like me or if I'm just a toy to play with while you're here," Zack yelled.

"I'm not sure what I'm supposed to say. I was just having some fun with you," Joann said.

"Not sure what to say? I wanted you to tell me your feelings about me. Just forget it. I'm going home," he said and turned to leave.

"Stop. Don't do that."

"Well, what is it then?"

Joann looked down at the ground, swinging her leg through the grass. She appeared shy and demure, things that he never associated with her. As Joann raised her head, she looked Zack right in the eyes. He could feel his chest start pounding as he prepared to get his heart broken.

"Zack, I love you," Joann said before hesitating. "Back in Wyoming, I really did decide that we weren't right for each other, and then when I got back here, things changed. I don't know why I've acted the way I have. I guess part of it is just my nature and part of it was that I was scared about us. That was the easiest way to deal with it."

Zack stood dumbfounded. His body felt so limp that he wondered if he would fall into a heap. Joann had surprised and thrilled him. The girl certainly never made for a dull moment. Silence hung in the air and he needed to speak.

"I love you, too," he said. Never had he said that to anybody other than his father and his aunt. As the words rolled off his tongue, he wanted to throw his hands in the air and dance. Saying it felt liberating. "The rest of it doesn't feel so important now, but let's just be ourselves. I'm going to quit worrying about trying to impress you. I am what I am and I can deal with all this a lot better now that I know how you feel. Not understanding where things stood drove me crazy."

He held out his arms and took a step towards her. Joann flashed her devilish smile and started running.

"If you want a kiss you're going to have to catch me," she shouted.

Zack tackled her before she had taken five steps, taking her down onto her back in the thick grass and pinning her with his weight. Her devil-may-care grin remained on her face as he peered into her blue eyes.

"You really are a brat and you're hell-bent for keeping me on my toes," Zack said.

"Guilty on both accusations," Joann answered.

He kissed her passionately. Emboldened by Joann's declaration of love, he no longer feared making some kind of mistake. He had an urge to walk through Last Stand and shout that he was in love with the woman of his dreams.

Breaking off from the kiss, Zack looked Joann in the eyes and asked, "Do you think that you would like to spend the rest of your life keeping me on my toes?"

With a coquettish smile, Joann said, "What are you asking me, exactly?"

"Joann, will you marry me?"

"Yes, I will."

Chapter 31

The engagement of Zack and Joann had sparked the idea for Abby to have a party. Her life consisted of sleeping, sitting, reading, and playing games. Conversations with Joann had kept her sane. She longed for a simple visit to Last Stand. Sarah and Doc were her only visitors outside of family. On his last visit, Doc had guessed that the baby would arrive in another week or two, and she wanted to have the celebration before then. Even though Joann would have to do the brunt of the preparations, she squealed with excitement when Abby had mentioned the idea. Gideon had been another story. The two women ganged up on him and wore him down to get their way. Sarah, upon hearing of the event, volunteered to help.

After conceding defeat, Gideon dug a pit in the yard and fashioned a spit from some wood and an iron rod that Blackie gave him. He already had plenty of firewood on hand that he had cut and split the previous fall. Lastly, he visited a farmer and bought a pig for the feast.

On the Saturday of the party, Abby had her strongest contractions to date. They had been coming more frequently and stronger for the past week. She wasn't overly concerned that she would go into labor. Both of her previous pregnancies had gone on in this manner for a couple of weeks.

Gideon already had the wood burning and the pig on the spit. He and Winnie were monitoring it as Sarah arrived early to help with the preparations. After walking over to greet Sarah, Gideon helped her down from the buckboard.

"It's going to be quite the shindig," Sarah said.

"I guess. It's easy being the host when you aren't allowed to do anything but boss," Gideon said.

"Be nice. Abby hasn't gotten to do anything in months and you played your part in making her that way."

Gideon grinned at her. "You women all stick together. You must love seeing me all domesticated."

"That I do. I better get inside and start helping."

Sarah found Abby and Joann trying to doctor up the basting sauce for the pig to their liking. Both knew that the sauce wasn't right, but couldn't decide what it needed. Sticking her finger in it, Sarah took a taste.

"It needs some more hot pepper sauce, vinegar, and sugar," Sarah declared before chuckling. "You know, Joann, those are three tastes for a good marriage. You need to add some hot sauce to keep things spicy, some vinegar to grab their attention and keep them on their toes, and some sugar to keep them sweet and to get what you want out of them."

Joann blushed and didn't say anything.

Sarah looked at Abby and said, "Have you had the talk with her yet?"

Abby looked uncomfortable with the question. "No, not yet. They haven't even set a date yet."

"Abigail Johann, I never pegged you for one to be uncomfortable about talking about sex with your daughter," Sarah said.

"Well I am," Abby said defensively.

Sarah had no problems with the subject and decided to offer her advice whether asked or not. "Joann, a lot of women think that sex is something that they are obligated to do and they don't like it. They hike their nightgown up and scrunch their eyes shut waiting for it to be over. It doesn't have to be that way. Your mother and I like it just as much as a man does. Shuck that nightgown off and let them see you naked. They love that. And don't be afraid to tell them what you enjoy. They can be a little dense about those things, but once they figure out that the happier they make you, the happier they will be, they can get downright enthusiastic about things. A happy bed makes a happy marriage," she said while continuing to add ingredients to the sauce and stirring.

Joann's face and ears were so red that it looked as if a drip of water would produce steam. "Yes, ma'am," she stammered.

Abby was looking down and had her hand on her forehead shielding her eyes.

Sarah glanced at her and said, "Abby, back me up on this so she doesn't think I'm some pervert. There'd be a lot more happy marriages if every girl got this talk and a lot less business for the prostitutes."

Abby looked up, taking a big breath, and exhaling slowly. "Sarah is right about everything that she said. I didn't get in this condition because it was forced on me, but for God's sake wait until you are married. We don't need history repeating itself."

Sarah let out a cackle and Joann managed a smile.

Joann stuck her finger in the sauce and tasted it. "This is better than I ever imagined, but I may never be able to look at you two the same again. I'm sure Zack will love it," she said, grinning at her double-entendre.

Abby jumped up as if her seat was on fire. "My water just broke," she exclaimed.

"We better call off the party," Sarah said.

"No, we are not. It's always been another day before I delivered anyway. I want everybody to have a good time. We won't say a thing and I'll tell Doc when the party is over," Abby said.

∞

All the guests had arrived by four o'clock. Doc came with Finnie and Mary by wagon. Ethan, Zack, and Benjamin rode together on their horses to the cabin. All of the men were sitting outside drinking beer that Mary had provided. They waited for Gideon to pronounce the pig ready while the women were all inside finishing the side dishes.

Doc took a swig of beer and looked at Zack. "Zack, have you got yourself an apron yet? Once you're married, she'll be bossing you around like a maid. You might as well get used to it, especially with that little filly you're marrying."

"Don't listen to him, Zack," Finnie said. "He's so old that he's forgotten the pleasures of keeping company with a woman."

"You're a fine one to talk. Mary set you straighter than a ruler," Doc said.

"Mary was the making of me. She is more enjoyable than any whiskey that I ever tasted," Finnie said.

"I suppose that you'll be teaching him the art of loving a woman like you did boxing," Doc said.

Gideon turned away from the pig and towards the men. "All right, that's enough on that. You are talking about my daughter. The pig is ready if somebody will go tell the women, Ethan and I can get it down from the spit."

Everybody gathered in the cabin. Gideon had rigged together another table and Zack and Joann sat at it with Benjamin and Winnie. Ethan said the blessing.

Gideon stood with his glass of beer in hand. "Before we begin, I want to make a toast. May Zack and Joann find all the happiness that this world has to offer. I can't think of anybody finer than Zack to be Joann's husband. This has been a special year and a special day. Cheers."

Abby tried eating the meal, but the contractions were to the point that she had no appetite. It was all that she could do not to show her discomfort. She would occasionally take a bite, but spent most of meal acting as if she were engrossed in the conversations.

Gideon noticed that her meal was barely touched. "What's the matter? Didn't I cook the pig to suit you?" he asked.

A big contraction hit her at that moment and she groaned. Unable to hide the pain any longer, she grabbed her belly. "The food is fine. We're about to have a baby," she said before disappearing into the bedroom.

Gideon remained seated, too surprised to move. He looked around the table as if searching for guidance while Doc and Sarah chased after Abby.

"You might as well relax and finish your meal. Doc and Sarah can handle it. I suspect that there will be plenty of waiting," Ethan said.

"Do you think that I should go back there?" Gideon asked.

"No, stay here with us. You don't want to go back there just yet. There's no need to break up a party over a little thing like a baby coming into the world," Ethan said wryly.

"Her water broke this morning and Abs made us keep it a secret. She didn't think she would have the baby until tomorrow," Joann said.

"She could have cancelled this. I guess having it tonight with all this company beats Joann, Winnie, and me here alone," Gideon said.

"I'm still hungry and I'm going to have me some more pork. We could be here all night," Ethan said as he flopped a large chunk of meat onto his plate.

"It's just like a Johann to come charging into this world and upstaging poor old Zack on his big night. Zack if you run with this crowd, you had better get used to playing second fiddle," Finnie said.

Mary elbowed Finnie in the ribs. "Don't talk badly about a poor baby that isn't even born yet."

"I'm just funning Gideon. I'm a bit excited about the baby myself," Finnie confessed.

Mary and Joann cleared off the tables after everyone had finished and began washing the dishes. The two women did not know each other all that well and began talking while they worked. They found that they both had a weakness for dresses and were soon discussing all the different styles that they loved.

Gideon needed to get his mind off worrying about Abby and the baby. He pulled a deck of cards out of a drawer. "Let's play some euchre. It'll occupy my mind."

Gideon teamed with Finnie, and Ethan with Zack as the four began playing cards. Mary and Joann went into the front room and continued talking while Benjamin and Winnie passed the time playing checkers.

Sarah came out after about an hour. "Abby is doing fine. The baby still isn't ready to make its entrance into the world, but Doc says that everything is going good," she said before retreating to the bedroom.

The games and conversations continued on for another couple of hours before everyone heard a baby crying. Gideon jumped up from his seat, almost knocking over the chair.

"Should I go back there?" Gideon asked.

"Just wait for Sarah to come get you," Ethan assured him.

Several minutes went by as Gideon stood nervously tapping his foot and rubbing his scar. Ethan and Finnie tried to keep him calm with little success.

Sarah finally came into the room. "Mr. Johann, you have a visitor. Come with me," she said and gave the others a wink.

Abby was propped up in bed holding the baby. "It's a boy. Come meet your new son," she said to Gideon.

Gideon had so many emotions coursing through him that he didn't feel attached to his body. He bent over and peered at the baby. "Is he fine? Are you fine?" he asked.

"Doc says that he's healthy and I'm fine," Abby answered.

Using his index finger, Gideon lightly brushed across the baby's forehead. The baby opened its eyes for a moment and Gideon saw the same blue color as his own. "He's got my blue eyes," he said before kissing Abby.

"Yes, he does. You'll never be able to deny that he and Joann are yours."

Doc sat in a chair by the bed. Gideon turned to him and started pumping the doctor's hand. The hand shaking was so vigorous that Doc chuckled.

"Thank you so much, Doc. You've been a good friend to me my whole life. I owe you a lot," Gideon said.

"Congratulations. That's a fine little fellow you got there," Doc said.

Gideon turned to Sarah, engulfing her in a hug, and kissing her cheek.

"Sis, you can't fuss on me no more. I've made good on all that you ever thought I should," Gideon said.

"Yes, you have. I knew I'd make something out of you," Sarah teased.

"Can I go show the baby to everybody?" Gideon asked Abby.

"Certainly. He needs to meet his sisters," Abby said.

"Sarah, will you pick him up and hand him to me. I'm afraid I'll break his neck or something," Gideon said.

Sarah picked the baby up and handed him to Gideon. At that moment, Gideon became overwhelmed with emotion and clenched his eyes shut, fighting off tears that would have embarrassed him. His mind flashed backed to the time in his life when he didn't care if he lived or died. Sometimes he had a hard time believing that life could be so good or that he could be so happy.

"Come with me, Sis," he said to Sarah.

Gideon and Sarah walked into the room to where the others were waiting, all standing together.

"Everybody, I'd like you to meet Chance Beneth Johann," he said and turned so that everyone could see the baby's face. "I owe everything that I have to Ethan, Benjamin, and Sarah. This day would not be possible without them. If the baby had been a girl, we would have named her Sarah Hope. However, since it is a boy, we stuck Benjamin and Ethan together and came up with Beneth. I thank everyone here for being a part of our lives."

About the Author

Duane Boehm is a musician, songwriter, and author. He lives on a mini-farm with his wife and an assortment of dogs. Having written short stories throughout his lifetime, he shared them with friends and with their encouragement began his journey as a novelist. Please feel free to email him at boehmduane@gmail.com or like his Facebook Page www.facebook.com/DuaneBoehmAuthor.

Made in the USA
Las Vegas, NV
24 January 2021